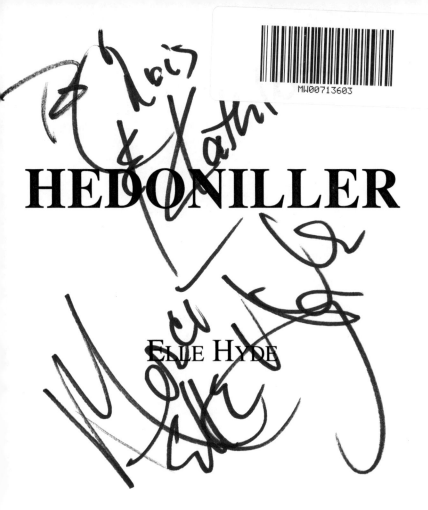

HEDONILLER

ELLE HYDE

PublishAmerica
Baltimore

Softcover 9781629076348
PUBLISHED BY PUBLISHAMERICA, LLLP
www.publishamerica.com
Baltimore

Printed in the United States of America

Dedication

This book was started when my father, Rudy Kardos, was diagnosed with terminal lung cancer. Through the course of writing this novel, he succumbed to this disease. This book is lovingly dedicated to him, his life, memory, and creativity. I love you dad.

Acknowledgements

It is due to Mark that I continue this arduous career. Thanks are inferior.

CHAPTER ONE

The Second to the Last Trailer on the Left

"Envy the confident, determined spirit of fire. For it is only contained when annihilated, it is never partially determined in its path." E.H.

The orange flames splintered and flickered around a large blue flame as if dancing a seductive tango, only visible for seconds before disappearing into the fading sky, as a seducing lover's absence when the sun rises.

Kitty looked out at the fire burning in the field, as several men stood attending to it. She allowed herself to become mesmerized for a moment before coming back to reality.

"Look Smithton, there is a sign on that last trailer saying it's fer sale." Kitty pointed with her finger, displaying a chewed down stumpy fingernail with a ring of dirt around the entire nail.

"There is a neighbor so close beside it. Maybe we should move on." she added.

"Kitty, shut the fuck up and let me make the decisions," Smith replied as he leaned forward onto the steering wheel and squinted into the distance. Smoke was rising from somewhere on the near horizon and Smith strained to see if he could determine where the smoke was coming from.

Kitty grabbed the roof of the rusted out, spotty red pickup that they hotwired from a garage two nights ago. Her dirty toes spread out and gripped the dashboard for stabilization as the truck sunk down into the ruts of the dirt road.

As the two navigated slowly around the loop in the densely wooded, holiday rental trailer park, they looked closely at each trailer.

"There," Kitty pointed again, this time jutting out her chin. "That one says 'fer sale'."

"I see it, Kitty," Smith replied in frustration.

They were tired, hungry, jonesing for a fix and on the run once again.

Smith reached one of his dirty, chafed hands from the steering wheel and ran his fingers through his long, oily strawberry blond hair.

"Kitty, make yourself useful and pull this off my fucking face," he snapped.

Kitty quickly reached back, pulled the black rubber hair band from her own ponytail, and tied back Smith's hair.

"I love your hair, baby. It reminds me of an old rock star's. You know, those ones you listen to: Guns n Roses and shit." She spoke as she played with his disheveled, greasy mane.

"Sweet child of mine," Smith sang out in a rough rock star karaoke voice, stretching the last word into four distinct syllables

"You know we coulda' kicked sweet ass in Hollywood," he said as he scanned each trailer in the small vacation rental park. "Those other fuckers are just luckier than we were." He paused and craned his neck to inspect a trailer to his left.

"I have a good feelin' about this one. I don't see many people comin' here this time of year. A lot of these look empty."

Kitty leaned forward and tilted her head up, looking at the white sky.

"It looks like it's gonna rain," she commented.

The tall, straight trees, with short branches draped in bright green leaves of various varieties, cast a backdrop of camouflage around the trailer park. Unless stumbled upon or intentionally sought out, the park did not receive visitors.

Each lot was cleared only enough for a small trailer, leaving enough trees in-between trailers to secure anonymity. The trailers in Fennely's Circle appeared old and worn as if they had little to no upkeep. The aluminum sided boxes of white, green, and gray trailers were dirty, dented, and unattractive.

Families and people of modest income rented the trailer to be within twenty minutes of the lake. The lake in Deep Creek, Maryland, was a beautiful manufactured lake that housed multi-million dollar houses around its banks. The wealthy, successful, and trust fund people vacationed here in the summer, boating and hiking around the lake and many state-run parks. The lesser income-based individuals rented small houses and various trailers. In the nearby areas of the lake, this rental trailer park was left for the individuals who did not fit in either one of the two categories.

The recreation activities in this area were hunting, camping. The vacationers to these sites did not hike, as the woods were very rocky and dense. The deer population was growing rapidly and becoming a backyard nuisance in addition to a road hazard.

"Why are we moving on all of the sudden? I don't know anything about this town, or Maryland," Kitty asked as she gazed out the window again at the scatter dilapidated trailers as they slowly drove past them, one by one. "I was beginning to like it there. It seems so quick this time to move on." She turned to look at Smithton, who was ignoring her questioning.

"Smithton, are you listening to me? Fer God's sake."

The tone of her voice got higher as she became annoyed by the fact that he was ignoring her.

"Fine. We'll just talk about it later, then." She made her displeasure known without pushing an altercation.

Drops of rain pelted the windshield as they navigated through the small community. Smithton reached over and rolled down the window of the beat up truck, giving him better visibility out of the driver side window.

"This one looks empty and beat to shit," he said as he nodded his head toward an insignificant white trailer that had a "For Sale" sign half taped, half falling off the window. The window was duct tapped from the inside, holding shattered pieces of glass in place.

Kitty stared, fixated as she watched the rain stream down the center of the rutted dirt and stone road. A small portion of the main stream broke away from the flow of the rushing water. She watched the water as it meandered street.

"I meandered away from every home I've had." She thought as she dreaded another move.

Kitty could not help but stare into the line of trees thinking of her life and how she and Smithton were always running away from these neighborhoods, making a new path to another one. Just like the water she was watching.

Smithton parked in front of the next neighboring trailer.

"Get out, Kitty," he demanded as he opened the door and exited the truck. He pulled the collar of his denim jacket up.

Kitty opened the door, stepped out, and her rubber flip-flop sunk into the mud as she put her weight down on her foot. Mud enveloped the sandal and onto her toes and as she stepped, the sandal was sucked off her foot. She bent down pick it up, slipped off her other flip-flop, and carried them carefully between her fingers.

Being barefoot in the mud was a common and comforting feeling to her. In Alabama where she was raised, she played for hours barefoot. In fact, Kitty only wore shoes to school.

Kitty raised her head and lifted her eyes to the gray sky. She opened her mouth and allowed the rain to fall onto her tongue. With her eyes tightly closed, she stopped and reveled in the moment, thinking of her childhood.

I outran the lightning bolts, in the thunderstorms, back home, she thought as she recalled the early years of her childhood. She thought about how she played for hours in the late summer rain, dancing and jumping through the puddles of water that collected in the low lying tall grass of the empty fields.

"Kitty?" She heard her name yelled at her, startling her from her quiet daydream.

She moved her head from the clouds and opened her eyes. Smithton was standing in front of her with a vexed expression on his face.

"What are you doing? Come on, we need to look around." He grabbed her hand and held it, not out of emotional bonding but to make an appearance for any possible onlookers. They were a happy couple possibly moving into the neighborhood.

As Smithton drug her toward the trailer, she placed a fatuous smile on her lips. This drill had played out four times prior. Kitty looked over at Smithton and asked, "This is move number five right?"

Smithton did not answer her. "Can't we rent one real like instead of always squattin' Smithton?" She nagged at him for an answer yet he did not acknowledge her.

Kitty tried to think of happier times when she had a home. She wasn't fully aware of the necessity for the sudden move from their last home. She had fixed up the inside of this last trailer with curtains and other items she bought at a local Goodwill store. She tried to make it a home, and in her mind was content with that effort but Smithton woke her up yesterday morning with news that they had to find a new home

"Why did we really leave Pennsylvania?" she thought as she was drug by the hand around this new, dilapidated white aluminum sided trailer. The bottom skirting was lifted, exposing the axel of the bottom. Two of the windows were busted and duct taped together. There was not grass surrounding the trailer, it was all muddy with holes filled with murky water. The deck that lead to the front door was relatively new but didn't have side rails, only steps and a deck. The screen door was ripped and the aluminum frame was bent preventing the door from closing.

"Kitty, a shed," Smithton said as he walked toward a small white building housed at the back of the property.

"There is a lock on it, Smithton," Kitty said as she inspected it.

"No, the lock is only through the one door;" he said, excited. "It's not through both."

He let go of her hand.

She stopped and looked down at her toes, wiggling them.

"Look, Smithton. I have mud in every toe." She laughed but he ignored her comment.

He pulled the door open with slight struggle, and then the two walked into the dark, small shed. They both raised their eyes and looked around as they slowly moved forward to explore the contents.

The shed was filled with untouched items. Smithton walked straight in, focusing on the push lawn mower, while Kitty gazed at the walls. Handmade fans made of turkey feathers bound by leather were hanging on the walls. One of them had a long wrinkled piece of leathery skin hanging from it.

She reached up and out, touching the feathers with her fingertips, her eyes fixed on the long plumes that formed a native looking headdress. She looked around at the numerous fan shaped feather arrangements.

"Smithton, what are these?" she asked as she continued to scan the walls.

"The guy musta' been a turkey hunter. They are from the ass. That one there is the beard, from the male." He pointed at the one fan that had the long hanging piece.

"But that's not important Kitty; there's at least $400 worth of shit in this trailer. We hit the jack pot, babe." He smiled, displaying his crooked, rotten front teeth. Despite his unattractive appearance, Smithton had a certain rugged, rough, and manly look. He had a straight bridge to his thin nose, lips that resembled a rock star's, and long thick hair that he hung tangled and unkempt. He had an insidious aspect to his smile, even when happy. Only Kitty knew the dark side to Smithton. In fact, only Kitty knew Smithton. Everyone else in his life is just an acquaintance.

"I think this is it, Kitty. We hit the mother lode. I feel good about this one. What about you babe?" He turned and picked her up at her waist and twirled her around.

Something caught his attention and he abruptly put her down. He stepped over to a tool that was eight inches in length, with the blade folded shut similar to a pen knife within an orange sheath. Smithton knelt down to pick up an old rag left on the floor, and then used it to lift the tool off the rusty nail that held it on the wall. He turned the saw over looking at it, as he was trying to figure out how to open it.

Smithton's low IQ was compensated by his street smarts. His most honed skills were ones of deviance and manipulation. Kitty noticed him looking at the saw and spoke up.

"It's a rose saw," she said as she walked over and reached out to take it out of his hands.

"No, not with your hands, Kitty," he said as he held the tool up and away from her reach.

"Let me see it, Smithton. I'll use the rag."

She grabbed the tool with the oily rag and searched for a small button that was concealed underneath it. She found it and depressed it. A long, deeply serrated blade fell out. She snapped the blade open by setting the tip on the floor.

"My Gram used to have a rose garden. She used this to cut them back. You know, prune 'em."

Smithton grabbed the tool back out of her hand.

"I don't care what it is supposed to be used for," he replied as he lifted it upside down to close the blade. He pushed the button himself as Kitty did, while trying to snap the blade open as if it were a switchblade. His first few attempts failed, but he persisted. After four or five attempts he was able to open the long rusty blade with one hand and in one flick of the tool. His eyes brightened up and he beamed with excitement.

"All right, let's go get high," he said as he turned and walked in front of Kitty, out of the shed. He didn't wait for her response. He kept the saw under his shirt and wrapped in the rag.

Kitty was several steps behind, left to close the doors the shed.

"I'm so not in the mood to get high," she thought to herself. "I get so sad when I crash. I'm sick of it."

Kitty knew, however, that her participation was not prerequisite for Smithton. He would reach get high with or without her approbation or participation.

Despite impromptu acts of humanity, Smithton's first commitment was to his addiction. He was in love with methamphetamine. The drug satisfied his needs, calmed his fears, and abated his insecurities. Smithton's inner demons were managed when his mood was high. Methamphetamine however, also kept him irritable, bipolar, and poor.

Smithton's timing was always curious. Kitty often wondered if he barked orders at her just to see how well she followed them. She didn't consider herself responding so much as obeying.

No sooner did she shut the door and turn that he yelled back to her, "Grab that box of candles outta that shed. I saw 'em on the floor to the left as soon as you walked in."

She sighed, gathered her physical strength, and pulled the rusty, bent doors back open. She glanced down at the obstreperous door, clogged with dirt, mulch, and sticks. She walked into the dark shed and searched for the candles in the vicinity that Smithton described.

"These are tapers," she thought to herself. "They won't stand unless he has a holder. I wonder if he knows that?" She said as she picked them up and turned to perform the same tiring task of closing the uncooperative door.

Once outside, she turned and walked to the truck, holding the candles under her shirt.

Smithton had the driver side door open, and his body was bent behind the driver side seat. He is either hiding that blade, or riflin' around for his drugs, she said to herself as she fixed her eyes on his back.

As Kitty looked at Smithton she was repulsed by his lifestyle, mostly from consternation. "If I just quite overthinkin' what he does, it'll be okay." She said as turned away from him. Kitty wanted to keep up a wall between her and her emotions, her longing for her past and her mourning over her father's death. Kitty knew that pondering her reality would challenge the morals instilled in her by her altruistic father.

"Aw, Smithton, I was hoping we could talk about this move before gettin' fucked up and not speakin' about it," she said with a discerning note of disappointment. "And I wanna know whose license you got," she added.

"What's there to talk about, Kitty? I say we are movin', so we're movin'. I say this is the one, now this is the one. The license is none of your business." He sat on the seat and closed the door to the truck.

Kitty hauled herself into the truck and pulled the door shut, not looking over to Smithton. There was a sick feeling in her stomach, a twang she got when she knew something was wrong. Smithton shifted his weight, reached his right hand into his right pocket, and pulled out a small plastic bag tied with a bread wrapper.

"What is it? Blow or meth?" she, asked pausing in between the two drugs. "I told you I am not doing meth anymore."

He looked at her with condemning eyes

"Then don't, Kitty. I don't have blow for you little Miss Higher-than-the-Rest. Anyway, we can't afford that Hollywood drug right now." He pulled out his wallet to pull out a Pennsylvania Drivers license. He placed the corner into the bag, placed a small amount of the powder onto the card, and brought it to his nose. It was gone in one snort.

"Where did you get a Pennsylvania drivers license?" Kitty asked, ignoring what he was doing and focusing instead on the card.

He ignored her. Once the rush from the amphetamine overtook him, he smiled reaching over to hold her hand.

Kitty raised her eyebrows at him. "Where did you get that man's license? Cause I can see that ain't you."

Smithton's high was taking affect and he was becoming annoyed with her intrusion into his escape.

"Fine, you wanna know?" he snapped at her.

"Obviously," she replied.

"Remember that cock sucker who was buyin' all the meth from me at that last place? The pill head?" he asked her.

Kitty stopped to think of the several derelicts purchased drugs from Smithton at their last trailer squat.

"Maybe. Did he have short black hair?" she asked.

"Yep, that one. Well, I found out from his dick suckin' old lady that he was a snitch." Smithton spoke as he dug the tip of the drivers license back into the baggie and snorted another dusting of powder.

He began to laugh cynically then replied, "I made him into a pill jar, and he was into pharma's, so it was fitting."

"What are you talkin' about, Smithton?" Kitty asked, perplexed. "You're not making sense."

"I stuffed some cotton into his mouth and nostrils and sealed him up with a security wrapper."

Kitty looked at him in shock.

"He sucked in for air harder than his whore did for cum." He chuckled to himself sinisterly.

"Why the fuck would you do that, Smithton?" she gasped.

"Well Kitty, if I am meant to keep you safe, that means I gotta keep me safe." His voice was soft, comforting, a vast change from the maniacal laughter just moments before. "He was gonna snitch on me and you would have no one left. I did it to protect you, just like I promised your Daddy I would."

Kitty atrophies with fear when she thinks of being left alone or without Smithton. He is all she has had since the death of her dad. Tears filled he eye as she spoke.

"What did you do with him?" she asked quietly, keeping her attention on the world outside the window. Kitty had to find comfort by removing her attention from her fears of abandonment. She went deep within her mind where she was removed her from pain, hurt, and loneliness. She visited this place all too often since her father died and their moves became more frequent. Kitty closed her eyes and focused her energy on escaping the stuffy truck. The thought of a lifeless body spiraled Kitty into a deep abyss of her father's death.

"Do you want to say goodbye to your father, Kitty?" the mortician said as her father lay on the gurney. His left foot fell to the right and outside of the sheet that they used to lift his body out of the bed in her home where he passed away.

Kitty just stared at his pale, white foot. It did not register in her mind that her father was actually gone forever.

"I guess so," she quietly replied as tears streamed down her cheeks. She slowly walked over to his head.

Mr. Roger, the mortician, pulled the sheet back to expose her father, emaciated and cold. In the time her father was being consumed by cancer, Kitty tried to focus on the tall, heavyset man that Bob once was. As he withered away to a mere 110 pounds, she still saw her Daddy as he was for the whole of her short life. This time, she saw her father as he actually appeared: with deep sunken cheeks that recessed into his jaw line. Gray whiskers extruded from his leathery skin.

Kitty reached out and touched his forehead as she always had, running her fingers over his sparse, matted hair.

"I love you, Daddy," she said the best she could speak the words through tears. She leaned forward and kissed his cheek. His skin felt like putty. There was no resilience or softness to it.

"Let a flight of angels speed you to thy resting place" She fumbled with his limp hand, reciting the phrase etched in her mother's tombstone. She did not know where it came from or who said it, but it comforted her to think that angels would lift up her father and carry him through the clouds and up into heaven.

"Kitty, for fuck sake. Are you listening to me?" Smithton snapped. "We gotta talk about what we're doing now."

Kitty was back into reality, despairingly. She very quietly asked Smithton, "What did you do with him?"

Smithton laughed, ignorant to her demeanor change.

"I took the fuckin' wannabe cock suckin' snitch to work."

Kitty had an idea of what this meant but in her innocence never imagined the grotesque manner in which Smithton disposed of bodies in carcass landfills. With this last comment, Smithton was done discussing the subject. He reached forward and turned up the radio.

"My baby's got blue skies up ahead," he sang out, following the words of the song. His voice was in tune and strong.

Smithton turned and leaned over toward Kitty, who sat stoic next to him. He turned her chin with his rough hand and gave her a gentle kiss on her forehead, then placed his forehead onto hers and looked into her eyes, which were deep, empty. His bright blue eyes looked down and into hers, strong and confident, as if he were her savior. He reached his hand over and grabbed the back of her head, stroking her hair as he sang quietly to her.

Smithton knew that only he could sooth Kitty. After her father's death he spent months consoling her. He made a promise to Bob before his death that he would care for his daughter. Smithton was capable of love despite his often being consumed with derelict survival instincts and actions. In his eyes, Kitty was a fragile scared child, regardless of her age. She would never grow old. He rationalized that all actions carried out by him, heinous and deviant, was done to protect his freedom so that he could in turn protect Kitty's.

"Come on Kitten; let's look at this as our new home," he whispered as he moved his arms down to her body and pulled her thin frame closer to him.

Kitty snapped out from her other world. "Yeah, baby," she replied, her voice devoid of enthusiasm. "To our new home,"

CHAPTER TWO

The Hook

"Familiarity forms a cocoon of comfort around weary, confused minds." E.H.

Kitty found it oxymoronic as she was a nomadic squatter. Her heart and soul longed to replace her childhood home. She longed for continuity.

As Kitty and Smithton walked back to the truck, the light rain turned to a constant drizzle and several residents returning from work passed by the two as they sat in the truck. They watched and waited. Smithton turned to Kitty.

"Here is what we're gonna do. You sit here; I will go slip the lock of the trailer. Slouch down so no one sees you, but keep an eye out. If you see someone comin' around, get out and stop 'em."

She looked at him, all too familiar with this plot. "What do I say this time, Smithton?"

This was known as the hook. Once they found a suitable, inconspicuous trailer, the two would meet the neighbors, telling the same story.

"I don't know, Kitty. Think on your own. Or try 'hello'. How about that one?" He pulled out the bag once again.

She just stared straight ahead. "Fine, I can handle it." She listened as he snorted another bump of meth.

He jumped out of the truck and walked to the door of the trailer. She watched him, and then scanned the grounds as she slumped in the seat, just low enough for her eyes to see out the window.

A man dressed in a mechanic's jumpsuit got out of his car, several trailers down. As he got out of his truck and slammed the door, a young girl ran up to him, throwing her arms around him. He hugged her and lifted her off the ground.

Kitty watched remembered past events that she had long since repressed. Memories she would not recalled if not for this vision. She recounted the endless summer days when she would color on the dark gray asphalt surface of the road with pastel colored chalk. She prolonged her play on the road that led to her small humble home, waiting. Every time she heard a car, she looked up to see if it was her father's truck arriving home from work.

When she saw him rounding the corner in the distance, she jumped up off the warm road and stood up, the truck moving impossibly slow through the summer haze Once it stopped in front of her, she stepped up onto the bumper grasping the tailgate, then sat in the trucks' bed, the wind whipping her hair around her head. She looked through the glass leading to the driver's seat and her father smiled, slowly driving on down the road to their house.

She looked back at the man and noticed he was walking toward the truck. Startled, she looked over at Smithton who was still working on opening the side door. She looked back up to see the man was still moving toward them. He was. She sprang up, opened the door, and jumped out, pushing her hair back with her hands.

"Howdy," she called out to distract him from looking toward Smithton.

She walked toward him.

He did not speak but turned and directed his young daughter, "Get on back home now."

Kitty tried to remain calm. "How ya doing?"

"Hello," he replied, "Are you alone here?" He was genuinely concerned, for Kitty was sure she looked too thin, sopping wet, and out of place still holding the tapered candles.

Kitty was nervous and unprepared because Smithton would be pissed if anything she did affected his plan. She looked over toward the unoccupied trailer with the hope of seeing Smithton; she feared he would be still trying to get in.

"No, my boyfriend and I are moving into this here trailer," she said, feigning confidence.

The man glanced around and toward the door where Smithton had been attempting to break the lock, but he was already inside.

"He's inside already," she said.

"I guess you're my new neighbor, then?" she asked as she walked him away from the truck and out of view of the side door.

"I guess," he replied, "I'm Jimmy. Nice to meet you." He held out his hand.

"Kitty," she said awkwardly as she held out her hand to shake his.

"Let me go fetch my boyfriend," she said as she quickly changed the subject and walked away from him toward the door where Smithton entered.

"Smithton," she called out.

As if the two staged the entire façade, the front door swung opened, and Smithton appeared in the doorway with a large grin placed upon his `lips.

"I'm in," he said with a look of accomplishment.

"We have visitors." She motioned with her head toward the neighbor.

"What the fuck did you tell him?" he hissed at her under his breath.

"Nothing. I didn't even know if you got in. I told him we were movin' in."

"Follow my lead Kitty, and don't fuck up." He walked sternly out the door, pushing past her toward the neighbor.

Kitty didn't have a high school diploma. Her father became ill and died when she was in 10th grade. She dropped out of school to care for her dying father; after Bob's death, she left Tuscaloosa with Smithton. Smithton had a habit of speaking to her knowing she had little education.

Smithton walked out of the trailer and to the front of the truck. Kitty was nervous that the man knew what was going on, that she and Smithton were breaking and entering. Kitty thought,

"Was he taking their license plate number? Smithton's rotten teeth are gonna give us away. Or his sallow complexion? Or the yellow-white tone to his skin with sunken dark ringed eyes?"

Kitty tightened her fist with nervous energy as she questioned the unknown.

Smithton noticed the man sneaking around his car, taking down the license plate number. This stirred him to action.

"Hey, bro," he called out as he got within five feet the man.

"Hey," the man replied as he looked at him. He man spoke without judgment, yet Smithton translated his body language to be questioning his intentions and judgmental. Kitty could tell Smithton was paranoid, and the drugs just made the paranoia worse.

"Looks like you smashed the front end of your truck," he said as he pointed to the front left fender of Smithton's truck.

"Yeah, my girlfriend and I got into an accident on the way here. Our trailer with all our stuff went over the hillside. We have nothin' left."

Kitty just looked on.

Smithton pointed to her arm. "Kitty got all bruised up."

Kitty awkwardly slid her right hand over the bruises on her left arm, left from Smithton during a drug-induced fight two nights ago, not from a fabricated truck accident.

Kitty's mind drifted to the incident. After Smithton pushed her over a nightstand and into the wall, then hit her in the face with a closed fist, she fled and roamed the neighborhood until she got so tired that she slept in the truck. At some point in the early morning, Smithton awoke and went looking for her. He woke her up asking why she had slept in the truck, as if the fight never occurred. Instead of reminding him of it, she simply said she had slept there because it was too hot in the trailer.

Kitty's reaction was unconditional, she snapped out of the flashback and made eye contact with the neighbor. She tried to convey a look that begged for saving, but she knew from experience that her eyes did not translate what her heart and soul were screaming.

"That's too bad. Can I help out?" Jimmy asked after hearing Smithton's retelling of the woeful adventure the two had while traveling from Pennsylvania to their newly purchased trailer.

"Well, that is right kind of you. Actually, I could use a few bucks to pick up my wife's prescriptions. We went to the ER and they gave her meds but we gotta pay out of pocket and can't get 'em right now." Kitty knew he was going for the sympathy card.

"Oh, no problem," Jimmy said as he reached into his back pocket and pulled out his wallet. Kitty felt a pang of guilt but knew they needed the cash.

Smithton look closely at the amount of money he had in his wallet as Jimmy shuffled through the bills. He pulled out two twenty dollar bills, folded them, and handed them to Smithton.

"Will this help?" he asked.

"That's perfect. I can't thank you enough, Jimmy. I'll pay you back once we get settled and I find some work."

Jimmy raised his eyebrows. "What kinda' work are you looking' for? I have a garage down the road. Do you know anything about cars?" he asked.

"No, not a fucking thing," Smithton replied as he reached out his arm and placed it around Kitty's shoulders. "I'll look for state work. Cleanin' up road kill." The neighbor replied, "Are you serious or jackin' me around?"

"Someone's gotta do it?" he coldly replied.

"Ok man, I wish I could help you there, but I can't." Trying to relieve the tension, Jimmy added, "You must have a strong stomach, I couldn't do it."

"Nothing so specialized as lying under cars all day, right?" Smithton spoke with a passive aggressive tone and a fake smile plastered on his lips.

Jimmy, sensing something not right about Smithton's demeanor replied, "Look, I got to get home. The wife always has something on for me to eat. Nice meetin' you both."

Smithton looked into the man's eyes and removed the smile from his lips. "Thanks man, for the money and all." His attempt at being sincere was transparent.

"It's all right; not a problem." Jimmy glanced toward Kitty. She merely smiled and nodded her head as he looked at her.

Once the neighbor was far enough away so that he couldn't hear them, Kitty turned and spoke to Smithton.

"What the fuck Smithton, an accident? She pointed at her bruises, "You did these, own it…" she stopped short of telling him to leave her alone for the rest of the night. She turned and walked toward the open screen door of the trailer. Smithton followed her without speaking, but once inside, he closed the door behind them and grabbed her arm.

"Damn it Kitty, don't ever question my actions." He walked over to her and grabbed her arm, "Bitch," he yelled as he squeezed her already bruised arm.

Kitty yelled from the pain and yanked it away. "Smithton, stop it! Maybe you should tell me your plans ahead of time if you want me to 'act right'." Her voice was strong and controlled. Kitty had not resolved his actions from, her response defiant against his violent outbreak. He backed off, but Kitty couldn't fight the nervousness that choked her. Smithton was becoming less predictable each day as if they were moving toward a major incident. This scared Kitty. Smithton lost control when he was drunk and high, he was irritable when he was coming down, and he was moody the next day so to medicate he would inhaled more meth. The spiral was becoming deeper and faster toward a decent.

In this occasion he was at the very early stages of being high so he did not continue with his tirade. He understood that she was right. He still had some sense of right and wrong in him before he totally lost sense of reason. The higher Smithton became, the more he thought like a psychopath.

Kitty knew that on bad highs, Smithton's mood was often due to an incident a few years ago. While driving his brand new pickup home one night in October when he was eighteen, he hit an embankment and then ran over his passenger. He was never brought up on charges, and he never saw a day of jail time. Smithton's father was a political figure in their small town. His family name and father's power saw to it that his wrongs were never brought to public or victim awareness. This was not for love of a son but love of oneself. This was acutely in Smithton's awareness.

Only Kitty knew the truth about Smithton and of his true demons, of all the times he relives the accident. She often wondered if this was another reason for the perpetual cycle they were in, running from one place to another. Smithton's nightmares were a life sentence that the legal system could never impose.

In truth, Smithton's personality had been developed by self important parents that had no time for a child. Kitty felt he was trying to justify his internal pain by his violent lifestyle and hedonistic gratification. Smithton tried unsuccessfully to erase his past with meth, sex, alcohol, and murderous rampages acted out at those who got too close to him or her.

"I just don't want to get too far into this lie, Smithton," Kitty said. "And how did you get in?" She asked him.

"I found a key hidden in the dirt." Smithton laughed then said, "Stupid fuckin' people."

The sun was falling beneath the thick tree line behind the trailer. Smithton turned and flicked the light switch, but the lights did not come on.

"Fuck," he whispered under his breath.

Kitty just stood in the middle of the empty room.

"Did you bring those candles in with you?"

"No, they're still in the truck. Want me to get them?"

"No, I will." He leaned forward and kissed her on the lips. "I love you kitten," he said lovingly. Kitty was never ready for the swift shifts in his personality. He turned on and off like a light switch. Ironically, with the lights, nothing changed; with

Smithton, everything within his persona did. He left quickly through the squeaking trailer door and returned in a few moments, dangling the tapered candles by their long wicks.

"Here, take one," he said, handing one of the candles to Kitty along with his lighter. He pulled his pocketknife from his pocket and cut the wicks as she held the candles apart, and then she lit them, moving over to an empty corner of the trailer. She leaned her back against the wall and slid down until she was sitting on the brown shag carpet.

"We can pretend we're campin', or better yet, the lights went out and we are roughin' it in our mansion," he said as walked over to her and knelt in front of her.

"Yeah, we can pretend, Smithton," she said with low spirits.

He turned and sat beside her, dripping hot wax from his candle onto the carpet until it formed a small puddle. He broke off the bottom of the taper and stuck it to the melted wax, holding it until it bonded.

"Here, give me your candle," he said as he held out his hand. She handed him the candle and he did the same to hers.

"Turn down all those blinds Kitty, and rip that sign out of the window," he said as she stood up and walked across the room. She did as she was told and returned to sit in the same spot. Smithton's lighter was on the floor and she picked it up, flicking the lever until a hot blue flame sprung to life, dancing against her light breaths.

This is how this day started, staring at flames, she thought to herself as she watched the flame. She remembered the winter, years before her father's death. When the lights went out, for days before being restored, she, her mother, father, and dogs lived in the basement of their house with the fireplace roaring every minute of the day for warmth. This was a fond memory for Kitty; she loved the time she spent one-on-one with her father. They listened to the radio every night for entertainment and her father told her stories about the Korean War.

"It was so cold I lost feeling in my feet and hands," he would tell her. "The little Korean children would come up to us as we stood guard at camp, we would give them bubble gum so they would go away." She recalled him telling her. This was one of her favorite stories. He had a picture of him at the age of nineteen handing pieces of bubble gum to small Korean children with hands held up high to the soldiers.

Smithton knew Kitty's father before he actually knew her. Smithton was hired as a laborer for her father. He had a small concrete company within their small town of Tuscaloosa, Alabama.

Her father was very skilled in one area, concrete. He did not speak with a verbose vocabulary. He did not express himself eloquently. He had two things in his life, his craft and his daughter. He spoke about Kitty none stop at while at work. This is how Smithton became familiar with her.

After working for Bob for many months, Smithton got up the courage to ask him if he could ask her out. Smithton's mother would drop him off at their house early in the morning on the days they worked. He would sit outside on their porch waiting for Bob. Smithton would drive to job sites with him whereas the other employee, or two, would meet them at the various job sites.

Kitty would open the screen door, pushing him off his perch. She would walk past him with a smug smile on her lips, coy and confident.

After Bob had given his consent for Smithton to take her out on a date, the dates multiplied.

What Bob never knew was that Smithton sold drugs. What Bob didn't know was that Smithton introduced his little Kitten, to drugs. He got most of the middle school neighbors hooked on drugs.

Another very important aspect to Smithton that Bob never knew was that he was violent. He repressed thousands of demons; Demons that stemmed from his vehicular homicide, to being the victim of his own father's hand, to being the sole witness to his mother's egregious domestic abuse.

At present, Smithton and Kitty were two of many, in the vicious cyclone of pain, regret, sorrow and denial. Unfortunately, Kitty would have healed and dealt with her father's passing differently if not for her association with Smithton. An association that became indelible.

She watched the flame and felt a hard lump form in her throat. Who was she now, sitting in a trailer in a state she did not belong in, and where had the young Katherine, the Katherine who smiled and laughed and was happy before her father's death, gone?

It took hours before Kitty fell asleep. Once asleep, she was back in her childhood bed, with her father in the next protecting her.

CHAPTER THREE

A Lower State of Consciousness

"If we hold our hand up to the wind, we feel the air's movement not consistent in its path. If we try to grasp at the energetic moving force, the futile attempt to control it fails. Inevitably, we lose feeling the essence of the air and can only feel our own clenched fist." E.H.

Kitty opened her eyes, then closed them several times wrestling with herself to stave off the reality that was the imminent day. She could no longer force her body to lay still, in the fetal position on the dirty brown shag carpet with strong odoriferous damp and stale overtones.

She opened her eyes sparsely to see if Smithton was still sleeping. She feared he would see her awake so she squinted. Kitty was certain that he would be asleep due to the amount of meth that he had snorted the night before.

History taught her that he would awake in the afternoon irritable and preoccupied with finding a local supplier to replenish his dwindling stash.

With closed eyes, Kitty went through a mental list of redundant steps that they both would need to perform in order to make this new move work, for the short term.

The highest aspirations that Kitty had for the duration of one of their last home, was not seen to fruition.

She longed for a Home, in structure, concept and emotion. Kitty had not experienced the feelings of the concept of a home since the death of her father.

Kitty succumbed to the light of morning and opened her eyes. She stood up and quietly walked over to the window. She looked out through the faded ivory LEVALOR blind. Her head lifted upward as she searched for the rod to shut the blind. The ability to close the blind was lost; the handle was gone.

She paused and looked out the window, past the dusty plastic slates and out onto the faded green aluminum siding of the trailer that neighbored the one they occupied. Fiberboard covered the windows of the adjacent trailer.

The skirting was buckled, exposing the ground underneath the long dilapidated structure. The roof housed an old circa 1970's TV antenna. The bent structure was weathered and dilapidated to the extent that it could no longer hold its stance.

Kitty shook her head in silent opposition to her surroundings. Her childhood home was not exalted in status but was a far contrast to the dwellings she occupied since living with Smithton.

She shut her tired eyes to envision the comforts of her childhood home, escaping the reality of her grungy existence.

She smiled slightly as she recalled the front porch where she played for hours. The wood tongue and grove boards of were meticulously painted grey, shining with years of thick glossy oil based paint. She saw the ghostly vision of a young girl playing with her pretty dolls. She glanced to the right of this faded vision and saw an empty rocking chair, slowly moving with the passing wind. She opened her eyes. As much as she tried to manufacture happy and fond memories, they were always transposed them to acrimonious ones.

She closed her eyes once again and brought her hands to her face. Her memories were more visual that therapeutic.

"Stop it Kitty. God, stop." She quietly said aloud before asking herself, "Why do I always go here? Just move on, fucking move on."

She turned, and looked at Smithton who was stirring as he was also losing the battle to the infiltrating sunlight.

He opened his eyes and took a second or two to focus on her frame behind the streaming light.

"What are you doin' over there?" He asked.

"Nothin', I couldn't sleep either. I thought I could shut this blind but the handle ma-jiggar is gone." She replied as she walked toward him.

She knelt down by him and kissed his forehead as she placed her fingers through his tussled hair.

"Can I find work at this place?" She blurted out, "I want to work and earn my own money."

The morning after partying, Smithton was not at his approachable best. She felt strong affirmation about her convictions to make her own money however, so she took the chance of his verbal repercussion.

"Kitty, come on now, it's too fuckin' early to talk about this. What are you doin?" He replied with a quiet tone instead of the anticipated indignant one.

"It's important to me Smithton. Daddy always wanted me to provide for myself." She no sooner finished the word, Daddy, when Smithton's demeanor began to change.

"Oh, here we go, fuckin' Daddy. Daddy wanted, Daddy's dreams for me, Daddy didn't know about you." He yelled at her as he turned over away from her. He pulled off his shirt and placed it over his eyes, blocking out the sunlight that poked at him.

He continued, "Don't go down this Daddy road now Kitty. I can't handle it."

Expressionless she looked on, waiting for his tirade to end.

Smithton was not yet done; he added,

"You're doin' my head in with all this."

She removed the languorous expression and screamed her emotions tacitly with her forehead and stance.

"I follow you around this damn country Smithton." She fired back.

"Who the hell do you think you are? I have a life also. I have dreams. I need worth. I'd think that you would stop and look at me." She yelled as she stared onto his bare back. He did not move a muscle. This enraged and fueled her rant.

"And, don't you ever talk about my Daddy in that disrespectful way." She walked over closer to him.

He did not move, respond or react in any manner.

Kitty became more incensed with every second she looked at him, ignoring her.

She cocked her foot back and kicked his back with a force strong enough to push his frame forward a foot or two.

This act incited a response from Smithton. He jumped to a sitting position and turned toward her.

"Don't start somethin' you can't finish Kitty." He said as he looked her directly in the eyes.

"Then don't defame my Daddy, Smithton." She yelled back.

Smithton had been with Kitty long enough to know that there were few subjects that evoked her to physical representation. One was her father. The second was the high level of respect she tried to maintain in the relationship. This innate pride was instilled in her by the same subject that rankled her, her father.

Smithton knew Kitty's father before he actually knew her. Smithton was hired as a laborer for her father. He had a small concrete company within their small town of Tuscaloosa, Alabama.

Her father was very skilled in one area, concrete. He did not speak with a verbose vocabulary. He did not express himself eloquently. He had two things in his life, his craft and his daughter. He spoke about Kitty none stop at while at work. This is how Smithton became familiar with her.

After working for Bob for many months, Smithton got up the courage to ask him if he could ask her out. Smithton's mother would drop him off at their house early in the morning on the days they worked. He would sit outside on their porch waiting for Bob. Smithton would drive to job sites with him whereas the other employee, or two, would meet them at the various job sites.

Kitty would open the screen door, pushing him off his perch. She would walk past him with a smug smile on her lips, coy and confident.

After Bob had given his consent for Smithton to take her out on a date, the dates multiplied.

What Bob never knew was that Smithton sold drugs. What Bob didn't know was that Smithton introduced his little Kitten, to drugs. He got most of the middle school neighbors hooked on drugs.

Another very important aspect to Smithton that Bob never knew was that he was violent. He repressed thousands of demons; Demons that stemmed from his vehicular homicide, to being the victim of his own father's hand, to being the sole witness to his mother's egregious domestic abuse.

At present, Smithton and Kitty were two of many, in the vicious cyclone of pain, regret, sorrow and denial.

Unfortunately, Kitty would have healed and dealt with her father's passing differently if not for her association with Smithton. An association that became indelible.

Smithton stopped, for reasons he could not explain, and looked at her sympathetically.

"We can talk about it Kitten. Now come and lay with me, for a lil' longer, my head is poundin'." He said with a quiet understanding.

Kitty looked at him and relaxed her stance. This was the Smithton that she fell in love with, the understanding, emoting, and gentle man that no one else, but she viewed.

"Thank you, honey." She said as her eyes danced and her smile was the rainbow back dropped by blue skies.

"Let's talk tomorrow about it, okay?" He said as he pulled her in close to his bare chest.

She punched his stomach as she replied,

"S M I T H T O N."

Kitty can speak to Smithton in way that only she could, in part because she had a level of empathy for him that no other had. No one but Kitty was aware that there was a descent human living inside the shell of an angry man.

Kitty did not push the work subject further. She was determined to be productive in this new neighborhood, in this new town, and in this new State.

Kitty had not been employed for two moves now. She did not think of her past in terms of years but in terms defined as places, number of moves and series of loses.

In the past two moves, she had not been employed. Three moves ago she cleaned houses for money. She quit when Smithton pressured her to inventorying the items of worth from the houses she was cleaning for street value.

Kitty didn't have a high school diploma. Her father became ill and died when she was in 10th grade. She dropped out of school to care for her dying father; after Bob's death, she left Tuscaloosa with Smithton. She hoped to run from the pain that invaded her dreams and tormented her waking mind.

While in the encompassing arms of Smithton she felt the pull of her morals. She wanted to reject the termination of the subject, but she did not. In a way, Kitty deeply resented Smithton and herself for her acquiescing behavior. Consistently for 5 years, Kitty remained in the relationship despite the nomadic temperament and instinctual belief of his psychopathic and sociopathic behavior. She lay still without movement; even the fear of deep breath petrified her.

Kitty's mind was long gone, back to the familiar comforts that she depended on; the ones that her entire short life were based upon. She knew a world with her father where she belonged, felt loved and was understood.

Kitty was able to survive in the relationship with Smithton without denial. The dichotomy was that in denial she would not survival.

Smithton tightened his grip on her attempting to show her he cared for her.

Kitty closed her eyes tight and whispered, "Daddy, please don't leave me on my own."

When she opened her eyes she accessed it was morning. Kitty saw Smithton through the light of day as it streamed through dirty windows and into an empty dilapidated trailer. Dust particles hung in the rays of light adding to dim light in the trailer. She realized she was without her father her world. She shook her head and closed her eyes, opening them once more to see Smithton again. Kitty was not in control of her destiny.

CHAPTER FOUR

Rolling

"The irrefutable ominous clouds overtook the sky as thunder announced the invasion proclaiming victory." E.H.

While Kitty was falling into her safe zone, Smithton was also falling but not into a safe place. Smithton closed his grip on Kitty as he shut his eyes and started to fall into his REM's Gehenna.

His dreams were neither imagined nor felicitous. Smithton relived Hell.

"Fuck you Damian, if you don't have a Ben, I don't have a bag." He yelled as he drove down the road.

Darkness was filling up the sky as it drown day light. The shiny new truck flew down the road on roller coaster tracks.

Smithton was skilled at shaking himself awake once this nightmare started to play. What he could not force from his mind was replaying the memorized version of the actual events.

The memory always started the same,

"It was a good day, I got paid, picked up the town whore, got drunk and high, from there it fucked up," He thought as he lay on the ground thinking about the accident.

He did not pay attention to Kitty when he relived the accounts of the night that ruined his life although she was instrumental in survival.

"Come on Cee!" He can here himself say as he laughed and pushed the barley sixteen year olds, head down and toward his penis. He remembered driving down the road with one hand on the wheel and the other on the back of his muse's, when high's, head. The last of the positive emotions play out. He remembered feeling young and invincible.

Bob, his new employer, had just placed him on full time work. He was making extra cash selling drugs and had just had a conversation with a beautiful young girl who saw him for who he saw himself to be, handsome both physically and superficially. Her name was Katherine. Her father Bob, his employer, called her Kitty and sometimes, Kitten. She was fifteen. She floated past him smelling like fresh summer air through the screen door after a storm. His mind drifts away from Kitty once again and back onto the road which was now dark.

"Give me one more bump Smithton and maybe you'll convince me to give you some of my special drug." Cee yells out to him, over the radio playing loudly.

He reached down and in between his legs and pulled out a small bag of white powder. He holds it up in the air and the young girl grabs at it as he pulls it away.

"Ahh, not until I get head, Cee. I know you by now you lil' coke whore." He says as he looks over at her frustrated reaction.

"Shut that dog up." He yelled as he can hear the high pitched bark of his mother's poodle from the back seat.

"Fuck her, I should'a told her to pick her own bitch up." He added before he yelled, "Shut the fuck up."

The young girl replied, "You should've dropped her off home before comin' to get me, it's your fault."

The baggie of coke floats overtop of his head and the young girl's hair brushes across his face as the truck made descended down the hill.

The sound of guardrail is the last sound he remembers. He never hit the brakes. There was no screeching of rubber, just the sound of the metal of his truck forcing through the metal guardrail.

Smithton opens his eyes to see the night sky in clear vision.

"There is no windshield." He thought as he looks to the right, "There is no window, there are no windows."

When Smithton dreams about the accident, he sees himself dragging the young girl behind him to safety. Outside of his denying thoughts, the truth is that he fell out of the truck, confused and scared, and ran into the tree line.

He does not look for the young girl or his mother's dog.

Hours later he stumbled onto the picturesque front porch of his parent's home and sleeps on the swing until he sees a bright light in his eyes.

"Smithton Taylore." The deep voice calls to him.

He opens his eyes to see two police men. They ask again, "Is your name Smithton Taylor."

Smithton opens his eyes and is finally able to stop the replay.

Kitty is sleeping quietly in his arms. He can barely feel her breath on his hair of his forearm.

He reaches over and puts his hand on her neck, at her pulse point, to assure himself that his angel is still breathing.

Smithton checks for Kitty's breathe every time he awakes before her.

He paused, his heart races and he holds his breath to feel for her pulse.

He feels the soft beating underneath of his fingers and lets out a sigh of relief.

He turns slightly over onto his back and takes her limp body with him.

As he stares up at the popcorn looking ceiling tiles of the trailer, he remembers once again, "the event."

He is standing on Bob's porch the next day, with the same cloths on his back.

He strikes the screen door as it reverberates back from the force of his knuckles.

"Smithton, we're not working today, it's Saturday." Bob calls out from behind the decorous ornate screen door.

"I need some help Bob." Replied Smithton.

Smithton blinks and looks over at Kitty. She is still.

He slides his arm from underneath her light frame, without disturbing her, and sits up.

"Fuck this." He says to himself.

He stands up and stretches his long slender frame toward the ceiling. He reaches into his pocket and pulls out the small amount of meth that he had been rationing.

He holds the baggie up to his nose and turns it inside out at the base of his nostril and snorts a strong breath.

He paces, and waits, to roll on and through, surviving once more, his personal Gehenna.

Kitty feels that she is laying on her own, she rolls over, then opens her eyes wide and focuses on Smithton; her angel.

"Hey," he says he turns and sees her sit up.

"Kitten, you are my white light." He adds, with all of the conviction within his soul; meth raging, emotions ebbing.

Kitty looks at him. She does not take time to register the sentiment he just gave her. She asks,

"Smithton, that nark, ya' know who I'm on about?"

Smithton's pupils as large as the full moon, focuses on her beauty and replies as if hypnotized.

"Ya, and?" He asks of her.

Kitty painfully extracts the words from her mind post dream.

"Did you fuck his old lady?" She asks.

Smithton saw Kitty as an angel that peered through his soul and exposed all of his sins. He awkwardly replied, "Why are you askin' me this Kitten?"

"I dunna know." She paused as she gathered more strength.

"I had a dream that you did."

Smithton looks at her omnisciently and asks, "Did you dream this just now? As I was holdin' ya?"

"Yes," she replied. "Well, did you? Is that why you were callin' her a whore n' stuff?"

Her demeanor was quiet and calm.

Smithton began to feel the pressure and guilt rise within him.

"Are you askin' me this 'cause of Cee, Kitty? I confessed to you 'bout that." He spoke with a stone flat expression. The irony was his eyes were emoting with guilt.

"I forgave you from all that stuff Smithton. I just need to know, 'cause we haven't been, like that...since leavin' that park." She spoke with forthright conviction.

Smithton's mind, tricked him, convinced him, surrounded him and ambushed him.

"She knows." He thought.

He did not reply. He looked past her and saw Cee, lifeless on the ground. Her left leg bent underneath her torso just as she landed after being flown from the truck. Her right leg bent out from the hip at a 90 degree angle.

He remembered kneeling down in front of open flowing wounds as they flowed with her scarlet red blood.

He saw himself as he leaned down closer to her lip. She no longer had two. The bottom half of her face had been partially removed from sharp glass as she flew through the windshield.

"Is she breathing?" He remembers thinking to himself as he leaned into to her heinous deformed face.

A large piece of glass was stuck into her skin where the point of her nose was.

Smithton reached down and removing it, thinking it would allow air to flow through the holes in face that were once her nostrils.

There was not air, no sign of life or breath with in her lifeless body.

He placed the shard glass into his pocket and fell to the ground beside her body. His hands instinctually reached for the ground for stability as he gagged and retched. Remnants of stale alcohol flowed from his mouth and onto the ground as he threw up beside her body.

"Smithton, are you gonna answer me?" Kitty yelled out.

He lost memory of the question. With a blank stare on his face he could do nothing but look at her. He stared, and then swallowed, as if he could choke down the memories.

All he could think of saying what was in heart. He spoke sincerely,

"Kitty, I love you."

After this one sentiment he turned away from her and walked out the door, slamming it behind him the tinny rattle resonated within the empty trailer. The sound echoed a scream of loneliness once again for Kitty.

She just looked at the closed door, then around at the empty room. She backed into the corner and sat cradling her knees with her forehead on her knees. She prayed for strength and guidance.

She prayed for guidance from her father. "I will go adventuring out tomorrow." She said as if the directive came from her father.

CHAPTER FIVE

The Last Trailer on the Left

"At this minute our destiny, unbeknownst, is moving toward an intersection." E.H.

Kelsey redialed Meadow's number a third time but was once again greeted with an annoying ring back tone. She held the phone away from her ear and looked down at it.

"Damn it, Meadow. I need you to pick up the phone."

She let out a loud sigh of disappointment as she dropped the phone onto the passenger side seat. Kelsey and Meadow met right after the end of Meadows marriage. Their friendship and love affair has endured time and crisis thrown at them by life. They are always connected be it mind, body or spirit.

A sudden loud car horn startled her away from her thoughts. She looked up to see that the red light had turned to green. She jumped up and sneered into the rear view mirror at the large SUV behind her. Just as she started to press the gas, her phone rang. She picked it up without looking at the caller, pressing her foot heavily on the gas pedal

"Meadow?"

"No, this is Lee, sorry,"

Lee was a close mutual friend of the couple. I'm sorry, I thought you were Kels," Meadow said jovially and warmly.

They both laughed for a second. Lee went on to say, ""I need to know if you want the trailer for this coming weekend or next, 'cause there is some friend of Mark's wanting it for hunting."

Kelsey replied, "No, We definitely want it. We wanted it from this Thursday until Sunday. Do I need to give you a deposit?"

Lee laughed, "Yes please, $5,000.00."

Kelsey replied as she laughed, "Okay bitch." The two laughed before Lee said,

"No, when you get back you can just settle up with me,"

"Great, now which one is it again, can you text?" me the address?" Kelsey asked, conscious that her car was suddenly going seventy-five in a sixty-five. She eased off the gas a little but stayed focused back on the phone conversation.

"It's the second to the last trailer on the left, 209, as you pull in and around the circle," Lee explained before concluding, "I can text you the address."

Kelsey was passing the car in front of her in the right lane as Lee spoke.

"Got it, it's at the end on the left," she blurted out, trying to navigate through the slower vehicles. Kelsey was not concentrating on the address as much as she was avoiding a car accident.

"Idiots. They're all idiots," she said loudly as she passed the slowest one.

"Alright Kels, I knowing your driving skills. I think you should concentration on driving instead of talking," Lee said with a smart but jesting undertone to her voice.

"Very funny. Hey, thanks for letting us have this for the long weekend. We need it. Things have been really rough since the failed IVF attempt. Meadow is stressed, I am stressed." She paused. "It will be good."

Lee asked, "Was this your third attempt?"

Kelsey groaned. "Yes. I am going to suggest that we move to adoption. This is one reason I wanted to rent the trailer from you. It is so beautiful there. We can relax, walk, and talk about adopting. It's crazy to keep putting Meadow, more so than me, through this." Kelsey explained. She knew Lee, being a mother of two, would understand.

"You two will find the right answer, and the rental is on me."

"No, really, you don't have to." Kelsey no soon replied when she was cut short by her friend.

"Yes, I want to. If you argue, I'll tell Mark to rent it to the hunters; I know how that would kill you, thinking of them skinning Bambi." Lee changed the tone again to one of levity.

Kelsey noticed her exit and jerked the wheel to the right, cutting off the driver in the right hand lane, to make her exit at the last second.

"Shit, thanks Lee, I've gotta go before I crash," Kelsey said, breathing a little too hard as she glanced in the rear view mirror at the driver whom she just cut off, giving her the finger.

"Okay, the key will be in the mulch area to the right of the door where the flowers are. I'll have the cleaning company do a quick cleaning before you get there. Love you two, have fun." Lee hung up the phone with these last words.

Kelsey made it to her office and drove into her parking spot. She shut off the engine and looked down once again at her phone to see if maybe she missed a call from Meadow. They had been partners for ten years and wanted to have a child of their own. After failed marriages, establishing successful careers, and surviving stigmas, Meadow decided that she wanted to have a private donor supply sperm so that she could have a child. Kelsey had two children that no longer spoke with her since leaving her marriage and living proudly as a gay woman. She longed to exercise her maternal skills once again.

The unfortunate reality was that Meadow was past child bearing age and having difficulty conceiving. She was physically at a stage in her life that was difficult for her to conceive and carry a child to term. Meadow felt that she sacrificed much of her life and missed her chance of having children. Meadow spent much of her adult life in an abusive marriage where she found escape working and traveling extensively with her job. Her measure of success was through financial and scholastic achievements. Meadows ex husband misused, abused and denied her of having children. Meadow carries anger and hostility toward her ex husband for his role in her childless life. Meadow mother's her clients now and finds great joy and fulfillment in this pursuit.

Kelsey was shocked back to reality when she felt cold water creeping into the crevasses of her shoe, soaking her sock.

"Shit!" Kelsey spat under her breath. She had opened her car door and stepped out and into a large puddle of water that collected in the low spot on the asphalt. Once again, her phone rang out and without looking at the caller she answered it anticipating it to be Meadow.

"Where have you been?" she blurted out before waiting to be greeted by the caller.

"Jeez back off, Kelsey. What's the crisis?" Meadow asked with casual irreverence.

Kelsey's relief in hearing Meadow's voice silenced her for a moment.

"Hello?" Meadow asked.

"Sorry. I spoke with Lee, and we can have the rental for this weekend," she said, stepping over the puddle and heading to her office building.

Meadow's tone changed dramatically, "I can't go until Sunday. I am committed to work Thursday through Friday."

"Well if we don't go this weekend, we can't go until the end of January. Once this holiday season kicks off, I have to work," Kelsey explained.

There was a short pause from both of them as they searched their minds for a solution to the problem.

"Why don't you go, relax, take walks and enjoy the good weather?" Meadow suggested. "It's supposed to be nice this weekend. I'll come down Saturday as soon as I can."

Kelsey was not impressed with spending any time off work without Meadow but knew that she needed the break as much as Meadow did, and if they didn't go now, they would not be going for months.

"Well, I guess that's better than nothing." Kelsey's disappointment was apparent. "Shit, I have to run, honey. I am running late and I have a meeting, five minutes ago."

"Okay Kels, call me when you have a minute. I love you."
***
After Kelsey had disconnected the call, Meadow placed the phone in her back pocket as she walked down the hall to perform her room and patient inspections.

"Hello, Timothy," she called out with an uplifting tone to her voice and bright smile on her beaming face.

The ninety-four year man pulled his head up slightly and turned it to look at his friend and caregiver. Timothy had features that reminded Meadow of her father. Her mind wondered for a moment as it did more often than not when she visited Timothy,

"I miss you Dad. I miss talking with you. I miss your advice," and just before emotion would take control of her demeanor she focused back on the frail old man.

"You look so handsome today, if I were a younger woman Timothy," Meadow joked with her patient as a visual wave of hope and sheer joy flowed over his physical posture. Timothy struggled to find the strength to sit up in his wheel chair. Meadow reached down to help him. Timothy's eyes spoke of the mutual sentiment. Meadow imagined him saying, "If I could get out of this chair and walk, I would embrace all of my visitors with open arm while and kiss them on each cheek."

Timothy was a proud Italian man who embraced people warmly with a hug and two kisses. The people who visited him looked past his white glazed cataracts and saw bright eyes shining through to a beautiful soul.

Meadow placed her hand on top of his, rubbing it gently as she asked,

"Let's go outside today, Timothy. Maybe I can get you get on up off those wheels and walk with me a little. The weather is beautiful."

Her mind had moved past all of her personal issues focused solely on the fragile old, dying man that she was committed to cheering up. Meadow often told Kelsey that the true gift of her job was how it gave her a sense of purpose and lifted her spirits on a daily basis.

"Alright," his small voice said. "But only if you'll dance with me." He paused for a second, and then added, "The jitterbug."

His comment surprised Meadow, causing her laugh out loud and have goose bumps on her arms rise. She tried to contain her thoughts and replied,

"Well alright, it's a date," she replied, wheeling him out of the room and feeling as if she just conquered the world's biggest crisis.

Meadow however could not deny her memory with Timothy's unexpected 'Jitterbug comment.' She felt happy as she recalled her father's words,

"Meadow place your hand on mine and follow my feet, let me led." Her father instructed as he taught her to jitterbug one Saturday. The two of them spent hours rehearsing the steps the week before Meadow's first Junior High School Dance.

Meadow heard the laughter, the music and felt the touch of her father's loving hand. This time she could not control a rush of emotion that surfaced unexpectedly from this one comment.

She looked up at the lights as she turned her patients wheel chair to wheel Timothy down the hall, battling to stop her welled up eyes from allowing tears to flow.

"Get a grip Meadow, we don't want to explain this one and look like a crazy woman." She said to herself.

She looked down at Timothy and decided to use this moment his benefit. She asked,

"What was your favorite song, to Jitterbug" to?

The two laughed and spoke as they made their way down the hall.

"This is my purpose." Meadow firmly said to herself as she smiled looking down at the beautiful old man sitting in the chair.

"This is how I chose to close today's nostalgic moment.

With this Meadow carried on with her day caring for others.

CHAPTER SIX

Pristine Adulation

"A harden heart is merely atrophy, not paralyzed." E.H.

Smithton pulled the aluminum chair out and sat down quietly, looking at the cluttered fiberboard desk, scattered with papers, paperclips, a football bobble head, and a picture of a gawky teenage girl in braces. He thought, "This place looks like every other shitty job center."

"This is a strange request for work, Mr…"

There was an awkward pause from the heavyset woman reading the application handed to her by Smithton's hand. His fingernails yellowed with black dirt under the nails and in the cuticles.

She began pronouncing her his name, "Smit

Smithton interrupted her, "Smithton Taylore."

"Ok Mr. Taylore," she could not conceal her annoyance with his interruption. "How is it you came to request such," she paused, "Well, nasty work?" She asked as she pushed up pink, square plastic rimmed glasses that were sliding off the bridge of her stout nose. Smithton glanced at the center buttons of her blouse exposing rolls of fat stuffed in her milk colored skin.

"It was the only work I could find Madame." he replied as he looked up and into her eyes as he replied.

She looked at his dirty hair and the soiled, wrinkled t-shirt that looked as if he had just woke up in it. The truth was that he did. He saw the job center while driving and pulled right in instead of going straight to the trailer park.

"Why did you leave that employ?" she asked with a condescending tone.

Smithton blinked once. "Because they had cut backs. Last one in, first one out. That whole thing."

"I can see if we have any openings for this specific field. It is deer season and not many people want to pick up road kill, and since this is rural Maryland, we have our fill of road kill this time of year." She placed his application into a manila envelope, wrote his name on the top tab and set it aside.

"Alright then." She did not reach out her hand or stand up. "I will call you if I have anything come up." She sat unmoving, staring at him.

Smithton thought to himself, I guess the fat bitch hog wants me to get up. He stood up and held out his hand. That'll give her some exercise.

She reached out with hesitation.

"Nice to meet you, Mr. Taylore," she said as she shook his hand. He smiled at her as politely as he could and then walked out of the office into the partially abandon strip mall.

"I need to get a real job," he told himself, unlocking his truck door a few minutes later. He got in and reached around under the seat, pulling out a single cigarette and lighting it with the cigarette lighter on the dash

He knew a little ways down the road was a concrete plant, and when he saw it, he pulled into the parking lot and got out of the truck. The plant was noisy and busy as concrete trucks were being loaded with concrete, sprayed down and supplied for the next run. He looked around for the office.

"Can I help you?" a thin man in a flannel shirt and jeans asked loudly.

Smithton looked around until he spotted the man speaking to him.

"Yes. Sir; I'm lookin' for the office?"

"It's around the other side. Can I help you?" He started walking toward Smithton, and Smithton headed in his direction to meet him halfway.

"As a matter of fact, you can. I am looking for an Industrial Supplier 'round here.". "I am here working from outta town and my boss sent me for some muriatic acid. We're doin' some expose aggregate work at an office park down the road there."

The man raised his eyebrows and whistled quietly. "Yeah, we don't sell supplies like that here, but you can go to George Wilkons."

Smithton put his hands in his front pockets. "I don't have a pen; can you write down an address for me and explain how to get there?" he asked.

"Sure, let me just run to the truck and get a pen and paper. I'll be right back." The man walked away and back to the concrete truck. Smithton stood kicking stones as he waited. After a few minutes passed, the man returned with a piece of paper. He held it out to Smithton as he spoke.

"Here you go. It's back on Route 68 back toward West Virginia. Then take 78. Follow it until you get into the town of—."

Smithton received the paper and placed it in the front pocket of his jeans. Smithton held out his hand and thanked the man, then headed to his truck. The man did likewise, but then turned to Smithton.

"What office park is doing exposed?" he asked, but Smithton was already in the truck, door closed, quickly pulling away from the plant. The man just shrugged.

Smithton drove to the interstate as directed, and once in West Virginia, he observed that he was in a rather derelict neighborhood. As he navigated through the town, turning his head to the left and right down side streets, he noticed a young woman, most likely a prostitute, standing on the sidewalk lazily. He quickly turned his truck down the street without braking. He drove up beside the young girl standing with her back to a garage door of an abandon auto body shop, and she eyed his truck down as he slowed to a stop.

He leaned over and rolled down the window. "Hey, can you give me some directions?"

She stopped texting and took short, unbalanced steps in the platform patent leather knee high boots she wore to the truck. She leaned in to take a closer look at Smithton.

Sure is handsome she said to herself as she looked at his face, lips, and then long frame.

"What kinda' directives are you lookin' fer?" she asked as she smiled and winked. "'Cause I can direct you to Tight and Hard for $150.00."

She replied.

Smithton looked at her and smiled.

"I wasn't lookin' for Tight and Hard but tell me about Suck and Swallow," he replied without blinking his eyes. The prostitute smiled and said, "Seventy-five. Fifty if I like it." She displayed a coy smile teasing on her lips. Smithton's mysterious and outsider aura intrigued the girl, who was so used to the town's regulars.

"Oh, you'll like it," he said as he reached over and opened the truck door. The young girl plopped herself down onto the seat and shut the door, then pointed in front of the car.

"Down here then to the right, then left."

Smithton drove and got hard thinking of the lips of the young prostitute on his dick. Smithton loved being sucked off. He never asked Kitty to perform such acts on him; he could never ask her to lower herself to such a level as Cee, the whore who he used for fucking, the whore that caused the accident that ruined his life. He made love to Kitty, but this did not fulfill his needs and sexual desires.

He reached down with his right hand and shifted his stiff penis away from the center zipper of his jeans. The young prostitute looked over as he touched his penis. She leaned over to him.

"Let me do that for you," she said as she placed her hand on the lump in his jeans. Smithton laughed and looked over at her. He saw Cee. The girl sat up and unzipped her purse. As she rifled through the small blue satin bag, she asked Smithton if he wanted a bump of heroin.

"It's gonna be another twenty-five for it, though."

Smithton laughed. "Twenty five for a bump of heroin? You must be on the stuff. That'll be the day; I'll fuck my hand first. Have any AMP?"

"Yup, but it's thirty fer that." She pulled out lipstick.

"Let's do some," he said as he contained his rush thinking about the drug and not the imminent blowjob. Although Smithton loved sex, he loved meth more. The thought of the drug surging through his bloodstream made him excited beyond what a hard dick could portray.

The young girl took the lid off the lipstick and turned it upside down. Two baggies dropped out: one pink, one clear.

She stuffed the pink one back in as she said, "My pink lady will have to wait."

She removed the bread tie from the baggie and turned her right pinkie fingernail over and into the bag. The fake, exaggeratedly long nail scooped up the powder, and she took a quick sniff.

She repeated the movements and reached her hand over to Smithton, who had pulled behind the building the young girl directed him to. Surveying his surroundings quickly, he knew it best to lock the door. The prostitute held out her hand and he took it, bringing her pinkie finger to his nose and taking a big sniff. He then reached past her and locked her door, as well. The prostitute looked at him with dismay.

"Relax, darlin'. I don't need to be jumped back here by the big bad wolf."

He leaned back over and placed his hands on the steering wheel. He laid his head back onto the seat and closed his eyes. The young girl touched his penis tentatively.

"Not yet," he snapped. "Let it peak first."

The young girl did as she was told, waiting while Smithton drifted and surged. He saw red fur. The poodle's white fur was blood stained. He ran past the small, still body that lay in the grass.

"Now," he said as he kept his eyes closed, as his mind stayed back in the past far away from his adulated Kitty. Minutes passed like seconds.

"Come on! Come on! Come on, Cee!" he yelled out as the young prostitute brought him to orgasm. He felt the rush of the drug simultaneously with the release from his orgasm. He opened his eyes after a few seconds to see the young strange whore. She looked at him with a grin on her face.

"That will be $50.00," she said with laughter.

Smithton grabbed a piece of garbage off the floor of the truck and a pen that was in the visor. He scribbled on the crumpled up paper, then handed it to prostitute.

"Here is your pay; now get the fuck out of my truck before I cut out your little serpent tongue."

The prostitute looked at him as she grimaced.

"Are you for fucking real? My Daddy will fuckin' kill you."

"I think your Daddy will want me more than your dirty lil' cunt," he shot back, a detached smile curling his lips. Smithton knew he could sell crank better than anyone else. This girl was merely the means to the source; the blow job was a bonus. What Smithton really wanted was to get to the person supplying her with the meth.

"Now get out of my truck before I get my blade and make my threat a fuckin' harsh reality." He reached over and unlocked the door and shoved it open with the palm of his hand. Eyes blazing, he gave her one last look before she jumped out of the truck. He pulled the door shut, shifted into drive, and spun out of the dead end street. Once he was back on the main road he gathered his bearings and rolled with the high, to the Industrial Supply store.

Trying not to raise attention at the supplier, Smithton purchased enough red phosphorous, hydiodic acid, and hydrogen chloride to cook enough meth for his own consumption. He knew that neither the trailer that they were squatting in nor Kitty would allow for enough production to sell. That's where the whore came in. Smithton would just sit back and wait to be hunted by her Daddy, his new employer.

CHAPTER SEVEN

Two Percent Milk

"Needs that becomes primary will keep one living as an addict."
E.H.

Hunger persuaded Kitty's conscious mind to abandon the replay of the visions of her father. Her regression was intrusively breeched by the pain in her upper abdomen.

Kitty thought as she acknowledged the twang of pain,

"When was the last time I ate?"

With her head still perched on her forearms, her mind moved past her father's memory as she concentrated on counting backward on her fingers to remember the date.

She lifted her head as conversed with herself.

Kitty's personality was fractioned. Cracks in her shattered personality revealed the past life she spent with her father, then those of the conflicting ones between her current life and the ones she wanted to become.

"God, I need to eat. I need food for Smithton." She thought as she stood up and reached into her pocket. She pulled out the cash given to them from the neighbor.

She shuffled through the worn used notes, counting up the worth.

She strained her mind, tired and malnourished, to remember the food store they passed while entering the neighborhood. Kitty did not own nor have the luxury of having a car so her mind worked in terms of converting minutes into miles that would be spent walking.

"Ten minutes, that is about a quarter of a mile." She thought as she stuffed the money back into her front pocket. She looked up and scanned the small damp room looking for her backpack. She remembered bringing it in when they first arrived.

Once spotted, she walked over and strained picking the overstuffed black nylon pouch. She was interrupted when she noticed a small blue object semi hidden between the fibers of the dirty brown shag carpet. She bent down and picked it up.

It was a blue LEGO piece. She handled the object and smiled as her mind once again regressed.

"God, I loved these." She recalled as she fondly saw her father handing her two quarters one long past bright and sunny summer morning.

"The McName's." She remembered, "They had a garage sale. I wanted the used box of LEGO's so bad."

She saw herself running through the various shaped yards of the neighboring lawns, through shrubs, leaving scratches on her ankles.

"Dad was asleep on the couch, on his back." She remembered, as her memory recalled the event in full vibrancy.

Kitty did not allow herself to enter real time. That would leave her destitute and lonely.

"Dad, can I have $.50, it's really really important." She whispered out loud.

She referred to her Dad's response as she shook his arm.

"What is it for Kitten?" She heard him say while his eyes remained closed.

"A really important tool," She replies weaving a story to convince the man who would have given her all the objects in the world.

"So I can build things like you do." Her lips whispered the words as she teared up, feeling a swell of pride and adoration for her father's talent, just like she did as far back as she could remember.

The LEGO piece tumbled around in her hand before grasping it so tightly that it placed red lines of indentation upon her pale skin.

She forced herself to move onwards leaving her past in the back of her mind. She picked up the backpack and walked down the hall looking into the other rooms.

She and Smithton had performed the invasion of others home several times making it routine. So much that when either arrived they did not bother to look into the other rooms of the trailer. It was standard for the trailers to have a kitchen, bathroom, bedroom, sometimes two bedrooms and baths.

Kitty opened the first door on left revealing a bathroom. She noted a soiled pink shag rug still remain around the toilet, on the toilet seat and on the tank of the toilet. A matching shag rug lay in front of the old green laminated cabinet. She opened each door scavenging for items, hoping to discover toothpaste or soap.

She opened and closed the first two cabinets with disappointment, finding them vacant.

She pulled open the drawer sliding an item to the front. She looked down and picked up a plastic box containing dental floss. She opened the lid, a thin white string wrapped around the metal cutter.

"Good, there is still floss in here," She thought as she set the container on the countertop and closed the drawer.

She lifted her backpack up and unzipped a small front pocket, put it aside items until she found her toothbrush.

She lifted the used toothbrush up, with abated bristles brown bristles, and turned the handle to the faucet on the sink as she wondered to herself,

"Will there be water, please let there be water."

When she opened her eyes, a small stream of yellowish brown colored water tapered from the tap. She placed her toothbrush under it, devoid of toothpaste, and brushed her teeth.

She laid the toothbrush on the countertop and looked into the mirror revealed white speckled dots from the last occupant. She looked up higher to the reflection of her face.

She reached up and smoothed her once shiny, curly, fresh smelling hair. She did not bother to find her comb. Her reflection revealed a displaced vision on her true appearance. In reality her hair was flat, greasy and saturated with the odor of Smithton's stale cigarette smoke.

She rinsed her mouth out then spit into the unkempt sink covered in a film of soap and dirt.

Kitty did not have the courage to see the reflection of a young woman who was living as a vagrant. She did not see the dark circles that had formed a puddle beneath her lifeless eyes, or the blemishes that dotted her once pristine skin.

Dismissively, she turned away from her reflection. She placed her arms through the straps of her backpack and walked out of the bathroom and out of the stranger surroundings.

Kitty walked for over 8/10 of a mile before reaching the Food King. The sight of the neon crown inspired her to push forth. The tennis shoes that she was wearing were a size too large, blisters had formed on the back of heals. The skin had fillet off exposing her raw skin that rubbed more and rawer with each stride.

Kitty approached the food store with a pep talk to herself to give her much needed confidence.

"Woman, with all shiny painted nails and COACH purses, set perfectly in their lil' carts are gonna judge me. Like I'm a nonperson or somethin'. Well f-you, I'm not." She said to herself as she walked through the parking lot watching women place bag, after bag into mini vans and SUV's. As Kitty walked abnormally close to the back of each car she thought,

"If one of 'em walk to the front, I can grab at least one bag and keep walkin'." She said as she tried to pick the right person loading their car.

Kitty's stomach ached, her mind raced, her confidence waned.

Kitty rolled the blue LEGO between her fingers, rotating the plastic piece diverting her insecurities.

"My life was this normal, better in fact." She thought.

"Who are they, I'll tell you, lucky."

She came within 10 feet of a middle age woman concentrating on the conversation she was having on her cell phone. Her new black BMW trunk flipped open and filled with groceries.

She turned and walked to the driver side door leaving her trunk unmanned.

Kitty saw a gallon of milk left in the cart. Ironically, she was experiencing nervous anticipation of the rush an addict feels.

She kept pace, did not stop, reached into the cart and grabbed the gallon of milk, and kept walking as she placed the cold, wet with sweat plastic carton under her oversized shirt.

She held the carton close to her skin, although she formed goose bumps along the forearm of each arm, she could only think of satisfying her excessive thirst.

"Walk to the back of the building." She said as she felt the anxiety of ambiguity.

"Is she behind me? Did she see me?" She repeated as she kept stride as she felt physically ill from hunger coupled with stress.

Kitty did not steal pearls, fur coats or other luxury items of inconsequence but yet she did; milk was a luxury item to her. Her need for food was consuming and primary.

She walked out of site and to the back of building. Once she felt safe she leaned against the cement block building and squatted to the ground, so she could appear even smaller.

She removed the milk carton that was concealed under the button down plaid print shirt she was given from GOODWILL. The days of Kitty wearing pretty pink dresses with satin bows ended, yet in her eyes she wore the floral patchwork smock dress she wanted for her 10th birthday. The one she wore until she outgrew the shoulder size.

She struggled to open the top as her soiled fingers lost grip. Dirt from her hands and fingers transferred to the wet diaphanous jug. She picked up the bottom of her shirt and used it to grip the plastic cap.

She opened the milk and lifted the opening to her mouth. She gulped down as many times as she could stomach.

Once she felt full, she set the jug beside her and lifted her head up to the blue sky above.

"Daddy, I'm just hungry." She said out loud.

She put the cap back and picked it up, she walked over to a dumpster and set it behind it, hidden from site.

"I have $40.00." She thought.

"I can buy 40—$1.00 items." She thought as she limped back in view of the population.

She stopped and knelt down to look at her bloody heal.

"Ouch," she said, as she breathed in air as if it soothed the pain. She placed her heal down onto the top of the shoe forcing the shoe to crumble under the weight of her foot.

She shuffled with her feet close the ground so the shoe would not fall off now that the back was not around her foot.

Kitty grabbed an abandon cart and pushed it through the doors and they welcomed shoppers into the store that embodied stress and insecurity to her. Her heart pounded as she felt fear. Fear she felt since being homeless. She looked anxiously at women passing her the aisles, answering her questions.

"She knows I am homeless. She's lookin' down at me. She is judgin' me."

She walked slowly through the aisles looking for 1 dollar items to fill her cart. The majority of items filling her cart were cans of soup and boxes of macaroni and cheese.

She checked out to the apathetic stare of the young cashier and walked out of the store carrying several plastic bags of heavy cans of food.

She could not afford the luxury of Band-Aids, shampoo or other items that she took for granted her entire life. She walked out of the store much different that she walked in. An exit, she was humiliated, hungry and dreading the painful walk back to the trailer park. At the time of her entrance into the store, Kitty dreaded what lay ahead. At the time of her exit from the store, she loathed what she had become. There still remained harden morals to her edifice when she had lucid moments of reflection of her actions. This was one of them.

CHAPTER EIGHT

Indian Summer

"Memories consume half of our heart." E.H.

The late day sun roasted the top layer of the striated leafy ground emitting the unmistakable smell of autumn. Kitty shook her head to the left quickly, shaking her hair from resting over her eyes and impeding her vision. She stopped and set down the numerous bags of grocery items. She reached into the heaviest bag and pulled out a can of condensed soup. She peeled the red and white label from the tin can and swung her torso behind her.

She lifted her heel and stuck the soup label in her shoe buffering her heel from the canvas shoe. She winced with pain when the paper touched her bloody heel.

She tried to softly slide her foot back into the shoe but the pain remained excruciating. She turned and picked up the bags, holding several to each hand and continued limping back toward the trailer park.

With her head bowed low, squinting from the bright summer rays, limping and struggling with every step. She reached a part of the road where it became narrow and bordered by a guardrail on each side. Over the roadside was a weed filled, stony and steep embankment.

She tried to pull her arms in closer to her body but the cumbersome weight of the bags caused her to bang the numerous cans into her knees, tripping clumsily. She lost her balance and her right leg slid uncontrollably away from her left.

The bags became uncontrollable and the heaviest one ripped open, spewing tin cans onto the road, which rolled down the hillside.

"No, please." She screamed as she witness her much revered cargo roll away.

She quickly dropped the bags onto the narrow roadside and leapt over the guardrail to retrieve the cans before the rolled to the bottom.

She slid onto her elbows, the stones scraped the skin from them.

"Ough," she screamed as she continued to slide several feel along her back.

She braced her bloody heel forward catching it on a large stone. The stone shocked every nerve ending but stopped her from sliding further.

She rolled over to her stomach and grabbed two of the cans before they rolled past her. She picked up the bottom of her shirt and cradled the cans.

Bleeding, in pain riddled with mental defeat she partially stood up. She limped back up the hillside on three of her four extremities. Her left hand holding up her shirt securing the few cans that she was able to salvage. The right grabbing at thorny, dried and sharp weeds to help pull her weary body back up to the road.

As she reached the top of the embankment, she immediate spotted a white police car with flashing lights pulled off the road and behind her groceries.

"Shit." she mumbled as she instinctually dropped back down to her stomach.

"Mamame." She heard a male voice call out. She did not reply.

"Can I help you? Are you alright?" The voice said as she kept her nose in the stony ground.

"This is car 725, I need medical assistance on Timmons Road." She heard the voice say.

"Fuck, fuck, fuck. It's a cop." She screamed within the confines of her mind.

"Think, Kitty think." She stopped herself from panicking although her heart raced and her throat stiffened preventing her from immediately responding.

"I'm okay, I don't need an ambulance." She yelled back as she lifted her head up.

The police office placed the radio back in his belt loop and stepped over the guard, spreading his legs, bracing his body. He allowed gravity to work in his favor, squatting low and sliding slowly toward her while he held out is hand toward her.

"Grab my hand." He called out to her.

Kitty reached up and grabbed his hand as he lifted her off of her knees.

The strong police officer towed her slender battered frame up the embankment.

He stepped back over the guardrail and reached his other hand around to assist Kitty over the metal obstacle. She was still holding the two cans of soup in her shirt.

"Miss are you shore you are not hurt, I have already called for assistance. You're bleeding." He said firmly without compassion as he profiled her.

His eyes looked over her dirty hair, soiled clothes down to the paper sticking out of her back of her shoe.

"No, I'm okay. Honestly." She quietly replied.

"Where do you live Miss?" He asked her with a slight tone of prejudice and assumption that she was homeless.

"I am just passing through town to my Aunt's house right over the Maryland border." She quickly replied wise and arrogant.

Kitty was determined to stay one step ahead of him.

The police officer spoke sternly,

"Miss, I will need to see some identification."

"What the fuck did I do wrong?" she thought while replying,

"I don't have any. Is that a problem? Did I break some law by falling over the hillside?" She added with strong dissent.

"Miss are these your groceries?" He asked without answering her question staying on focus to his own agenda.

"Yes, they are." She replied impetuously.

"Can you show me your receipt?" He asked as he stood with his legs slightly apart, hands on his hips, right one inches away from the 9mm pistol loaded in holster.

"Kitty watched his right hand movement. She looked at the butt of the gun and noticed that the leather strap was still snapped behind it.

The police officer noticed every eye movement that she made. He watched her as she surveyed his gun. This only caused his stance to stiffen and his suspicions to purport.

"Miss, I have to ask you again, do you have a receipt for these groceries?" He glared at her and waited for her response.

Kitty shifted her weight and leaned her butt against the guardrail. She did not respond.

"Fuck this, fuck him. Let him wonder, God, I hope I didn't lose it over this fucking hillside." She thought as her bloody right hand reached tentatively into her front pocket.

She felt a piece of paper and sighed with relief.

She pulled out the folded paper and handed it forward without speaking. She looked up and directly into his eyes.

He reached out and removed it from her hands. He did not open it,

"Miss, will you please follow me back to the car." He directed.

"Why?" Kitty asked, "I just gave you the receipt. Would you like to tell me what I did wrong? Or is being poor a crime in MARYLAND?"

The police officer coldly once again dismissed her question.

"Miss, if you don't want to talk from my patrol car we can talk from the station. It's up to you."

"Fine, I did nothing wrong." She said as she stood up from the guardrail.

"Smithton will kill me. This can't be happening,'" She thought with intensity and self-composure while internally she was in a state of pandemonium.

The police officer pulled out his radio and spoke.

"Cancel that ambulance to Timmons Rd. Copy."

The scratchy reply affirmed his request as Kitty listened with vigor.

"Thank God for that." She thought as she stooped her body down and into the back of the patrol car.

The door shut and she sat back, terrified of the possibilities.

The police officer opened the driver side door and sat down. The radio constantly turning on and off with replies and requests that made no sense, as the dispatcher communicated in code.

She watched the back of the police officer's head. She heard him open the receipt and look over it.

He turned his head and spoke to her through the metal mesh screen,

"Miss, stay put and let me look through your bags."

"Whatever." Kitty replied as she glared at him without blinking.

She watched as he walked over to the disheveled, scattered bags. He reached behind his back and pulled out his batten, snapped it forward and extending it. As he riffled through the bags Kitty was devising her responses and excuses.

"Wait and see what he asks. Maybe he will leave this alone now." She tried to think positively although she had looming doubt.

The police officer walked back over to car, opened his door and sat down.

This time he questioned her as he pulled out a metal boxed clipboard from the dashboard. He pulled out a pen from the top and asked,

"What is your first name Miss?"

"Why? Why are you writing a report? I have rights." She affirmed.

"Miss, you can make this easy and answer my questioning or I can take you in." He replied.

"Why?" She screamed this time, in opposed to the level demeanor that she had been portraying.

The robotic police officer reached forward and put the car into drive.

Kitty panicked and reached for the door handle. Her hand felt a smooth surface devoid of a door handle. She burst out in tears and sobbed as she asked, "What did I do?"

The officer finally spoke to Kitty.

"Miss, I am questioning a few things with your groceries. One, why do you have crystal drain cleaner? Two, you said you have a receipt but this receipt does not have a gallon of milk on it and your bags contain milk." The officer spoke cryptically.

Kitty froze. She did not stop to think about the milk. She was so focused on the crystal drain cleaner being her only trap. She thought to herself, "Fuck. Smithton—fuck." She spoke up, "Let me explain." She started with as her emotions gave way, "I can explain."

"You can explain when get to the station." He answered as the patrol car inched forward until it closed the gap between it and the groceries. The car jerked forward into park and the officer stepped out. He walked up to the bags and picked them up. He walked to the back of the patrol car to the driver side. He opened the door and placed the bags on the floor.

"Oh my God, what is gonna happen to me?" she said in a soft almost inaudible voice.

When the officer got back into the car he put it back into drive and made a u-turn, away from the trailer park, away from what she currently knew as home. It was however a place that she would never be able to admit too and with a person she would have to deny. Smithton lived as if he were a ghost. Kitty lived as if she was a ghost.

She sat back, cried, listened and questioned her fate.

CHAPTER NINE

Kathern Hepburn

"Lies protect the undeserving in our heart denying the righteous."
E.H.

The patrol car drove through picturesque tree lined roads. Kitty laid her forehead against the window and watched as the steam from her breath fogged up the window muting the canvas, then disappeared. She did this repeatedly trying to occupy her thoughts. Kitty wished she could disappear. She was becoming detached to the reality that she was going into a police station, was guilty of theft and possessing questionable items.

"Daddy, please come help me. I was so hungry and thirsty. I didn't think it was wrong. If I'd ask'd that lady for milk or a hand out, I'd be disgracin' my name." She thought to herself as she tears fell from her glazed eyes.

Kitty knew that she could never expose their life. She could never tell her real name or Smithton's or where they were staying, illegally.

"Smithton will go to jail. Who will take care of me?" She asked herself when she thought about his actions. The same actions she dismissed and ignored.

Kitty was aware that the Pennsylvania Drivers license belonged to the neighbor of the last trailer park. She put together various inconsistencies and variable that led to her to suspect that Smithton killed the husband of his last sexual fling, the supposed informer. Kitty's father still lived very much with her from day to day. This was a protective measure for herself preservation. Knowing Smithon's actions was also a matter of self-preservation for Kitty.

Kitty heard that Smithton killed the dealer that screwed him over on $40,000.00 of income for product he cooked. This was at the trailer park before the last trailer park. The theme just kept repeating. She could not get out of the clothes dryer as she put it.

"Daddy, Smithton is my only family, the only one I have left in the world, I know he does wrong but would you rather I be alone?" She asked as she looked upward at the graying sky.

"Oh God, what time is it? She thought at the sight of the suns disappearance."

"Smithton must be in a hell of a fit, freakin' out on me fer sure." Her stomach rumbled and panged from hunger and nerves.

"I can't call him. He'll freak if he finds out I was arrested one block from the trailer." She looked down at her fingernail and raised the stubby dirty, frayed nail to her mouth and chewed on it.

As the patrol car pulled into the police station Kitty looked up at the large ominous structure.

"I better start thinkin' of what I'm gonna say." She said to herself as she prepared to descent the car.

The officer got out and walked back to open her door.

"Let's go." He said as he held open the door.

Kitty got out of the car.

"Turn around." He demanded of her.

"Why?" She asked.

"I'm handcuffing you." He replied.

"Fer what?" She asked.

"Miss, you're not getting it are you? You're being arrested for theft, vagrancy and loitering." He informed her.

Kitty did not respond. She was processing the allegations he just made.

"Loitering? Vagrancy?" She repeated to herself as she led her into the police station.

Kitty thought through the possibilities of what she was going to say.

"I did take the milk. I'll tell them the girl must'a missed it. I was not loitering, I was walking, to my Aunts. I need an address. Shit, I need an address. Wait, if I give them an address they'll check it. Shit."

The cold metal cuffs dug into her petite wrist bones and into existing bruises suffered during the fall.

The police officer walked behind her nudging her in the direction of a small brown metal door that was open. The inside was sparse with only a small metal table and two metal chairs.

"Hey Jimmy, what do you have there?" Another police officer called out as she looked up from a desk as they passed.

"Theft, vagrancy, loitering—all the fun stuff." He replied as he laughed.

"Have a seat." He said as he pushed her down. He walked over to the other side of the desk and slid the metal chair out, clanking it on the ground clumsily.

He threw the metal clip board on the desk and let out a sigh before sitting down, hands on the desk, staring in her eyes.

"Miss, what is your name?" he asked in a firm low voice.

Kitty looked up at him and into his eyes. She hesitated then replied,

"Katherine Hepburn."

"Is that so?" He replied.

"Yes, it is my birth name." Kitty said.

Kitty entered survival mode. She now successfully detached. She was replying and responding based on a movie that she was watching, not as a person in danger of maintaining their freedom. Her inexperienced had been transformed. She was now strong, impermeable, and experienced.

The police officer replied,

"I suggest you think before answering this next question Miss. What is your name?"

Kitty did not hesitate this time.

"You know, "On Golden Pond?" My name is Katherine Hepburn."

"Well Ms. Hepburn, you are not on Golden Pond you are in Deep Creek and I need you to answer my questions. Or, we'll see if Judge O'neil is a fan of yours." He set a pen down on the table and rolled it toward Kitty. "I am going to uncuff you, I want you to write me your statement and you can even put your big fancy autograph at the end."

The officer stood and walked over to Kitty. She did not look at him. Her face remained stoic and emotionless.

When her hands were released, she placed her hands on the desk and focused on what she was going to write.

"Fuck," she thought, "I was going to my aunts, taking her food..." Her mind stumbled through explanations as she siphoned the plausible from the non plausible excuses.

Kitty held the pen and stared at the scuffed worn wall.

She saw her father sitting in front her on the fake suede sofa. She was sitting on the rocking chair that his mother gave him at her death. The inanimate object was the only thing that she ever gave him; it was the only thing Kitty had that resembled a Grandparent.

Kitty never had the stereotypical holiday with Grandma and Grandpa. Kitty did not have a mother. She had her father and her father had scars left from his mother.

Kitty was taught that Bob's mother gave him up for adoption in 1950, not from poverty or addiction, she was devoid of instinctual love. The cause was adoption "just because", "just because" a mother does not want a child, maybe an anomaly from motherhood. Bob lived his entire life trying to forgive a woman who would not be granted absolution from the masses.

Instead of internalizing animosity, Bob externally played the role of the deferential son. Kitty was filled with negative facts that were made positive through the lesson of forgiveness.

This is where she learned that everyone has events or circumstances which turn otherwise normal acceptable behavior into behavior we would never anticipate or believe we were capable of doing. Survival instincts obscured acceptable behavior with Kitty.

"If I only forgive and work through anger and resentment, I can be like my Dad, he always did the right thing." She mumbled out loud in the quiet solitary room.

"Daddy, I am just trying to survive. Smithton's just like Grandma Busche. He's just doin' the best he can. I'm just tryin' to survive and have some good things."

Kitty picked up the pen and wrote,

"I did not steal, I am not a thief."

###

As Smithton loaded the truck with the last bag of red phosphorous from the industrial supply store his cell phone rang out from his back pocket.

"It's about time I heard from her." He thought as he reached around and pulled the phone to his ear.

"Ya." He answered

"Is this Smithton?" A lady on the other end asked.

"Who is callin'?" He replied with paranoia in his voice.

"This is the job center. I made some calls and have an immediate opening for you. Can you work today?" She asked.

Smithton's head was not ready to start working on areas outside of cooking his drugs. He hesitated,

"What kind'a work?" He asked.

"Well," She hesitated, "it's what you wanted. Garret County road kill patrol." She responded with reticence as she was trying to justify her job offer.

"Ya, I'll take it." Smithton accepted as he thought about a hypothesis of imminent need.

"How soon can you start?" She asked with the same uncertain tone.

Smithton assumed she was calling due to immediate need.

"Tomorrow, I guess." He replied.

The job placement woman surmised that Smithton was able and available now she changed her tone,

"You are needed today, as soon as you can. You need to show up at the municipal maintenance shed on 217 Fishal Road. Do you need directions?" She asked.

Smithton did not know his way around the area that well.

He responded with uncertainty, "Can I get directions?"

"Can't you map it on your computer?" She asked with annoyance. Any time spent doing extra work was not welcomed. She already looked down at Smithton for his job request. Her instincts told her that there was something off about him. She wanted to rid herself of this assignment as soon as possible.

She hesitated.

Smithton asked, "Can I stop by and git the directions?"

"I guess." She acquiesced.

Smithton disconnected the call with her affirmation. She was merely a step in securing his and Kitty's security.

As he placed the phone back into his pocket he looked at the graying sky and thought,

"Where the hell is she?"

The woman hung up the phone and failed to shake a consuming feeling of trepidation.

She looked up, and at the photograph of her child. She felt an unexplainable feeling of distress.

She thought to herself,

"There is something not right here."

Her phone rang and she answered it. Her mind moved on and off Smithton and the instinctual badgering of peril.

CHAPTER TEN

Burnt Orange Roses

"Would we begin if we knew the end?" E.H.

"I have to get started down to DEEP CREEK honey." Kelsey said as she stood up and picked up her and Meadow's coffee mug from the kitchen table.

"Can't you wait an hour or two? We can take a walk or hang out a little. I'll go into work a late." Meadow begged of Kelsey.

"Sorry honey, I can't, I have to get there to get the key. I told her I would get it before 10:00 am.

Meadow stood up and placed her arms around the back of Kelsey's waist as she washed the two mugs.

"I'm really bummed about this Kels. I wish you would wait and just go with me." Meadow said as she hugged her soul mate.

Kelsey turned around and looked Meadow in the eyes,

"I need a break from all of this failure. I never expected IVF to be so difficult, then in turn heartbreaking." She said as she looked down at the ground.

"We need to pursue adoption avenues then Kels. We can adopt some cute little girl who is just dying to be raised by the crazy lunatic lesbians." They both laughed and kissed each other lovingly and supportively.

"We will make it through this and it will all be worth it. Nothing that is valued in life comes easy, you know that Kels. Hell, look at the journey we had to take and endure before our souls found each other."

"Ok, let's get this going. I am going to get down there and buy groceries to make you a wonderful dinner the first night you arrive." Kelsey said as she walked out of the room toward the bedroom.

"Awe, don't go to all that trouble, I'll take you out to dinner that first night." Meadow screamed through the walls so that Kelsey could hear her in the other room.

Kelsey screamed back, "It will be fun. I can play domestic goddess. I even have a maid's outfit and all."

Meadow started to laugh, "You do not."

Kelsey appeared in doorway holding a duffle bag in one hand and a maid's outfit in the other.

Meadow burst into laughter.

She walked over and took the outfit from her hand as she held it up.

"Where on earth did you find this?" She asked as she examined the garment.

"It was one of the new Halloween costumes we got in the store. You do know Halloween is this weekend." She replied.

Meadow held the outfit up to Kelsey's torso,

"This is going to look great!" She smiled then commented,

"But what am I going to wear?" I didn't know we were going trick or treatin' around the trailer park." She laughed loud again held her stomach from laughing so much.

"You're causing my AB muscles to hurt Kels." She said as she tried to stop laughing.

"Well maybe you shouldn't do 200 crunches before bedtime, every night Meadow."

Meadow held the bottom of her shirt up exposing her 6 pack,

"Yea, but then you wouldn't get this." She pushed her stomach out and walked over to Kelsey as she stood in the doorway.

"I know you want to feel how tone my Abs are Kels, come on." She taunted her by moving her Abs from side to side.

"Come on Meadow, we'll play games later, I have to get going." She winked and pushed past her.

Meadow put her shirt down and agreed to be rejected,

"Awe, you're no fun." She said in a small voice.

Kelsey walked through the kitchen and picked up her purse and car keys and talked to Meadow as she walked out the door.

"Ok, call me every second you have Meadow. The directions are on the side of the fridge. It takes about 3 hours to get there, so I'll be there around 1:00 barring me stopping for energy drinks, and peeing."

Meadow followed her, closing and locking the door behind them.

"Be safe honey. I love, love, love you." She yelled out.

"Don't pull out of this drive until you kiss me Ms. Kelsey." She added.

Kelsey was eager to go, she had her bags in the car, purse on the front seat, navigation set and engine on.

"Come on Meadow, I'm waiting." She yelled out of the window.

Meadow walked over and kissed her.

"You can't leave until I do, your trapped. My car is in front of yours. Ha, ha, ha." She teased.

Kelsey looked up at her tall lean mate and rolled her eyes.

"I am patiently waiting love." She replied.

"Ok, God, all business today." Meadow said as she walked to her car, got in and started the engine.

She stuck her head out the window and yelled back at Kelsey,

"I love you and miss you already."

Kelsey yelled back,

"I love you miss you more."

With this exchange Kelsey drove away from their home following the directives from the navigation system.

Kelsey relaxed and admired the beautiful fall foliage that portrayed the hills as works of art. Up and down winding roads she traveled through the picturesque Pennsylvania topography.

She passed tractors with pumpkins stacked on a flatbed, hay, apple cider and corn stalks.

"Won't that be fun if I decorate the trailer for Meadow?" She thought as she passed up the farmers market. She pulled off the side of the road and stopped the car.

She crossed the road running in front of a car traveling at a rate of speed that she did not anticipate.

The driver sounded the horn as she started and ran quicker.

She looked back at the taillights of the car that did not slow down. It was a truck, a beat up truck.

"Asshole." She screamed out at the driver whom she could not see.

The farmers and other shoppers looked up at her as she screamed at the obscenity into the quiet bright day.

She walked over to the market and merely said,

"Crazy people around these parts."

She was not greeted with a response.

She pointed to the tall bundled stalks of corn,

"I'll take 2 of those."

She pointed to the bales of hay and said, "I want 1 of those," she bent down and picked up a large pumpkin, "and this."

The farmer replied, "That'll be $25.00, want any cider?" He asked.

Kelsey replied, "Sure why not," as she reached into her purse and took out the money.

She started to turn and walk back toward her car carrying the pumpkin and looked back to see that the farm was not following her with the corn stalks, or hay.

She turned back around and mumbled, "Thanks for the help Homer."

She returned to make two additional trips carrying the items that she stuffed into the truck and back seat of her car.

Once she had all items safely secured, stocks sticking out of the open window in the back, she drove away.

"Wow, that was weird." She said as she opened the cider and drank out of the carton.

"This stuff is pretty good." She added.

Three hours later and one additional stop for coffee, Kelsey saw a sign for the trailer park.

She slowed down and drove into it slowly. It did not prevent the front of her car from hitting the dirt though.

"Damn it." She yelled out loud.

"What's with this road?"

She pulled around the circle to the last few trailers on the left.

"Damn, is it the last or second to the last on the left?" She asked out loud as she pulled over in between the two. She noticed a pumpkin on the doorstep to one the trailers, it had been hollowed and an arrangement of burnt orange roses and lantern flowers filled the inside.

"I bet that's the trailer." She said as she got out of the car and walked to the trailer that had the arrangement.

She leaned in and looked at the card housed on the arrangement.

The envelope read, "Kelsey."

She opened it up to reveal a small card that read,

"I miss you already and counting the time until we can see each other and spend quality time alone together. Whatever happens in life, I want it to happen with you as my partner."

Meadow

She smiled as she held the note card.

"She is so sweet, and loving, and thoughtful." She thought as she paused and felt the warmth flow over her body.

"Well this must be it. I could've sworn she said the second to the last trailer on the left though."

Kelsey walked over to the car, unloaded all the items, including the bale of hay, pumpkin, and stalks. She laid all items at the door to the trailer and looked for the key.

"Right, flowers, mulch." She repeated as she looked down for anything resembling this description.

The area to the right of the cement pad was just dirt. There were once flowers there but they had long died.

Kelsey bent down and felt underneath the flowers for a key. There was not one.

"That's strange." She thought as she stood up and tried the door.

The door opened.

"Oh, maybe she left it unlocked for me. This won't help though if I don't find the key." She thought as she started moving her items into the trailer from the porch.

"I need to call Lee and ask her where she put the key," She said to herself before she stopped in shock as she looked around at her surroundings.

The trailer was dirty and barren except for miscellaneous items in the center of the living room. She walked over and to examine the items. She saw a large filled garbage bag, a small card table, a propane tank, camper's hot plate, empty liter soda bottles and plastic tubing.

Kelsey walked over the bags to see what they were. She read them with confusion.

"Lime, red phosphorous?" This can't be the right trailer." She said into the quiet strange atmosphere. She felt an eerie wave of unbalance karma and oddity rush over her causing the hair on arms to rise.

She turned and walked back to where she assumed the bedroom would be. A torn black backpack, tennis shoes and some clothes lay scattered on the floor.

She stood in the back room and held her phone up to her eyes to see if she had service.

"Thank God, I have to call Lee." She thought as she scanned through her last few calls received.

The phone rang several times.

"Shit Lee, it's gonna be her voicemail." She thought as she heard a door slam.

Kelsey jumped and dropped her cell phone dislodging the battery from the back. She turned fell to the dirty musty brown shag carpet and reached out for her battery.

"Hello." A male voice said.

She turned while still on her knees and looked up at a tall, thin ominous looking young man with spurious smile.

She quickly stood up from the inferior position, leaving her cell phone on the ground.

"Are you a friend of Lee's?" Kelsey asked.

"Yea, I am, sorry to startle you mamame, my name is Smithton." He spoke with fatuous maladroit politeness.

Kelsey was disbelieved that he was a friend of Lee's. Lee was an older lesbian friend of theirs. This was not the profile of one of her friends.

"Are these your things?" She questioned him.

"Yes, they are, why?" Smithton was immediate on guard and paranoid.

"She is a member of the FBI, sent from the last trailer park. This fuckin' cunt will not bust me. Watch her every move." He thought as he grinned at her through his black edged, rotted teeth.

"What is your name Mamame?" He asked her as he leaned against the doorframe blocking her exit.

Kelsey sensed the defense posturing of the man and attempted to assuage the atmosphere.

"My name is Kelsey. I am a friend of Lee's. I am sorry if she rented this out to you. I thought she rented it to me this weekend. It must've been next. I am so sorry. Let's call her and straighten it out." She turned and kneeled down reaching out for her phone.

Smithton saw her move and allowed her to pick up the phone.

"Here, let's use my phone, I have her number right here. Let me give her a ring a ding." He said with failed humor.

Kelsey picked up her phone and quickly connected the battery. She started to turn the phone on when she heard Smithton speak,

"Lee, your friend Kelsey is here, do you want to speak with her?" He said as he handed the phone to Kelsey.

Kelsey looked at him with disbelief.

She reached out for the cell phone and held the phone to her ear.

"Hello, Lee she said."

Smithton swung a piece of plastic tubing around her face and onto her neck in one quick move.

The last thing Kelsey remembered was feeling desperation for air, eyes bulging as if they were going to pop out our her sockets. She reached up reactively to grab at the plastic noose, with no success.

Darkness was drowning out the light. She saw an endless field of gold wheat stocks swaying in the breeze. She dropped her hands from her neck and reached out toward the glowing metronome.

"Bitch, you think you're so smart. I saw you followin' me, all day." Smithton yelled out as he choked her enough to have her body go limp and pass out from lack of air.

Once Kelsey fell to the ground, he dragged her into the spare bedroom of the abandon trailer.

He walked out to this truck past the two dead deer that lay in the back bed and to the driver side door. He pushed the seat forward and grabbed a roll of duct tape and the rose saw he found in the shed, still with the oily rag wrapped around it.

He quickly walked back into the trailer, slammed the door behind him and locked it.

"I'm gonna get me some satisfaction fucking the feds." He said to himself as he smiled while pulling out the remaining meth he had from the whore he encountered earlier that day.

"God damn, it's been a good day Smithton." He said out loud echoing in the trailer as he walked back to the room where Kelsey lay unconscious.

CHAPTER ELEVEN

No One on the Other Side

"Keep those who are gone living within your mind all the days of your life, you will never know a day without them." E.H.

"Sergeant Simpson," The trooper called out.

"Sir, can I speak with you?" he called again from across the noisy barracks.

The tall large framed Sergeant walked over to the trooper who brought Kitty in.

"What is it?" he asked with the presence of superiority.

"This girl I picked up. I found her with bags of food walking along Timmons Rd, out there by Rt.68. The thing is she had a receipt all but for a gallon of milk. She had several containers of crystal drain cleaner." The trooper explained.

"We've had an alert from the other barracks about Blood Ice. These tweakers are cooking up red colored crank and selling for Halloween." The trooper was well spoken and educated on the subject.

"If they were only so creative in productive ways. Jeese." The supervisor replied as she shook his head.

"Should I talk to Trooper Mason about it?" Trooper Cantoniski asked.

Trooper Simpson added another sentiment before replying,

"That would be just great if this gets out around here with all these trailer parks in the area, and the young trailer rats that go trick of treating and I don't mean the teenagers."

"Where is she?" Trooper Simpson asked.

"I put her in interrogation B. She was timid when I picked her up but then her demeanor changed when I called for an ambulance. She clamped up and got an attitude real quick. She refuses to give me her real name, address or explain the drain cleaner. She made some excuse about walking to an Aunt's house in PA." The trooper explained.

"Isn't that convenient?" Sergeant Simpson responded as he picked up the phone and hit an extension number.

"Trooper Mason, this is Sergeant Simpson, I need to see you now for a few minutes, at my desk." He spoke briefly then hung the phone up.

"Almost immediately the undercover drug specialist walked over. He was a muscle clad large man with long black hair, pulled back into a ponytail. His bulging triceps sleeved with bright tattoos.

"Yes sir?" He responded to the supervisor.

"Seems Trooper Cantoniski here picked up a possible cooker or girlfriend of one." Trooper Simpson explained.

"Oh ya, where is she?" Trooper Mason asked as he looked at his co worker.

Trooper Cantoniski responded,

"She is in interrogation room B."

"What's here statement?" He asked.

"I don't know, I left her with it, I don't think she is gonna talk thought. She got a real attitude since I started questioning her." He explained.

"I think we should keep her the minimum, shake her up a little more. She'll never tell us or the cooker she was even in here, we'll let her loose then I can keep tabs on her." Trooper Mason proposed.

The sergeant looked at both and nodded his head in affirmation.

"Move on with it Cantoniski." The two men scattered and the sergeant was pulled in another direction.

Trooper Cantoniski opened the door and walked back into the interrogation room where Kitty sat with her hands at rest on the desk.

"Are you done?" He called out as she shut the door.

"Yea, I'm done." Kitty replied.

The trooper walked over and slid the piece of paper off the desk and picked up the pen and put it in the front pocket of his shirt, buttoning over it. He had a crank head once stab him in the hand with a pen left on a desk.

He read the statement with expectations of the content.

He did not speak, he stood up, slid the metal chair in with his hand, pushing it loudly along the floor.

"Stand up." He said as he reached around and removed his handcuffs.

"What are you doin' with me?" Kitty asked with a noticeable look of fear in her wide eyes.

"I am locking you up until the judge can hear your charges." He said very factually.

Kitty stood and with the flick of his wrist the trooper aggressively slapped the first cuff around her battered wrist causing the metal cuff to force its way around her petite bone.

Kitty grimaced and bent over slightly from the pain.

He grabbed her other wrist overlooking her discomfort and held it by the cuffed one, in front of her body. He walked her out of the room and down a dimly light cluttered hall. Boxes of files and papers were stacked on both sides.

Kitty quietly followed with her head low, trying not to look around at her surroundings.

Tear had won the emotional battle raging within her head. The detached indurate side of her personality collapsed under heavy weight of her insecurities and fear.

The trooper led her into a room framed by a long metal bar four feet off the ground. A bench spanned the three walls just below the bar.

The trooper pointed to the far corner.

"Sit down." He said.

Kitty did not look at the others in the room sitting on the bench. She sat with her left knee bent in front of her face to the bar, back to the others in the room staring at her.

"Raise your hands." He commanded.

Kitty raised her swollen wrists and the trooper opened the left cuff and pulled her arms closer to the bar that was at eye level to her.

The trooper secured the cuff around the bar. Kitty looked at the area in which she had to slide the cuff. One foot to her right was a cross bar and one foot to her left was a cross bar. She could only slid the cuff or move her body within two feet of where she was secured.

The high was uncomfortable. The bar was too high to allow her to relax and bend her arms and the bench prevented her from standing up.

Kitty's emotions abated even further and she began to cry, out loud and uncontrollable.

"You might want to control that, I can't sit in her and blow your nose for you." The trooper sarcastically commented as he turned and walked out of the room, locking it with a key from the other side.

His comment did not affect Kitty one way or the other. She was hungry, in pain and terrified.

Two men to her left continued talking to each other ignoring her. A woman sat cuffed to the bar six feet or so to her right. She stared at Kitty, making a cracking sound with the gum in mouth.

Kitty cried and leaned the left side of her face on the bicep of her left arm. Her bent leg fell asleep forcing her to move it to the ground.

Her bruised body ached yet she endured the pain keeping her head to the wall.

"You think your too good to be here or what?" The woman called out to Kitty.

Kitty did not answer and the two men fell silent.

"Answer me lil' bitch. You think you're too good for us? Can't you look at us?" She yelled even louder at Kitty.

Kitty did not look despite the taunting.

"Hey you, I'm talkin' to you." She yelled even louder.

Kitty kept her silence and position, like a cowering battered dog under the intimidation of its master.

"hhmmm." The woman commented before becoming silent again.

"Daddy, when are you gonna come git me?" She cried loudly within her mind.

"Ppllleeease Daddy." She cried as tears once again fell from her eyes tumbling down onto the worn wooden bench.

"Ms. Smithton, when's my Daddy comin' to git me?" She remembered saying on her first day of kindergarten.

This was the first time Kitty can remember being away from her Dad for so long, it was the only time she could remember feeling so terrified and abandoned.

"Get, Kitty, not Git." She remembered her new teacher constantly correcting the way her father taught her to speak.

"When is my Daddy comin' to get me?" She mumbled as the others in the room watched her mumbling to herself.

"She's on somethin'." The woman to her said.

"Hey, girl, throw sum of that drug over here so I can zone out." She yelled at Kitty as all three of the other detainees laughed.

Kitty did not hear them.

She was back in Kindergarten.

"Kitty, your Daddy did not abandon you, he will be back soon to get you. You are here just for a few hours to learn and play." She said, answering for her teacher.

Kitty can only remember sitting in the coat room corner crying, until her father walked in.

She smiled at the wall as she remembered his appearance.

Work boot, red worn front pocket tee shirt, brown canvas pants covered in concrete dust.

She rubbed her arm with her left cheek envisioning hugging her Dad so tight that she never wanted to let go.

Her mind stopped here as she heard a key open the metal door to the holding room.

She listened without moving her eyes from the wall.

"Miss Katherine Hepburn." The man called out.

The three others in the room busted into laughter.

For the first time since being led into the room, Kitty looked up and spoke.

"That's me." She said quietly.

"See you all didn't know you were detained with a celebrity." The trooper said with banter.

He walked over to her and uncuffed her from the bar.

"Follow me." He directed as he placed the cuff back over her left wrist.

"Bye Ms. Hepburn, love your work." The woman yelled out at Kitty as she left the room.

Kitty asked the trooper,

"Where am I going?" Kitty was terrified of being in front of a judge.

"It's time for you to see the Judge." He said.

"Can I go to the bathroom?" Kitty asked.

The trooper looked annoyed at her and replied,

"After your arraignment."

Kitty replied, "I really have to go now."

The trooped led her to a door that said "bathroom."

"You have 1 minute, don't make me come in after you." He instructed as she opened the metal door.

Kitty walked in with one hand cuff dangling off and one still cutting into her skin. Her left fingers were now going numb. She walked over to the faucet and turned it on.

She looked into the mirror and leaned forward, splashing cold water onto her face and into her eyes.

She looked up at her red swollen eyes and red nose.

She grabbed a paper towel and blotted her face dry.

She did not have relieved herself, she wanted to contain herself before speaking to the person who would or would not believe her story.

"I can't screw this up. Don't screw this up Kitty Schode." She thought to herself.

She walked out the door and was immediately greeted by the police officer who picked up her right wrist and placed the handcuff back over it, securing a slightly less tightly this time.

He walked her down the same hall that she entered. At the end of the hall he turned her to the right and down to an open door. She could hear a man speaking.

She walked into a large room with a judge sitting on a raised platform behind a wooden desk. He was wearing a black rob. He was older and heavy set.

"$1000.00 bail Mr. Swain," he said as she stuck his gavel down startling Kitty causing her to jump at the loud banging sound it made.

Kitty and the trooper waited right inside the door until another trooper led a man in handcuffs, waist chain, chained down to his feet and ankle cuffed, out of the room.

As the man walked past Kitty he grinned and winked at her. She looked away.

"Next." The judge called out as if he was a clerk at the meat counter in the food store.

Another man sat at a small worn office desk with dented metal drawers. He called out,

"This is Ms. Katherine Hepburn your honor."

"Oh, is it now?" The judge replied looking up from the papers on desk and through his reading glasses.

"Ms. is this your name?" He asked in a loud voice that carried through the entire room.

"Yes it is, sir." Kitty replied.

"It's your honor." the man in the suit snapped back at her.

Kitty corrected herself, "I'm sorry, your honor."

The judge asked the district attorney,

"Is this the name on her identification?"

"Well, that is one of this issues your honor, she does not have any, or did not have any with her when she was picked up." He replied.

"What are the charges?" The judge asked.

"Loitering, vagrancy and theft." The DA called out.

"Ms. Hepburn, how do you plea?" He asked her.

"I don't understand Kitty said. I've never done this before, I'm not sure what is goin' on and no one explained it to me, sir. I mean your honor." Kitty stumbled, choked up and spoke softly.

"Ms. I did not hear you. Can you speak up?" The judge yelled out at her.

Kitty spoke up, this time yelling.

"I'm not sure what to say, no one explained this part to me." She asked this time paraphrasing her last comment.

"It is not our place to instruct you Ms. Hepburn, if that is your real name, if not, I will add impersonation charges and perjury onto your charges, now, how do you plea? Guilty or not guilty?" He asked with annoyance in his voice.

"I am not a vagrant nor a thief and I was not loitering." Kitty proudly replied.

The judge spoke this time with even less patience than the last time.

"I will give you one last chance before I have the nice trooper over there take you back to the holding cell for contempt. Now, how do you plea?" He asked, then added,

"AAaaaa," just as Kitty started to speak.

"One word or two, guilty or not guilty." He said as he glared at her with his face stoic.

"Not guilty," she said then paused for efficacy before saying in a slightly impudent tone, "your honor."

"See, you can play ball Ms. Hepburn. They taught you well in drama school." He said as the others in the room chuckled.

"Bail set at $1000.00." He said as he lifted his gavel.

The district attorney spoke just before striking it down.

"Your honor," He said.

"Yes, Mr. Miele?" He replied.

"If it pleases the court the state would like to waive bail for Ms. Hepburn." He said.

The judge looked at him and asked,

"Can you please approach the bench?"

The district attorney walked a few feet to the rudimentary wooden stage and leaned in. The two briefly conferred before the DA turned and walked back to his humble station.

"The offer to waive bail is accepted." The judge said before banging the gavel down once again causing Kitty to jump from being startled.

"Go Ms. Hepburn." The judge added.

Kitty looked over at the trooper with a bereft look.

"Next," the judge called out and Kitty followed the trooper out of the room.

The trooper did not speak to Kitty. She followed him perplexed with what just transpired.

The trooper walked her through a metal door that led to an entrance area where the main door to the outside was. A woman sitting behind a glass enclosure was filling out papers.

"She'll process you out." He motioned with his eyes to a woman in a trooper uniform sat behind a glass enclosure. The trooper removed the handcuffs from Kitty's swollen wrists. With this last act, he turned and walked back through the metal door, leaving Kitty for the first time on the outside and without supervision.

Kitty looked around.

"Is this really it?" She thought to herself.

She slowly walked over to the glass booth.

The woman did not look up, she slid a piece of paper and a pen underneath a small gap in the glass.

"Sign this and you are free to go." She said without emotion.

Kitty slid the paper out and picked up the pen. Kitty's left hand could barely hold the pen and as she gripped it, could not feel her fingers from the tight handcuff that she had worn for over 6 hours.

She scribbled her name and slid the paper back under the glass. She stood and waited for instruction.

"That's it." The lady replied.

"Don't I get anything, a piece of paper or anything?" Kitty said.

"No. You will need to come back here in a week to receive your court date unless you have an address to give us." She replied.

Kitty stopped and hesitated,

"When I know my Aunt's address I'll call and give it to you." She said.

The woman trooper replied, "I bet you will."

Kitty was so nervous and afraid that she started an issue with the address comment that she walked out the door not remembering her groceries.

Kitty did not know where she was. She just kept walking through the sparsely populated parking lot and toward the road that led to the parking lot.

Once on the road she felt as though she was forgetting something. She stopped and thought,

"Shit, my groceries." She stood her ground.

"There is no freakin' way I'm goin' back in there." She said as she shook her head.

She looked forward at the long road ahead.

"I wonder where the Pennsylvania border is." She thought.

"There won't be anyone waitin' to help me, on the other side." She said as she started to walk back down the road and away from the police barracks.

CHAPTER TWELVE

The Left Side

"Avoidance is a misnomer; an action of avoidance negates avoidance." E.H.

"Time is runnin' down." Smithton said to himself as he walked into the kitchen. He looped the rose saw over his left arm and picked up one of the four aluminum chairs from the kitchen.

He walked back into the bedroom where Kelsey still lay unconscious. He lay the chair down on the carpet with the back tipped over forward, onto the rug beside her body.

Smithton quickly removed her shoes, socks, tee shirt, bra, jeans and underwear. He placed her body over the back of the chair face down.

Kelsey's arms hung down onto the shag rug to the sides of the chair, her legs still left straight down.

Smithton placed her right leg down onto the right leg of the chair and the left leg onto the left leg of the chair in the same position.

Working quickly he pulled at the end of the duct tape. He bound her wrists and slipped her arms over the back of the chair and bent them in front of her. He began taping her back, under her shoulder blades and around the chair securing her forearms.

Her chest pressed into the back of the plastic coating of the orange vinyl chair back.

Once her torso was secured, he turned her head to the left and taped her head to the top of the chair back.

Kelsey moaned quietly as her hair and skin were covered in the grey sticky tape. Smithton did not consciously leave gaps for air at her nostrils or mouth. There were gaps in the tape due to the mercurial pace in which he worked.

Kesley stirred but Smithton did not notice. He grabbed her left leg and taped her calf muscle to the leg of the chair.

He repeated the act with her right leg and drug the chair framing her body into the bathroom.

Smithton stopped once the chair was fully into the bathroom. He leaned his back against the small green Formica cabinet to get his breath and calm his heartbeat.

"You're tweakin' hard dude." He said to himself as the chemicals from the methamphetamine rushed into his brain. The meth coupled with his natural adrenalin generated from the violence caused his pulse to race his mind and onto the impending excitement.

He bent down and spun the top of the chair where Kelsey's head was taped, up and tipped onto the edge of the tub. He pushed her framed body forward until the chair and her head tipped forward and into the tub.

Smithton walked over to the door and slammed it shut with his foot. He locked it quickly. He started the water in tub and unbuttoned, then unzipped his pants.

His jeans dropped to the floor exposing his hard penis. Smithton did not own underwear. The least amount of clothes he had to carry and wash the better for him and Kitty. At this moment in time Smithton had only one intent, to please himself.

He spread his legs wide enough to so he could force his penis into Kelsey from her backside. As he entered her with force, she opened her eyes.

"What is happening?" was her first thought.

"I can't open my eyes. God, I can't open my eyes." She tried to scream out but could not. Her screams were mottled moan by the duct tape over her mouth.

She had no choice but to succumb to terror that now paralyzed her. She felt herself gag for the fractional amounts of air available to her. The horrific, surreal realization entered her failing conscious mind,

"I'm being rapped, from behind." She thought as tears soaked between the spaces of the tape exposing her pain.

Kelsey's last vision was of a field of wheat. The same field she ran through as child.

She raced forward as she turned and looked behind her to assess the distance between her and her father's tracker. His tracker was not, there although seconds ago she jumped off, running ahead as her father smiled.

She stopped and looked ahead with confusion. The sun glared at her blurring her vision.

"Speak to me." She screamed out.

The proud field sprawled into the horizon. The magnificent sight reflected every ray beamed down by the supervision of the summer sun hung in the glorified the blue sky.

A soft breeze gently swayed caressing the wheat.

The center invited Kelsey inward.

She ran forward.

Smithton grabbed the sides of the chair to brace the force of his hips thrusting into Kelsey. She was faceless and un-human now. He relished the fleeting moment as he was entering his euphoria. He tightly clenched his teeth together and closed his eyes as the drug over took his mind and his orgasm overtook his senses.

Once Smithton allowed all the semen to exit his extremity, he fell to his knees. The water splashed, the moans stopped as the water collected to the center of Kelsey's face.

After a minute, or two, Smithton got up off the floor. He stood and unlocked the door. He walked out and into the bedroom to collect the rose saw.

He walked back into the small bathroom and closed the door behind him, this time by using the doorknob. He pushed in the center button of the tarnished brass knob and turned, stepping into the partially filled tub.

He skillfully flipped open the rose saw's serrated blade with a quick flick of his wrist and smiled at the accomplishment of the skill that he had just recently learned.

He placed his left knee and the palm of his left hand onto the Kelsey's back. He looked at the back of head and leaned harder onto her back bracing his weight as he placed the blade onto her neck. Smithton sawed through her hair with long swift back and forth motions. Her skin ripped and frayed from the deep points and recesses of the blade. The muscles in her neck separated and her blood flowed into to the tub as it intertwined with the hot water, diluted and seemingly endless.

Kelsey's head fell forward held to her body only by her spinal cord.

Smithton stood up and lifted his right leg out of the water, with his work boot drenched and dripping, he thrust his foot down onto the back of Kelsey's tittering head separating life and death.

Her head fell and slid, still facing to the left, down to the drain. The water now plugged by Kelsey's severed head started to collect.

Smithton grabbed the chair quickly and flipped it to the side, then to the back. Kelsey's headless torso flowing blood faced upwards for the first time.

Smithton working with a quicker pace grabbed her bound hands with his left hand and sawed each one at the wrist until they both fell into the pool of dark pink water and floated toward her head.

A black shiny object caught Smithton's attention and shifted his sporadic attention span.

As Kelsey's left hand lodged against her other severed body parts, a ring on her left ring finger beckoned through the colored water.

Smithton reached his right hand into the water and picked up her hand, admiring the ring on her finger.

"This would be a great ring for me to give Kitty." He said with total ignorance to the fact that the titanium ring was secured onto his victim hand. Smithton was in complete hedonistic focus, ignorant and oblivious to the fact that there was emotional heartfelt attachment to such a seemingly material object.

He tugged at the ring trying to dislodge it from Kelsey's ring finger. The ring did not budge.

Smithton reached down and dipped her hand into the water, saturating her fingers. He pulled at the band once more and twisted it as he pulled.

The thin black band slid off Kelsey's finger and into the palm of her murdered. He shut his fists and placed the ring into his left pocket.

Smithton jerked his head up as he heard the sound of the main entrance door slam shut. He jumped up and unlocked the bathroom door and walked out into the narrow hall.

He looked into the empty room. His eyes scanned his cooking supplies. The corners were devoid of another presence. He quietly walked into to living room to see who was in the kitchen.

Smithton walked sideways down the hall, sliding his back along the floral paneling. He prepared himself as he viewed a shadow fading in and out on the opposite wall. He sprung around and surveyed the kitchen exposing an empty and quiet room.

He turned and looked over at the closed door.

"Get it THE FUCK together dude. You are fuckin' seein' shadow people. Get this fed the fuck outta' her and fix up some ice." He said to himself as he refocused his attentions.

He walked over to his supplies and grabbed one of several empty plastic shopping bags that lie on the floor.

He briskly walked down the hall with his mind set of cleaning up the wastes of wasted life he used and discarded of.

Smithton kept used plastic shopping bags and valued them more than the lives that he used for his pleasure or for in his paranoid dopamine deprived mind, survival.

CHAPTER THIRTEEN

Disposable

"Beware of disposal items that challenge your values." E.H.

Smithton placed the shopping bag containing Kelsey's once emoting brown eyes and artistic hands into the back of his stolen truck.

He jumped up and into the bed, pulling the blue plastic tarp off of the deer carcass' and over the bag. He picked up the cinder blocks and placed one down on the right end of the tarp. He repeated the act with one of three remaining blocks.

He jumped down and looked at the street and surrounding trailers. Vacancy occupied his adjacent properties.

Smithton reached into his back pocket and pulled out the car keys. He got into the truck and drove to the landfill outlined to him by his new supervisor, Phil something or other.

The township had a specified landfill for animal carcasses. Smithton was one of two employees that had knowledge and access to the land.

Smithton drove up to the aluminum gate. He got out and entered the code and swiped his employee card on the keypad housed just outside of the gate. Smithton had an arrogant air of authority to him although his privileges to the municipal landfill and dump as limited. He did not stop to consider the hour of his arrival as deviant to these privileges.

This was the first time that Smithton was at the landfill. He assumed it was similar to the last municipal carcass landfill.

He drove slowly up the road traversing the manmade hill. He reached a stop sign beaconed a surveillance area.

He looked around for any straggling employees. He saw a truck weigh station with an unmanned kiosk. He pulled past the check point and drove up the hill within feet of decomposing cadavers.

Smithton placed the truck into park and turned off the engine. He reached under the seat and pulled out a large hunting knife with a deer antler handle.

He looked briefly at the material object smiling at the grandeur.

"What a Christmas gift this musta' been for him." He said to himself as he recalled his fourth victim.

"Stupid fuck shoulda' kept a tighter leash on his bitch." He added before exiting the truck.

He placed his left boot onto the back wheel and jumped into the bed. He walked over to the doe carcass, the one he picked up first. It had been decomposing for days.

He placed the tip of the sharp blade onto the swollen chest of the motionless animal.

He aggressively pushed the blade penetrating the white fur.

Air, maggots and fluids fell onto the bed of the truck. Smithton did not cringe or reach from the stench.

He pulled the tarp back and reached into the plastic bag grabbing Kelsey's long blond blood soaked hair. He stuffed her duct taped head into the opening in the doe's abdomen.

He reached back into the bag and grabbed her right hand stuffing it and then her left hand into the parasite ridden corpse.

Once he had disposed of Kelsey's identifiable body parts, he walked behind the doe grabbing one front leg and one rear leg, stiff with rigor mortis pulled the both relics off the truck using the height and thrust to swing the body around as he was taught.

The doe held Kelsey's severed body parts and rested in between two deer cadavers. The foggy glazed over eyes of the one deer and one buck stared onward, mouths open, tongues slightly out. Death stared at death and more death.

One of the bucks had his antlers removed; the others were dangling down upon its bloodied face. All that remained on the side of the once beautiful and majestic buck was the splintered bone of his jaw, fur, fat and muscle had been torn away from being drug underneath the vehicle. Smithton took the remaining antler and hid it in the back of his cab. The four sharp points intrigued his macabre side.

Smithton turned and walked to the front of the truck, his mind consumed with addiction. He had all the single items needed to fix his withdrawal waiting for him back at the trailer.

He did notice that the doe carcass tumbled down several feet from its perch. The swollen stomach expelled Kelsey's bare left hand and naked ring finger.

Smithton drove back toward the home, tired and drained. He wondered about Kitty.

"She must he up to some shit of trouble or I'd have heard from her." He wondered but did not worry. He was confident that Kitty could handle herself in a crisis and not get him busted.

The air was chilling, leaves had all since abandoned the trees and the sun's endurance slowed down by late afternoon.

He drove slowly through the winding roads navigating back to the trailer and to the task that awaited him as a cooker.

His phone rang, with his left hand on the wheel he reached down into the fold of the seat with his right hand. He lifted out his phone and held the screen up to his line of vision. The caller displayed himself as "private", Smithton he broke from habit and answered the call on the hopes it may be Kitty.

"Yea." He said loudly.

"What up bitch mother southern fucker, your game to crank me is green. So what the fuck up?" The caller said with rough street slang.

"Back down Pitbull. I'm your new gold dealer didn't your whore tell ya?" Smithton replied with arrogant coyness.

Smithton had a set modus operandi that he followed in every trailer park community that they lived in. Find a whore who sales dope, stiff her and her pimp will call within hours. He had not taken into consideration that he was the new man in town. The paranoid group would automatically view him as a nark or a cop.

Smithton needed to establish himself as a user and dealer and not an undercover. He had a list of references though that carried hefty respect within the methamphetamine biker monopolized community.

Smithton made the right friends, paid off the right hands and murdered anyone who had a better than 10% chance of blowing his cover and risking Kitty's safety.

"Hey simple fuck, I have my boys, I don't know you. I don't want to give my bitch a Grant." The caller said.

"Grant? Wow, know who loves the southern fuckers? First it was an Andrew. No prob on that, I'm about to do some quick cook of my own. How about I give you some of my quick AMP and your Andrew and you see that I am your new boy." Sanguine and sly, Smithton terminated the conversation.

"I'll be round for another cleanin', tell Sharon she can clean it out again tonight. I'll hit you back on the block when my cake rises." With this comment Smithton started to disconnect the call before he remembered that his victim's car was still parked by the trailer.

"Hey D, you want a free strip down? Go to this address, free on me, just git it out within the hour. No owner." He gave the address and quickly disconnected the call. He knew that during this call he would not be given the dealers number and a person such as him would not have caller ID's that were legitimate.

He wanted and needed to gain the dealers confidence. He could only do that face to face without asking the wrong questions. He had the right names to drop and the right curriculum vitae.

Smithton drove back to the trailer watching every passing car, noticing every face that turned and took notice of his face, truck or license plate.

1,140 minute of every day was uncertain and suspect for Smithton. He saw shadows on concrete that disappeared in human form when he turned around. When he was on the road, cars followed him, when he spotted the one it would suddenly get lost in a flood of silver, white and black cars, resurfacing just before he arrived at his destination. Smithton saw the secretive drivers who pulled up beside his truck at red lights and take their visual photographs of his profile. He had been on nervous, on guard and edgy for 5 years. In his mind he was no fool.

Once Smithton was within 1 mile of the trailer park, he made a left hand turn without signaling into a small housing development. He pulled over and turned off his engine. Then he ducked down onto the seat as if he had got of the truck. He lay on the seat for a few minutes before popping his head back up and starting the engine.

He drove out of the development and back to where his supplies were waiting. He needed to get started if he wanted to take a sample of his AMP to the local supplier.

Smithton pulled his truck into the sparsely grassed area of the turn off, at their temporary home. He shut the truck off and got out, slamming the door shut.

"Hello there." A voice said from a yard away.

Smithton's guard rose and he squatted down behind the truck as he looked around.

"Hey, over here." The voice said.

He looked to where the voice resonated from and saw the mechanic neighbor that he and Kitty had saw when they first moved in.

"Oh, ya, hey." He said trying to smooth over his paranoid reaction. "You startled me." He added.

"How are you two doing? Are you settling in?" He compassionately asked.

"Where is your wife, I haven't seen her around." He inquired.

"Are you takin' notes?" Smithton acerbically replied.

The neighbor was jovial and did not take affront to the latent insult of the comment.

"No, no, I just want to make sure she was okay. I know you guys had at that accident n' all." He replied as he walked in closer to Smithton's face and the driver side of his truck.

"Ya, ya man, she's fine. She is visitin' her ma fer a few days. I'm goin' it solo." He said as he walked toward the neighbor away from his truck that had bloodstains in the bed.

Although blood from the deer carcass was a plausible excuse, Smithton did not want to have to talk about any of his personal affairs.

"Ya, man look its real nice n all but I have to get some hamhelper in me. I'm about a zombie here." He brushed off the neighbor and turned toward the trainer.

The neighbor looked at him with confusion as he tried to figure out what he had just said.

"Okay man, take care." He replied as he turned and questioned and attempted to decipher the conversation that had just taken place.

Smithton walked through the stony barren yard and up the rotting deck step. He reached into his pocket and removed the key that had become his property through deceit. He opened the door and entered the through the door way, surrounded by two walls that screamed of the horrific events that had just transpired between them.

Smithton was not in touch with the intangible. He had just set of an emotion preponderance of unbalanced karma. The once abandoned, quiet and serene trailer is owned by an aging 80 year woman who had not visited it since the death of 30 days from her husband of 75 years.

2 children had spent decades running in the yard cluttered with big wheel tricycles and other childhood toys. Dogs romped in the yard while their father grilled countless dinners.

The slates of the redwood picnic long unused and falling through the center of the table that once housed cherished but overlooked formidable family dinners.

He opened the door and walked over the card table that he had set in the corner of the once lived in room. The same table that facilitated card parties with the other members of the trailer park in a harmonious setting.

Smithton unpacked, cut, opened and set up his mobile meth lab. He opened the bags and measured out the chemicals with the skill and efficiency of an experienced cooker. After hours, he slumped down to the ground high with the pernicious odoriferous effect of the fumes.

This once revered family retreat trailer was no longer suitable for dwelling. The pernicious fumes had now penetrated into the walls, floors, fabrics, wood and plaster. Demolishment would be the only salvation for the family retreat. The mourning widow would experience one more form of loss and death.

CHAPTER FOURTEEN

White Rapids

"The river rushes forth determined and forceful. Yet it fragments and strays from the set course becoming lost and stagnant in collected puddles, waiting to be thrust forward and out of languidness." E.H.

A sudden unexpected current of air pushed Kitty into the rut along the side of the road; she stumbled, with sore heels and feet. She looked up as the 18-wheel tractor-trailer disrupted her course forward.

She looked around her surroundings and thought,

"There aren't no phone booths anymore." A force of panic overcame her as she felt desperate and isolated.

"Thanks to people like Smithton." She thought to herself as she side stepped the back draft from a passing vehicle. The all-consuming sound of the truck's deep throttle distracted her thoughts. She found concentration hard as she walked along the narrow noisy interstate.

Her weak, frail and malnourished body was easily thrown around by the back draft of the tractor-trailer.

"How and am I going to find my way back to the trailer park?" She wondered.

"This isn't even home and I am wandering a strange highway trying to find it. What has become of me Daddy?" She thought as fatigue won the battle on her psyche.

She reached into her front pocket and pulled out the only remaining bills, crumbled and disorganized. She unfolded them to count their worth. She had 3 dollars.

"I have nothing to show for the money that the neighbor gave me. Smithton knows how much he gave me. What am I going to tell him?" Kitty thought to herself with consternation.

She knew that she would have to explain her whereabouts and lack of money or items to show for the money.

A believable plausible excuse equated to Kitty's self preservation with Smithton. She was the victim, she had the experience, she was suffering, yet she would have to downplay all the emotional turmoil so make the event less of an event.

She walked, following the interstate. She knew that it eventually lead to roads that meandered through the hills and ultimate led to the trailer.

The lights of the cars grew brighter as day faded behind the hills. She knew her safety also faded as she would continue to walk a dark interstate road. The sound the cars rushing past toward their destination evoked thought and envy within her heart.

She looked at each car as they rushed and pushed past her without acknowledging her existence. She watched happy children waving out the back window on their way home, businessmen anxious to arrive home to their loved ones, and there was Kitty; but once again alone and lost.

She looked down onto the side of the road and saw a smashed plastic jelly packet. She bent down and picked it up, holding it tight in her palm as tears welled up in hers.

Kitty saw herself playing on the hot summer asphalt road that led to her home. She intentionally lingered around 3:00 pm, the time when her dad would be arriving home from work. She rode her pink bike up and down the road pacing the pavement until the right time. She looked down the hazy road and in the distance she could see her father's silver work truck.

She pulled over and straddled her thin legs holding tiptoe to the ground on the driver side of the road. She stuck out her thumb as if thumbing for a ride.

Kitty's father repeated this ritual every available summer day. He would stop and smile. Kitty would laugh and giggle as she walked her bike to the back of the truck. Her dad would get out and place the prized Christmas gift into the truck and she would climb aboard and sit down, facing the road behind them as Bob slowly drove the remainder of the way home.

The warm breeze blowing her long hair onto her face, as she held the tailgate of the truck, bouncing up off the bed alongside her bike at the same bump just before their home.

Once Bob pulled into the driveway and shut the truck off, he would get out and walk to the back of the truck and lift her off the bed with a big jump and swirling turn.

"Kitty, I have a present for you." She could hear him say.

"What is it daddy?" She whispered the words as she did when she was the excited child. She knew what the present was; it was the same present every day.

Once her dad placed her safely on the ground he reach into his pocket or sometimes when he had several gifts he walk back to the cab and gather up several plastic containers of grape jelly from the dashboard.

Bob would keep take purple jelly packs from that morning's breakfast where he would meet his laborers. 6:00 am every morning Bob would gather his crew at the local diner so they could ride with him or follow his truck to the job sites.

"Thanks daddy." Kitty replied with true heartfelt gratification of the gift. The jelly cost her dad nothing but was priceless for the heartfelt meaning. It Kitty felt special and loved in the world.

Kitty tripped and stumbled onto the road. As she sat on the crumbled asphalt road she looked back at where she had just walked from, looking for her daddy's work truck.

It didn't come, she knew it wouldn't come yet somehow the act comforted her. Kitty turned her attention forward and squinted at the large structure off into the distance.

"That looks like a gas station." She thought as she brushed the small stones from sticking to her jeans. She looked behind her, cars rushed onward. Her past was there, for her to close her eyes and feel. She stopped and turned forward. The back of the cars faded into the hillside. Her future did also. She could not see where the cars were going or where she was going. She was afraid to turn back and she was afraid to walk forward into ambiguity. Off to the left somewhere was Smithton. He was in the middle of the metaphoric juncture of her life.

Kitty stumbled, limped and tracked forward imaging herself as an explored of the Antarctic. She was injured, hungry but determined. As a child, she was enamored with everything about the North Pole. She would stand on a piece of cardboard box and whip a string tied to a stick forward yelling "mush," to her imaginary dogsled team.

Kitty looked down to the ground as she smiled at the thought of her 7 dog team leading her through the blinding snow.

She stopped as she saw a half filled bottle of Old Grand Dad bourbon.

"That's almost full, why would someone throw that out?" She said as she picked it up. She stopped and unscrewed the plastic cap and drank down the liquor without thinking of the contamination.

Within minutes Kitty felt the rush of the alcohol to her head. With little food in days, little water and no sleep she was victim to the mercurial high.

Kitty continued to drink down the dirty bourbon that housed a cigarette butt in the bottom of the bottle. She traipsed along the side of the road. The gas station was now steps in front of her. She was suddenly unprepared. When she was sober, she rehearsed asking a woman, pumping gas, for a ride and directives. Now that she was intoxicated, she was extemporary. She dropped the now empty bottle onto the side of the road.

Kitty stumbled into the door of the gas station and fell into the store, catching her balance before falling into the rack of candy bars.

"Can I use the bathroom?" She slurred her words out loud.

The cashier looked at her and replied,

"No, it is for customers only."

The young man who was paying for gas spoke up,

"She is with me, give her the key."

The cashier looked at him with embarrassment and handed over a large stick with a key tied to it.

The man paid and walked over to Kitty and ushered her out of the door.

"Her you go honey." He said out loud for the rest of the patrons to hear.

Kitty did not fight the strange man lifting the weight of her feet as he pushed open the heavy glass doors to the gas station.

He ushered Kitty to the ladies bathroom. He wedged her against the wall as she teetered to stay on her feet. He fumbled with awkward stick and key until he was able to unlock the dirty, dented metal door.

He pulled her into the bathroom.

"Here, I'll turn my back, do what you have to do." He stood at the door with his back to her.

Kitty looked at him, she had to relieve herself, she would never go into or to the bathroom in front of a strange man but in this case she could not refrain.

She pulled her jeans down and squatted down to the dirt toilet. She lost her balance,

"Shit," she called out.

The man turned around.

"Don't look." She yelled out as she fell against the wall then braced herself.

He turned and looked back at the door without saying a word.

Kitty relieved herself and pulled up her jeans. She walked over to the sink and turned the handle of the hot, spinning it without the release of water. She turned the cold and water splashed out.

She washed her hands and shut off the valve. She looked around for paper towels but there were none. The hand dryer was pulled off the wall and only holes remained where it was once housed. She wiped her hands on her jeans.

"I'm done. Do you know where Timmons Road in Deep Creek Maryland is?" She asked with a childlike innocent voice.

The man turned and looked at the drunk, young, frail and dirty girl,

"I'm going that direction, I can take you." He smiled at her.

Kitty did not smile back but yet she did not resist or say no. She followed him.

"Here, let me hold your hand." He grabbed her hand and led her out of the door. He walked over to a large black SUV parked at one of the gas pumps.

He opened the door.

"Here, sit her, I'll drop off the key." He said as he sat Kitty onto the seat and closed the door only after he placed both of legs forward.

Kitty's head slumped to the side as her eyes slowly faded out the car in front of her.

She could hear the driver side door open and shut. She heard the engine start yet she could lift her head nor open her eyes. Her head bobbed like a lure on the surface of a pond as the car drove away.

Kitty did not know where she was going. She did not know who she was with. She had never taken a ride from a stranger yet gone into the bathroom with one.

She did not feel threatened. Within her heart, she did not feel this man was a stranger. She did not sense imperilment, without personal struggle, she allowed herself to pass out in the passenger seat as it drove her away from the past.

CHAPTER FIFTEEN

Spies

"The weight of his glare sunk my courage. I floated to the surface gasping for air, after shedding my confidence." E.H.

Kitty opened her eyes as her head lay restfully on his lap, while his hands stroked her hair back, soothingly.

She looked up expecting to see Smithton but saw a stranger.

He looked down at her; not lovingly, not perverse, just looked at her.

She lifted her head to see the steering wheel within inches of her nose. She sat up and moved back over to the passenger seat.

"Where am I?" She asked as she checked the security of her jeans and felt her back, for her bra strap. Everything was intact and she was confused.

She looked over at the stranger.

"This is Timmons Road. You passed out and I did not want to wake you. I have some food here. It's in a bag to go, so you can take it with you." He handed a bag over to Kitty.

She looked at him, then at the bag, then around to see if she was in fact where he said she was. She was in fact in front of the food store where the whole ordeal started.

Kitty thought to herself,

"This man is my guardian angel. He did not harm me in any way. My daddy sent him."

She leaned over and kissed him on his cheek.

"I can't thank you enough, for everything." She said as she turned and opened the door and stepped out of the SUV, still surprised at the outcome of recent event.

She did not turn and watch as she heard the truck pull away. She kept walking, grasping the bag. Once she was back on the main road and felt she was at a safe distance, she reached into the bag and pulled out a breakfast sandwich.

She ate the sandwich so quickly heartburn interfered with the gratification of feeding her stomach. She ate the sandwich, reached back into the bag, and pulled out a hash brown in a paper bag. She ate it as quickly. She crumbled up the bag and stuffed it into her pocket.

"I can say I spent some of the money on this here food." She thought as she prepared herself for Smithton's interrogation.

As she reached the entrance to the trailer park a white sedan sped past her. She tried to look at the license plate to see if it was an undercover cop but could not tell.

"That looked like a cop." She said out loud.

"Shit, what do I do?" She thought as she panicked, "If I bring cops to Smithton, he'll kill me."

She ran behind a large pine tree and fell to the ground. She crawled underneath the long reaching branches. Dried needles fell into the back of her jeans and pricked her hands as she lay close to the trunk underneath the large sheltering pine.

She lay still although her skin was irritated and itching. She waited to see if the sedan came back down the road.

After what seemed to her to be half an hour she crawled out and ran through the back yards of the trailers until she reached their home.

Smithton's truck was parked off to side as if it belonged there. She felt a wave of comfort and safety overcome her until she got to the front door and took a deep breath and turned the knob. The door was locked.

"What the fuck Smithton." She said to herself. "I don't want to knock and I sure as hell can't stand here."

She tapped lightly on the door with her knuckles then paused for a response, within seconds the door swung open.

"Smithton," she cried as she threw her arms around his neck and fell into his thin frame.

Smithton embraced her back and held her close breathing in her presence. He stepped back after a moment and said,

"Where the hell ya been Kitty?" He looked at her with suspicion and concern.

"I thought I was being followed so I didn't come home after shopping, then I got to party'n with this girl I met behind the food store. I crashed at her hole for awhile." She looked into his eyes to gauge his veracity.

"Why, did ya miss me?" She quickly changed the tone of the conversation, attempting to move away from the dubious conversation.

Kitty heard a car in on the front road; she could not help but turn her head away from Smithton to see if it was the sedan.

"Kitty, your acting sketchy, what doin?" Smithton refused to ignore his gut instinct telling him that Kitty had been arrested.

"Were you pinched?" He yelled out after her hesitance and refusal to answer his last question.

"I'm 'bout to do some cookin' here, I don't need the boys comin' after me." He asked as she looked at him as she tried to force her tears from flowing.

"Smithton, no. I'm urched, can I just go lay down?" Kitty attempted to act like she was going to be sick. She put her hand to her stomach and walked to the bathroom.

She walked down the short hall and into the small bathroom. She closed the door and leaned her back against the door as she placed her hands to her head.

"Shit, shit, shit." She said to herself, "What am I gonna do?" She thought to herself, "He so knows."

She turned and locked the door.

"I need some space here." She thought as she turned to the sink.

Kitty's eyes briefly looked down to the floor.

"I never noticed the floor was so scuffed and dirty." She said, as she looked closer at the black marks all over the surface of the cream linoleum floor. Long black hairs were on the floor. Kitty thought, "The woman that lived her must've had long hair."

She looked away and turned the handle of the faucet. She held her hands under the water and bent toward the sink to wash her face. She splashed warm water over her tired, heavy eyes.

She looked at her reflection and looked away back to the door. She unlocked the door and walked out resigned,

"Stick to your story. No proof, suspicion only, proves nothin'." She said to herself as she walked back down the high to Smithton who was sifting through powdered chemicals.

"Tell me when you're cookin', I don't want fumes." She walked over to the corner where she and Smithton had first laid. She placed her hands on the carpet and bent down. She curled up in a fetal position and placed her left arm under her head.

Smithton looked down at her with distrust. He reached into his pocket and felt the ring that belonged to the "assfuck", as he coined her.

"If she'z thinkin' of rappin' on me I need to act now and turn her." He thought as he slid his forefinger through the graphite band.

He walked over to her,

"Kitten, I bought you somethin'," He hesitated for efficacy, "to show you how much I'm committed to ya." He knelt down in front of her.

He pulled his hand out his pocket with the ring around his forefinger. He turned his hand and held his palm to his face displaying the shiny black ring.

Kitty just looked at the band with surprise.

She sat up and reached out to remove it from his finger.

"This ring is beautiful Smithton." She tried it onto her left ring finger but the ring was too large.

She removed it and slid the ring onto her thumb.

"I've always wanted a thumb ring." She said to him as she moved over closer to him and grabbed his hand to pull him into her.

"This was a good line up." She smiled indicating that he had done the right thing.

Kitty pressed her lips to his and slid her tongue into his mouth. Smithton was always ready and eager to have sex with Kitty whenever she was assertive. He was quick to take over the lead role however, once she indicated to him that she wanted to have sex. Smithton was very primal but never desecrated the virginal figment of his imagination that saw Kitty in the purest light.

Smithton pushed her down on the rug and tugged at her jeans with raw, passionate and aggressive moves. He did not bother with her tee shirt. He pulled the button of his jeans open and shifted his legs jockeying his pants off.

As his jeans fell he pushed his left knee between Kitty's legs and had a brief vision of his last victim tied to the chair in the bathroom, feet away.

He shook his head as if the motion would push the vision out of his mind.

He placed his lips firmly upon Kitty's and kissed her with a closed mouth. He saw the backside of the much heavier woman that he had just sodomized. Smithton felt his erection dissipate.

"How the fuck am I gonna explain this." he thought.

"I can't do this now to my bright star." He said as he lay his body down on top of Kitty's.

"What's he doin'?" Kitty thought as she realized that he was not entering her.

"What's up?" She said softly.

"I just wanna luv you, you know, eye fuck for awhile. Besides, I feel sketch about the pigs watchin' us." He replied.

Kitty was surprised at his honesty and lack of sexual desire. There have been only four or five times in the past few years where Smithton had and lost an erection.

What Kitty did not know is that those were the time where he sodomized then murdered his victim.

Kitty wanted to console and assuage Smithton instead of make him feel inadequate.

"Your just bein' paranoid, there are no cops watchin' us. I shouldn't have said anythin' to ya. I was just trippin', now you're all noid and shit." She said as she ran her fingers through his hair the best she could before getting tangled at the matted ends of long locks.

"Kitty, I have to go out. I have to meet up with a d-boy. I have a job pushin' my ice." Smithton said as he pushed off of her body and stood up, buttoning his jeans.

It was standard that one of the first connections Smithton made in a new town was a crank dealer, then to make the methamphetamine, then sale some of the product he does not use himself.

"Alright, I'm gonna crash." She said as she also pulled up her jeans and buttoned them. She turned the ring on her thumb and felt comforted that he gave her the ring.

"He did not buy this, he has no cakes. I wonder who he stole this from?" She thought as she continued to fondle the oversized ring.

Smithton gathered his hair and pulled it back into a ponytail and pulled a rubber band out of his pocket and tied it back.

"Just thinkin', why didn't you burn up my cell with calls?" He asked as she turned toward the door.

"I worried about you Kitty." He added as he paused at the door for her response. "What are you gonna make up now?" He thought to himself.

"Smithton, I did call you. When you didn't pick up I hung up. Didn't a blacked out number show up?" She asked as she thought quickly once again saying,

"Stick to your story. No proof, suspicion only, proves nothin'."

"Funny, there are no blacked calls. See you in a few." He opened the door and yelled back at Kitty,

"Lock the door and don't talk to strangers." He slammed the door and walked out to his truck as he pulled out his cell phone.

He pulled up the last number incoming and hit send.

"What do?" The voice said.

"I'm movin' now. Where your chicken head hangs in a dime."

Smithton said meaning he would meet him in 10 minutes where he met the prostitute.

He opened the door to the truck and drove slowly away from the trailer looking behind him. When he was satisfied that no one was following him or watching the trailer, he glanced to both sides and in front of him, to see which neighbors watched him, what cars were following him or passing him.

As Smithton drove through the outskirts of town, he could not block the vision of the last victim's naked back on all fours.

As he saw her hair and face taped to the chair his penis now became hard. He was harder than when aroused by Kitty. He rubbed his penis through his jeans as he scouted the street for the same whore who serviced him the last time.

The bright plastic blue platform shoes stood out flashing in front of him. He pulled over and reached over to the passenger window. He rolled it down and smiled at the prostitute.

"Hello Armstrong." He called out.

"Armstrong, who the fuck are you talkin' to, I know it's not me." She yelled back as she turned her head and looked away from Smithton.

"You, my little astronaut, come on, ride this rocket, it's waitin'." He laughed loudly, "It's counting down. I can't do anymore zipper sparks here." Smithton rubbed his hard penis at the thought of her giving him head.

The prostitute could not help but laugh. She turned and looked at him.

"My boss wants to see you." She yelled back as she smiled and walked closer to the truck.

"I'm here for you first, d-boy second. Come on now honey, don't keep Daddy waitin'." He winked at her as he tried to charm her into the truck.

She opened the door as she also thought about how sexy this John was. The prostitute also craved Smithton.

She opened the door and sat down and looked over at him as she opened her purse.

"And do I have a bag of sunshine for you, if you give me some of that rocket launch." She said as she pulled out a baggie of powder.

"Crank not candy." Smithton said as he unzipped his zipper pulling out his stiff penis, displaying it to the eager girl.

She leaned over and wedged her body closer to Smithton. She opened the bag and stuck in her pinky fingernail. It was airbrushed bright pink with diamond crystals at the tip, with blue rays around it.

She turned her nail over and dipped it into the bag. A large amount of the powder scooped onto the curvaceous fatuous fiberglass makeshift spoon.

She lifted it to Smithton's nose.

"Daddy first." She said as Smithton inhaled the power.

The girl repeated the gesture and snorted the same amount of powder before turning her body toward Smithton.

"Pull into that garage at the end of the street." She pointed to an abandon auto body garage at the end of the derelict street.

She reached down and fondled Smithton's hard penis. He pushed his hips forward as he moaned with pleasure.

He put the truck in drive and drove to the garage.

He pulled in and stopped the truck and turned it off.

"Hold on their Armstrong." He said as he reached forward to assure himself that his 9mm gun was at his feet.

Once he felt it, he leaned back and unbuttoned his jeans.

"One more for the rocket fuel Armstrong." He asked the prostitute.

She obliged him and gave him another large spoon of meth.

"Now, I'm riding, not pulling, yanking or sucking." She shifted her short skirt up and threw her blue plastic shoe around Smithton and straddled his body.

She placed her body down on his large penis and rode him until he pushed her off.

"You're not gonna launch me this way ho." He grabbed her by the back of her head and forced her mouth onto his dick.

She tried to life her head but he forced her down onto him.

She did not fight him once she realized how strong he was.

The girl sucked Smithton until he came, she tried lifting her head off of penis right as she felt his dick contracting but he held her head with both hands down gagging her.

Once he came he pushed her off and pulled his pants up.

"Fuck you." The prostitute screamed at him.

"You did cunt, now where is D." He said as he looked at her coldly.

Although she felt manhandled and used, she also felt excited as her pelvic throbbed for more. His rude, aggressive and confident mannerism turned her on.

She looked at him as she spit on the floor of the truck.

"Fuckin' don't be rude." He said as she wiped her mouth with the back of her hand.

"Why, old bitch smell it and wonder what you been doin'? I think I need to be your lil' bitch." She said with full intent.

"Not today Armstrong, now get out and get your old man." He said as he pushed her body toward the door.

He rolled down his window and bent forward picking up his small handgun and placing it between his legs.

He sat back as she walked over to the large metal garage door. She lifted her arm up and pulled down on a long piece of rope hanging from the door.

She pulled with all of her weight as the door slid down the tracks and closed behind Smithton, while his truck remained parked forward.

He sat back and waited with confidence for the impending visit from the drug dealer. He had been in this power play situation many times before and always came out getting what he wanted. Smithton's hierarchy of needs was sole fulfillment of his desires, sexual releases, drugs and into this cocktail, Kitty.

CHAPTER SIXTEEN

Preservation

"The only cause which effects love is preservation." E.H.

Time moved forward but Smithton's attention stayed fixated and focused. "Come the fuck on, you mingin' cunt," Smithton uttered quietly within the confines of his truck.

Let's do this, I'm crawlin', he thought as he glanced at the left right and rear view mirrors, twitching his hands and shaking his legs.

The garage was dimly lit but outlines of clutter and stripped down car parts littered the floors. The door along the side of the garage wall, where Smithton's instincts had him fixated, was distinctly stained with soiled oil outlines of several fingerprints along the edge. Smithton's gut spoke virtuously to him. He saw the grungy door open and slam shut, allowing access from the anticipated business prospects.

Smithton's eyes focused and mentally photographed a short, heavy set Hispanic, twenty-something in age accompanied by three large gang fuckers.

"Bloods wear red," he said to himself as he looked at the characters, responding defensively and offensively recording their appearance and analyzing the bandana hanging out of the pocket of one of the bangers.

Fucking ego dick, he has three bangers with him as if he was the president of the fuckin' world, he thought.

Smithton did not change his stance. He slowly drew in a long, slow, and deep breath, taking mental control of a possible self-inflicted inferior situation. He held stance as he glared through the thick passenger side window.

The gang leader walked over to the passenger side window and stopped. He slowly moved his arms behind his waist and grasped his hands behind his back. He stared forward with over-inflated confidence. His boys placed their hands into the waist of their over sized jeans, grasping at their tools of salvation: 9mm handguns.

Toxic, tense paranoid emotions from all players sucked the air out of the small space, causing muscles to tense and egos to flare.

Smithton slid his fingers around his gun and slid it over with him as he leaned over to roll down the passenger side window.

"So you're Big D. What's up?" he said calmly but loudly with his foreboding cooker's smile.

The gang leader smiled slightly and yelled back,

"I see truth in the saying, crackers are white. Do you see sun or slither behind rocks all day?" His boys smiled and chuckled slightly.

Smithton felt no disrespect. He rebutted,

"I am flattered you know where I comin' from. You? A hole in a fence between El Paso and Juarez?" His humor did not amuse the leader. You are no better than the invasion of cockroaches or rats into this country, he added to himself as an afterthought.

"So what do I call you? Ass Peddler or Pedro?" Smithton called out.

"Just D. I'll call you doped out or Doped for short, being you let your job affect your mind," the leader said.

"Can we stop the dance and get to order?" Smithton asked.

"I have product to make and as you say, do, and you have product to sell, no?" Smithton asked.

"Stay away from my ass, hear?" D said.

"Why D, I think that should be a throw in for our deal. You want my amp, I have grade A to D meth. Dude it is wired. So place an order, front up and I can get cookin'," Smithton said as he leaned forward, talking out the window while holding his gun and watching the body language of the boys.

The gang leader reached into the front pocket of his red and white flannel cut off shirt, exposing big but not well defined arms, and pulled out a wad of bills bound by a rubber band.

He drew back and threw the bundle through the open window of Smithton's truck. It landed on the floor under his left foot. He through the money as if it were a mere trinket and Smithton ignored it, as he is not hired ass. Both men inadvertently exposed their weaknesses and psychoses in their behavior.

Smithton did not dare reach for it and expose his backside. He watched where it went them commented,

"I'll jet and count then spit at you for real. You get what I get, no more, no less. I'm straight up. See you here on the twenty-four from now," Smithton said as he leaned back, placing himself behind the wheel.

The three boys held out their pieces and aimed them at the car while the leader spoke.

"I fronted you Dope. He spoke with a strong Hispanic accent, strongly opposed to Smithton's laid back, slow southern drawl.

"I have some cookin' and liftin' to do. Later." Smithton looked back at the garage door and waited for it to open.

Smithton's mind raced with addiction to see the winner of the finish. He reached down and picked up the roll of bills.

He had money, supplies and housing. He needed to start cooking for real now.

He looked through the rearview mirror at the garage door that still imprisoned him. He did not look over at the bangers. He sat staring ahead waiting still until suddenly he heard the clanking of the garage door mechanisms churning and winding the chain of the large aluminum door.

Smithton started his truck and back out of the garage feeling confident and victorious.

Once back in light of day, he relaxed his stance and allowed his mind to take nominal steps away from life or death consequences of what he just experienced. He watched the red lights, stop signs, cars following him and pedestrians on the sidewalks taking down notes of his license plate, as he drove slowly back to Timmons Rd.

Smithton reached the trailer and parked the truck. He grabbed the wad of money and victoriously strode into the trailer looking for Kitty.

He opened the door and called out into the barren space, "Kitten, Daddy has some milk."

There was no reply. He walked down the short hall and looked into each room, including the bathroom. When he looked into the bathroom he stepped in and shut the door. He walked over to the toilet and unzipped his jeans. As he positioned himself over the toilet and began to urinate, his mind flashed back to his victim.

He turned and looked at the toilet where he had the chair positioned. He could see her body swollen, bruised, and duct taped to the chair. He could not control the arousal of his penis.

He knelt back into the same position and simulated the violent sexual act while satisfying his own erect penis. Smithton stopped and stood up out of frustration. He would not reach climax with the mere replay of the forced sexual act.

Fuck it, I need to get iced, he thought as he stood up and zipped his pants.

Smithton had disrupted his body's natural serotonin and pheromones levels to react only to chemical stimulus. Smithton looked at the wall where he cleaned down Kelsey's blood. His groined ached for release but he wanted that release to be with his Kitten.

Smithton's and Kitty's relationship had evolved into one of adulation and idolization. He saw Kitty as the innocent victim he could have saved. He sees all other women as the figure of sin causing him to commit acts of treachery against Kitty.

His frustration mounted and he felt no control, he screamed out into the quiet space, "Fuck! Fuck!"

He turned and walked back to the living room lab with new convictions. He reached into a box on the floor in the corner and pulled out a plastic jar of ephedrine tablets, then pulled out a thick plastic bag and dumped two handfuls into the bag. He pulled out a meat tenderizer and let his aggression out on the pills, crushing them down into particles.

He dumped the bag of white pebbles into a cleaned out commercial mayonnaise jar, fitted with the lid. The lid secured plastic tubing that ran a short distance over to a commercial ketchup jar. This jar was rimmed with a coffee filter.

Smithton with, great concentration, lit the camper's burner with his disposable lighter. At the point of ignition he felt like a scientist solving, creating, and making the world's cure for all that ails it.

He stepped back and watched closely as the solids liquefied, as the vapors traveled to their destiny.

He heard his phone ring twice before acknowledging it. The tone was disrupting his attentiveness to the vapors and control of the temperatures.

He looked at the caller ID and saw Jamison. This was his supervisor at work.

"Not now, dick," he told the ringing phone.

Smithton knew though that if he did not answer it, his only job and means of legitimacy would be in jeopardy. Just as the fumes from the air he was cultivating started to affect him, he reluctantly answered the phone.

"Yeah, Jamison," he said.

The voice on the other end was short and curt, "Pick up at 2338 Ellison Way. Death approximately twenty hours ago, so get it going. Oh, and when you get to the fill, see me." Jamison hung up as Smithton tried to recall the address.

"Shithead," he said to himself. "'Twenty-three somethin' blah blah Ellison Way. What the fuck?" He looked at the chemicals starting their transfiguration and knew he knew he had to stop it. He walked over and turned the knob to the burner and removed the plastic container,

"Shit," he said as the plastic molded onto is forefinger. He shut down the process and made his way to the site of the carcass.

Smithton drove through the picturesque hills acutely aware of his surroundings. He compulsively checked his mirrors, waiting to fulfill his prophecy that he was being followed, and watched, by someone.

"Where the fuck is Kitty?" he thought as he followed the navigation system given to him by his new employer.

"Turn right next 100 yards onto Ada Dr.," the voice of a robotic woman instructed.

"Yeah, yeah, what the fuck ever," he replied to the inanimate object.

"Where the fuck it Kitty?" he said again.

He was not worried for her well being as much as he was worried about her naiveté being the snowball to their demise.

She's been pinched and doesn't have the 'nads to 'fess, he thought. I promised Bob to take care of her. I am not doing that now, Bob. I'm sorry. I am failing you. These women are breakin' it down. I'm just bein' silly. I care for Kitty. I wouldn't diss her like I spend them. She is an angel.

As Smithton approached the road, Ellison Way., where the carcass supposedly laid, he scanned the sides of the roads looking for the dead animal. Within seconds he saw a large doe on the side of the road, intact, swollen, and rigid.

He pulled his truck off the side of the road and turned the car off. His mind fixated on his surroundings, as methodical as brushing one's teeth in the morning.

Standing over the body, he kicked it solidly, determining it to be swollen with an infection of parasites. He placed his right hand on the stiff leg of the doe and his left hand on bottom right leg that protruded forward. He easily slide the body along the asphalt until reaching the end of the truck bed.

Just as an Olympic shot-put thrower displays technique, Smithton bent forward with the required amount of leverage, started with a slide of the stiff body, and then created a whirl of current between the ground and the doe. He continued to lean back with all of his body weight and build higher lift between the doe and the ground. After three spins, the doe was high enough to reach the tailgate of his truck. He threw the body, sliding onto the metal and away from his grasp. The once beautiful, grace animal snapped her neck on the deep ridges of the truck bed, disrupting its movement forward. Her neck stayed fixed as the momentum from her weighted, swollen, and infested body moved forward. A large crack resonated from the metal truck bed. Her neck was turned an unnerving 180. Her glazed, milky wide eyes were glaring into Smithton's.

He noticed the obscure position of the doe's head but did not attach any emotion to the mutilated condition or consider any oddity of her eyes now fixated upon his.

"You're not the first lifeless female to stare me down this week, bitch," he said with a laugh as he spit brown saliva tinted by tobacco onto her neck.

He slammed the gate up with a screech of metal on metal, then turned and walked back to the truck with one thought consuming his mind.

"I need to dump this shit, I'm fiendin' a high and need cheese."

He reached the gate of the dump yard flashing his employee pass at the guard at the gate.

"Hey, Jamison wants to see you," the guard called out.

Smithton held up and out his forefinger and middle finger positioned in a v, with the palm of his hand to his face and waved at him. Smithton drove through the gate and up to the trailer adjacent to the dump.

He jumped out of the truck and headed toward the back, dropping the tailgate and leaning in to turn the doe's legs to face the tailgate. He grabbed the left front leg that was down on the bed and grabbed the back right leg off of the bed. He slid her as close as to the end of the bed as he could without tilting her balance, causing the stiff carcass to fall off. Throwing from the bed was preferred; the body already had lift, Smithton just has to product velocity.

He struggled slightly due to the cracked vertebrae of the doe; this caused a feeling of inferiority and inadequacy within him.

"Come on, stiff bitch. You cunts like it stiff, now you're just fuckin' with me." He spoke out loud enough for anyone standing within ten feet to hear his obscenities.

Phil Jamison had seen Smithton's truck pull up to the carcass dump. He was on the phone but was observing his behavior.

Smithton placed the dead doe at the right place, grabbed the body at the right balancing points and was skilled at the leverage and speed needed to now thrust the 130 pound carcass from the truck, up and onto the pile of decomposing animals.

The air smelled of rotting meat. The undesirable job was refused by most, selected by Smithton and questioned by Phil as he watched this new young, thin employee throw a large, heavy, and dead animal from the tailgate of a pickup truck. He hung up the phone and walked over to Smithton who was wiping his brow with the sleeve of his faded and torn flannel shirt.

"Smithton, can you come over here a minute?" he asked.

Smithton looked up without regard and nodded his head in affirmation, then walked over to the aged, overweight, and slovenly man. "What's up, Phil?"

The man disregarded Smithton's irreverence and replied, "I understand that you were here the other night, after working hours. I took the liberty to look up the records and you had not been called to go on a pick up." He stopped and waited for Smithton's response.

Smithton's impulsive reaction was controlled although he felt his heart race and skin start to sweat. He looked ahead with conviction and focus while replying, "Phil, Phil, Phil. How do I put this? Well, let me ask you this is: your Jammy bein' serviced?"

Phil was not accustomed to street slang. He looked at Smithton.

"What are you talking about, man?"

Smithton shifted to the left and right and back to the left, then replied, "Is the old ball and chain givin' your cock lip service? Giving you head?" He didn't laugh or even break a smile.

"Well," Smithson said when Phil didn't respond. "Mine sure ain't, but my ho ass is. I thought I could git some quick service here, no Jakes and such."

Phil rubbed his receding hairline with his fat stubby and dirty fingers.

"Look, you seem like you want this job, God only knows why. My fat ass is on the line for you." He stopped and stared at Smithton who was fidgeting a bit.

"Let's say you dumped a carcass late after a call, but you can't do it again." He stopped again and surveyed Smithson's body language.

"And no, my Jammy is not getting any lip service. It gets my greasy fingers if I'm lucky these days. So, set me up with your girl; and I will overlook this infraction this time." He smiled and nudged Smithton with his right elbow.

"Oh ya, boy. I'll be settin' your Jammy jamming tonight, if you want. And my ho ass is a total hoover." Smithton winked at him as he moved his hand as if he was holding his penis and thrust his hips forward into the air.

"I've been on this job for thirty years, son," Phil said. "No one would believe you over me. And if you were to lose your job over this or any other indiscretion, you will never work for this city again. Understood?"

Smithton spoke up quickly.

"Sure thing. Oh, I have to show you this, a dismantled twelve-point rack from the other day. I don't need that shit, I know you collect them." He spoke as he walked to the back of his truck.

He leaned his stomach over the side of the bed as his right leg lifted off the ground and grabbed two twelve-point racks from the back of his truck. He stood up and started to walk back to from his truck, still talking to Phil.

"I get what you're saying, Phil, it's understood. Be here at six tonight. Have the gate open so I don't have to use my pass, and I'll bring her in my truck like I'm dumping a carcass."

Phil listened to Smithton but was focused on the two beautiful, large, and developed antlers that Smithton had in each hand.

Phil changed the subject and commented, "Not a point broke, huh?" he moved closer to Smithton to get a better look on the rack.

"Nope, none broke, they're perfect." Smithton said as he lifted up his right hand. He tightened his grip around the base of the antler and as Phil walked in closer. Smithton was quick to pick up on an opportunity to remove a threat quickly and easily. Phil presented himself as easy prey. Smithton gripped the base of the antler tightly as he quickly leaned into swinging the antler around in a hook-like punch manner. The longest point of the antler pierced Phil in the neck while one of the other point punctured his eye. Phil reeled backward as he reached up to remove the antler that had opened the veins in his neck.

Phil choked and stumbled as he removed the antler and tossed it aside. "Ahhhhh, wha?" Phil was attempting to question Smithton, who scrambled to retrieve the antler.

The heavy set man still on his knees was fighting for life.

"Fuckin die," Smithton thought to himself as his endorphins raged. He wildly swung the antlers to the face of his opponent. The points pierced his cheek, lips, forehead, skimming over the thin skin pulling it from his bone structure.

Phil's face became unrecognizable. Smithton stumbled away from the bloody man attempting to catch his breath from the great excursion of energy. Phil quit struggling and lay limp on the ground.

Smithton acted quickly, stepping through the stream of blood that was flowing from his neck. He dragged Phil a short distance over to the dump zone. He grabbed the long legs of the decomposing deer and pulled them down. A fowl smelling of rotting flesh overtook Smithton. Although gagging and spitting up fluid from his stomach he moved quickly without hesitation. Thrown up fluid dripped from his lower lip and onto his shirt as he pulled Phil's body to the area he had just cleared.

Once Phil was face first in the carcass cavity he covered him up with the surrounding deer, raccoon, fowl and ground hogs. He used pieces of fur, bone removed from leatherized skin and fur, bodies crawling with beetles, maggots, flies, and ants soon covered the large man until he was not visible.

Smithton looked for the rack used to impale Phil. He ran over to them and threw them up into the air. He watched them fall onto the pile of bodies before turning to make his getaway.

Once Smithton was safely in his truck he started the engine and drove out of the landfill thinking to himself,

"It's gonna take forever for this fat fuck to decompose, lots of fat on that fucker." He laughed as he thought about it.

Smithton reached the gate and the guard was walking away from the small glass box carrying a thermos.

Smithton called out the window while driving slowly. He was careful not to stop his truck.

"Hey, I have another call and dump to make. Phil wanted me to ask you when the scheduled burn is."

Little did the guard know that Smithton was bloodied and smelled of the decomposed animals he touched.

The middle age man looked up and said, "I don't know that off the top of my head, man. Phil should know that." He looked confused and annoyed. "Anyway, I'm going home," he said as continued to walk in the direction of his car.

Smithton replied, "Hey, I'm just doin' what the man tells me; now, the day of the burn?" He looked at the guard without facial expression.

With a sigh and throwing of his arm downward, the man turned and walked back 5 feet to guardhouse. He removed keys from his pocket and shuffled though them. He placed a key into the hole and opened the door. The light went on inside the guardhouse and Smithton watched as the man shuffled through papers on a clipboard.

The clipboard was hung on the wall and lights went out. The man descended the small shelter, closing and locking the door. He walked back to his car, pulling out his car keys.

"The burn is scheduled for tomorrow," he called out to Smithton as he reached his car.

Smithton replied this time with a smile, "See you later."

Smithton drove back to the trailer to shower then finish what he started, cooking his meth for use and distribution. His mind wondered away from the plots, back plots and schemes and finally to Kitty.

"I need to reel her in. She is out there bein' watched. We can't have that." He said to himself as he drove.

"It's time to reel the lil' bitch in." he said before turning his thought to getting high.

"Come the fuck on you mingin' cunt." Smithton uttered quietly within the confines of his truck.

"Let's do this, I'm crawlin'," He thought as he glanced at the left right and rear view mirrors, twitching his hands and shaking his legs.

The garage was dimly lit but outlines of cluttered with stripped down car parts littered the floors. The door along the side of the garage wall, where Smithton's instincts had him fixated, was distinctly stained with soiled oil outlines of several fingerprints along the edge. Smithton's gut spoke virtuously to him. He witnessed the grungy door open and slam shut, allowing access from the anticipated business prospects.

Smithton's eyes focused as he memorized a short, heavy set Hispanic, twenty-something man. He noticed three of his gang members walking assertively by his side.

"Bloods wear red," he said to himself as he looked at the characters, responding defensively and offensively recording their appearance and analyzing the bandana hanging out of the pocket of one of the bangers.

"Fucking ego dick, he has 3 bangers with him as if he was the president of the fuckin' world." He thought.

Smithton did not change his stance. He slowly drew in a long, slow and deep breath, taking mental control of a possible self inflicted inferior situation. He held stance as he glared through the thick passenger side window.

The gang leader walked over to the passenger side window and stopped; he slowly moved his arms behind his waist and grasped his hands behind his back. He stared forward with over inflated confidence. His boys placed their hands into the waist of their over sized jeans grasping at their tools of salvation; 9mm handguns.

Toxic, tense paranoid emotions from all players sucked the air out of the small space causing muscles to tense and egos to flare.

Smithton slid his fingers around his gun and slid it over with him as he leaned over to roll down the passenger side window.

"So you're Big D, up?" He yelled out with his foreboding cookers smile.

The gang leader smiled slightly and yelled back,

"I see truth in the saying, crackers are white. Do you see sun or slither behind rocks all day." His boys smiled and chuckled slightly.

Smithton felt no disrespect. He rebutted,

"I am flattered you know where I comin' from. You? A hole in a fence between EL PASO and JUAREZ?" His humor did not amuse the leader. "You are no better than the invasion of cockroaches or rats into this country." He thought as an afterthought.

"What do I call you? Ass Peddler or Pedro?" Smithton called out.

"D is all. I'll call you doped out or Doped for short, being you let your job affect your mind." The leader said.

"Can we stop the dance and get to order?" Smithton asked.

I have product to make and as you say, do, and you have product to sale, no?" He asked.

"Stay away from my ass, hear?" He said.

"Why D, I think that should be a throw in for our deal. You want my AMP, I have grade A—D meth. Dude it is wired. So place an order, front up and I can get cookin'." He said as he leaned forward talking out the window while holding his gun and watching the body language of the boys.

The gang leader reached into the front pocket of his red and white flannel cut off shirt, exposing big but not well defined arms; and pulled out a wad of bills bound by a rubber band.

He drew back and threw the bundle through the open window of Smithton's truck, it landed on the floor under his left foot. He through the money as it was a mere trinket and Smithton ignored it as it he is not hired ass. Both men inadvertently exposed their weaknesses and psychosis in their behavior.

Smithton did not dare reach for hit and expose his backside. He watched where it went them commented,

"I'll jet and count then spit at you for real. You gets what I gets, no more, no less. I'm straight up. See you here on the 24 from now." He said as he leaned back placing himself behind the wheel.

The three boys held out their piece and placed it at the car while the leader spoke,

"I fronted you, Dope, the juice on the street it your git. Prove it." He spoke with a strong Hispanic accent as opposed to Smithton's laid back slow southern drawl.

"I have some cookin' and liftin' to do, later." Smithton looked back at the garage door and waited for it to open. Smithton's mind raced with addiction to see the winner of the finish. He reached down and picked up the roll of bills.

He had money, supplies and housing. He needed to start cooking now.

He looked through the rearview mirror at the garage door that still imprisoned him. He did not look over at the bangers. He sat staring ahead waiting still until suddenly he heard the clanking of the garage door mechanisms churning and winding the chain of the large aluminum door.

Smithton started his truck and back out of the garage feeling confident and victorious.

Once back in light of day he relaxed his stance and allowed his mind to take nominal steps away from life of death consequences. He watched the red lights, stop signs, cars following him and pedestrians on the sidewalks taking down notes of his license plate, as he drove slowly back to Timmons Rd.

Smithton reached the trailer and parked the truck. He grabbed the wad of money and victoriously strode into the trailer looking for Kitty.

He opened the door and called out into the barren space,

"Kitten, Daddy has some milk."

There was no reply. He walked down the short hall and looked into each room, including the bathroom. When he looked into the bathroom he stepped in and shut the door. He walked over to the toilet and unzipped his jeans. He positioned himself over the toilet and began to urinate. His mind flashed back to his victim.

He turned and looked at the toilet where he had the chair positioned. He could see her body swollen, bruised and duct taped to the chair. He could not control the arousal to his penis.

He knelt back into the same position and simulated the violent sexual act while satisfying his own erect penis.

Smithton stopped and stood up out of frustration. He would not reach climax with the mere replay of the forced sexual act.

"Fuck it, I need to get iced." He thought as he stood up and zipped his pants.

Smithton had disrupted his body's natural serotonin and pheromones levels to react only to chemical stimulus.

Smithton looked at the wall where he cleaned down Kelsey's blood. His groined ached for release but he wanted that release to be with his Kitten.

Smithton's and Kitty's relationship had evolved into one of adulation and idolization. He saw Kitty as the innocent victim he could have saved. He sees all other women as the figure of sin causing him to commit acts of treachery against Kitty.

His frustration mounted and he felt no control, he screamed out into the quiet space,

"Fuck it, fuck it." He turned and walked back to the living room lab with new convictions.

He reached into a box on the floor in the corner and pulled out a plastic jar of ephedrine tables. He pulled out a thick plastic bag and dumped two hands full are into the bag. He pulled a meat tenderizer mallet and let his aggression out on the pills, crushing them down into partials.

He dumped the bag of white pebbles into a cleaned out commercial mayonnaise jar, fitted with the lid. The lid secured plastic tubing that ran a short distance over to a commercial ketchup jar. This jar was rimmed with a coffee filer.

Smithton with great absorption light the camper's burner with his disposable lighter. At the point of ignition he felt as a scientist solving, creating and making the worlds cure for all that ails it.

He stepped back and watched closely as the solids liquefied, as the vapors traveled their short destiny.

He heard his phone ring twice before acknowledging it. The tone was disrupting his attentiveness to the vapors and control or the temperatures.

He looked at the caller ID and saw, Jamison.

This was his supervisor at work.

"Not now shirt." He screamed out.

Smithton knew though that if he did not answer it, his only job and means of legitimacy would be in jeopardy.

Just as the fumes from the air he was cultivating started to affect him. He reluctantly answered the phone.

"Ya Jamison." He asked.

The voice on the other end was short and curt, "Pick up at 2338 Ellison Way. Death approx. 20 hours ago, so get it going. Oh, and when you get to the fill, see me." Jamison hung up as Smithton tried to recall the address.

"Shithead, `23 somethin' bla' bla Ellison Way. What the fuck?" He said to himself as he looked at the chemicals starting their transfiguration.

He knew he had to stop it.

He walked over and turned the knob to the burner and removed the plastic container,

"Ouch, he said as the plastic molded onto is forefinger.

He shut down the process and made his way to the site of the carcass.

Smithton drove through the picturesque hills acutely aware of his grotesque surroundings. He compulsively checked his mirrors waiting to fulfill his prophecy that he was being followed, and watched, by someone.

"Where the fuck is Kitty?" He thought as he followed the navigation system given to him by his new employer.

"Turn right next 100 yards onto Ada Dr." The voice of a robotic woman called out directives.

"Ya, what the fuck ever." He replied to the inanimate object.

"Where the fuck it Kitty?" He said again.

He was not worried for her well being as much as he was worried about her naiveté being the snowball to their demise.

"She's been pinched and doesn't have the nads to fess." He thought.

"I promised Bob to take care of her. I am not doing that now, Bob." He thought. "I'm sorry. I am failing you. These women are breakin' it down. I'm just bein' silly." I care for Kitty. I wouldn't diss her like I spend them. She is an angel.

As Smithton approached the road, Ada Dr, where the carcass supposedly lay, he scanned the sides of the roads looking for the dead animal. Within seconds he saw a large doe on the side of the road, intact, swollen and rigid.

He pulled his truck off the side of the road and turned the car off. His mind fixated on his surroundings as methodical as brushing ones teeth in the morning.

He walked back, kicked the body, which he determined to be swollen with an infection of parasites.

He placed his right hand on the stiff leg of the doe and his left hand on bottom right leg that protruded forward. He easily dragged the body along the asphalt until reaching the end of the truck bed. The rough asphalt removed his exposed skin now displaying a pink edifice.

Just as an Olympic shot put thrower displays technique, Smithton bent forward with creating leverage. He started the momentum by sliding the stiff body toward him. He began lifted the doe by putting his full body weight into lifting the limp body up and off the ground. After spinning twice he had enough thrust and lift to reach the pass over the tailgate of his truck. The once beautiful, grace animal snapped her leg as it slammed off the side of truck.

"FUCKER." Smithton yelled as he dropped the doe on the bed of the truck. He walked to the tail gate and jumped it and onto the ground. He opened the gate and grabbed hold of the lifeless doe. The swollen and infested body moved forward. Smithton did not notice the glazed, milky wide eye stare. He was determined to remove the doe from his truck bed stoically.

He noticed the obscure position of the doe's head but did not attach any emotion to the mutilated condition or consider any oddity to the position of her eyes now fixated upon his.

"You're not the first lifeless female to stare me down this week bitch." He said with a laugh as she spit brown saliva tinted by tobacco onto her neck.

He slammed the gate up with a jarring screaming of metal on metal. He turned and walked back to the truck with one thought consuming his mind.

"I need to dump this shit, I'm fiendin'(needing) a high and need cheese (money)."

He reached the gate of the dump yard flashing his employee pass at the guard at the gate.

"Hey, Phil wants to see you." The guard called out.

Smithton held up and out his forefinger and middle finger positioned in a v, with the palm of his hand to his face and waved at him. Smithton drove through the gate and up to the trailer adjacent to the dump.

He jumped out and over the back of his truck. He dropped the tailgate down and he jumped up onto the bed so he could turn the legs to fact the tailgate.

He grabbed the left front leg left leg that was down on the bed and grabbed the back right leg off of the bed. He slid her as close as to the end of the bed as he could without tilting her balance causing the stiff carcass to fall off. Throwing from the bed was preferred; the body already had lift, Smithton just has to product lift and velocity.

He struggled slightly due to the cracked vertebrae of the doe; this caused a feeling of inferiority and inadequacy within him.

"Come on stiff bitch, you cunts like it stiff, now you just fuck with me." He spoke out loud enough for anyone standing within 10 feet to hear his obscenities.

Phil had seen Smithton's truck pull up to the carcass dump. He was on the phone but was observed his behavior.

Smithton placed the dead doe at the right place, grabbed the body at the right balancing points and was skilled at the leverage and speed needed to now thrust the 130 pound carcass from the truck, up and onto the pile of decomposing animals.

The air smelled of rotting meat. The undesirable job was refused by most, selected by Smithton and questioned by Phil as he watched this new young, thin employee throw a large, heavy and dead animal from the tailgate of a pickup truck. He hung up the phone and walked over to Smithton who was wiping his brow with the sleeve of his faded and torn flannel shirt.

"Smithton, can you come over here a minute?" He asked.

Smithton looked up without regard and nodded his head in affirmation.

Smithton walked over to the over aged, overweight, slovenly man and said,

"What up Phil?"

The man disregarded Smithton's irreverence and replied,

"I understand that you were here the other night, after working hours. I took the liberty to look up the records and you had not been called to go on a pick up." He stopped and waited for Smithton's response.

Smithton's impulsive reaction was controlled although he felt his heart race and skin release sweat. He looked ahead with conviction and focus while replying,

"Phil, Phil, Phil...how do I put this? Well, let me ask you this is your Jammy bein' serviced?"

Phil was not accustomed to street slang. He looked at Smithton,

"What are you talking about man?"

Smithton shifted to the left and right and back to the left, then replied,

"Is the old ball n chain givin' your cock lip service, giving you head?" He said without laughing or breaking a smile.

"Mine sure ain't, but my ho-ass is. I thought I could git some quick service here, no Jakes n such."

Phil rubbed his receding hairline with his fat stubby and dirty fingers.

"Look, you seem like you want this job, god only knows why. My fat ass is on the line for you." He stopped and stared at Smithton who was fidgeting a bit.

"Let's say you dumped a carcass late after a call, but you can't do it again." He stopped again and surveyed Smithson's body language.

"And no, my Jammy is not getting any lip service. It gets my greasy fingers if I'm lucky these days. So, set me up with your girl; and I will overlook this infraction this time." He smiled and nudged Smithton with his right elbow.

"O ya, boy-a. I'll be settin' your Jammy Jamming tonight if you want. And my ho-ass is hoover." Smithton winked at him as he placed his hand making it as if he was holding his penis and thrust his hips forward into the air.

"I've been on this job for 30 years. No one would believe you over me. AND if you were to lose your job over this or any other indiscretion, you will never work for this city again. Understood?" Phil added.

Smithton spoke up quickly,

"O, I have to show you this, a dismantled 12 point rack from the other day. I don't need that shit, I know you collect them." He spoke as he walked to the back of his truck.

He leaned his stomach over the side of the bed as his right leg lifted off the ground. He grabbed two 12 point racks from the back of his truck. He stood up and started to walk back to from his truck. He continued speaking with Phil,

"I get what you're saying Phil, it's stood. Be here at 6:00. Have the gate open so I don't have to use my pass, I'll bring her in my truck like I'm dumping a carcass."

Phil listened as he glared at the two beautiful, large and developed antlers that Smithton had in each hand.

"Not a point broke, huh?" He said as he walked forward to see the rack.

"Nope, there perfect, minus the head." Smithton said as he lifted up his right hand. He tightened his grip around the base of the antler, as Phil walked in closer Smithton swung his right arm around with disciplined hook punch technique. At the same time he thrust his left arm forward following perfect uppercut technique.

9 of 12 points from the lower antler contacted with Phil's skin, muscle, blood vessel and organs.

3 of 12 points from the hook contacted with Phil's juggler.

The heavy set man slumped down to his knees. His limp body fell, face-first to the ground.

Smithton acted quickly stepping around the river of blood that was flowing from his neck. He pulled the man over to the dump zone and let his body lay on the side of heap, face down in corroding bodies crawling with cock roaches, maggots, flies and ants.

Smithton lofted the antlers into the air and allowed them to fall onto the head. One landed and stuck where he threw it, the other tumbled downward slightly following the curvature of the shape of the horns.

Smithton went back to his truck and sat down, waiting. He thought to himself,

"It's gonna take forever for this fat fuck to empty." He laughed and said, "How's that service to your Jammy Phil?"

After 5 or 7 minutes, Smithton walked back over and kicked Phil whose face was now resting in on red, blood soaked 20 day old deer skin, still attached to the bones. The bugs ate the organs and most of the meat and flesh by now. Soon the pile would be burned.

Smithton walked back and got back into his truck and drove back toward the gate. The guard was walking away from the small glass box carrying a thermos.

Smithton called out the window,

"Hey, I have another call and dump to make. Phil wanted me to ask you when the scheduled burn is."

The middle age man looked up and said,

"I don't know that off the top of my head, Phil should know that." He looked confused and annoyed.

"I'm going home man." He said as an afterthought.

Smithton replied,

"Hey, I'm just doin' what the man tells me; now, the day of the burn?" He looked at the employee without facial expression.

With a sigh and throwing of his arm downward, the man turned and walked back 5 feet to guardhouse. He removed keys from his pocket and shuffled though them. He placed a key into the hole and opened the door. The light went on inside the guardhouse and Smithton watched as the man shuffled through papers on a clipboard.

The clip board was hung on the wall and lights went out. The man descended the small shelter closing and locking the door. He walked back to his car pulling out his car keys.

He called out to Smithton as he reached his car,

"The burn is scheduled for tomorrow."

Smithton replied this time with a smile,

"C ya later."

Smithton turned his truck around and drove back up the hill to the dump site. He pulled his truck up to where Phil lay and stopped. He jumped out of his truck and walked back to the bed of his truck.

He grabbed a mattick out of the bed and walked over to Phil. He raised the mattick with the spade side up above his head and swung it down into the pile of bodies. He lifted and pushed away bodies.

He walked over to Phil and drug him over to the hole that he had just created. He lifted his right boot, and kicked Phil as far into the hole as possible.

He used the sharp end of the mattick and pierced bodies and lifted them on top of the hole, covering up the body.

Once Smithton covered Phil with 10 or so carcass composing of deer, raccoon and possum he turned and threw the mattick back into his truck, got in and drove back down the hill.

"Phil is gonna have some serious service tonight." He said as he quickly detached from the incident.

Smithton drove back to the trailer to finish what he started, cooking his meth for use and distribution.

His mind wondered away from the plots, back plots and schemes and finally to Kitty.

"I need to real her in. She is out there bein' watched. I can't have that."

This was as much sentimental as Smithton was able to give while preoccupied and paranoid.

CHAPTER SEVENTEEN

Behind Blue Eyes

"Memory evokes a smile when our heart completes the grieving process for only when we pass through pain will a memory become pleasurable." E.H.

Meadow walked past an insignificant room during an insignificant moment of her day on her way back from a break. Without provocation, her attention focused on one of the many open doors. An elderly woman gently combed her husband's hair as he stared vacuously out the window in his small room. The leaves were tumbling downward, raining bright red maple leaves from the maple tree standing outside his window. Sparrows dropped from the branches and fell to the ground, rummaging and pecking for seeds left over from their last feeding.

The woman was dressed in a bright red wool blazer and a plaid red, green, and blue skirt. She wore a blue silk blouse with a beautiful gold brooch of a seashell.

Meadow smiled and paused, imbibing on their aurora. Her memory brought up a vision of Kelsey laughing as the pillow tumbled from the bed.

"Get up, it's our day off," Kelsey laughed as she jumped up and proceeded to bounce up and down on the bed like a child, jumping around Meadow's still body.

Meadow opened one eye without moving, planning her subterfuge. Once Kelsey was close enough, she reached out and grabbed her ankle pulling her down onto the bed.

"Ahhh," Kelsey screamed as they both laughed like school children.

The vision fell from her mind as the woman in room motioned for her to come in. She smiled and walked into the room.

"Hello, Mrs. Marino, how are you and Mr. Marino today?" Meadow asked cheerfully.

"We are wonderful. Today is our seventy-fifth wedding anniversary!" she proudly proclaimed. "This stubborn old man and I have seen it all together. I just wish I could take him home for the day," she added with an inflection of disappointment in her voice.

"Mr. Marino loved his front porch rocking chair. We spent many bright sunny mornings there. Warm and brisk nights, too." She laughed with a twinkle in her eyes. "If you know what I mean."

Meadow laughed as she replied and looked at Mr. Marino, "You Casanova, you, Mr. Marino. Why don't you sign him out for a couple hours?"

Mrs. Marino responded, "I broke my hip over the summer and I can't handle him alone. I don't have anyone else to help me, so we will spend it here," she paused. "Away from his home."

Meadow walked over to the elderly woman and spoke with inspiration. "I will help you take Mr. Marino home for a couple hours."

The elderly woman's gray eyes filled with tears and she reached out and grabbed Meadow's hand, clasping it with a rose printed handkerchief rumpled within hers.

"Thank you, my dear. Thank you," she replied, her voice breaking up.

"I have a few things to finish up, and then I will come back and we will celebrate your beautiful anniversary the way it should be, in your home, sharing your love and being surrounded with a lifetime of memories to comfort you." Meadow's emotions swelled as she said the words. She held it in the best she could and brushed off her pants, attempting to distract herself.

"It's a date. I will be back within thirty minutes." Meadow stepped forward and hugged Mrs. Marino, who was also moved to tears.

"Mr. Marino, we are taking you home to celebrate our anniversary." She spoke loudly and closely to his ear.

With these words, he smiled with full, open, shining brown eyes as he turned his head and looked at Meadow. She turned and walked out the room feeling overwhelmed with love and respect for the institution of love, unending, unwavering, and timelessly committed.

She felt this love for Kelsey and knew Kelsey felt this for her, without the need for a formality of paper instituting a legal marriage.

Shit, I have to call Kelsey and tell her I will not be there until tomorrow, she thought to herself as she realized her rapture of heart for the two slightly conflicted with her plans to leave work and go to Maryland late that night.

She pulled out her cell phone and hit Kelsey's picture on her main screen. She smiled without fail every time she saw the picture of Kelsey's smile, all teeth, within an inch of the camera.

The phone rang and on the fourth ring Meadow knew it was going to voicemail.

I'll try later. I don't want to leave a voicemail yet, she thought. Kelsey will totally understand, she would do the same thing. In fact, she would fuck me up if I didn't do it. She giggled at the vision of Kelsey pushing into her stomach with her shoulder in one of her playful football moves.

Meadow's mother and father were both deceased but Kelsey's were still living. They served as her surrogate parents. Kelsey's parents lovingly and openly accepted her lifestyle and embraced the relationship that she had found with Meadow. The two had a deep, meaningful, and transcending yet diametrically opposed frivolously blissful relationship.

When Meadow looks at Mrs. and Mr. Marino, she envisions what her parents could have been, what Kelsey's parents will become and what her and Kelsey have yet to experience through the course of life.

Lately, her inability to have children and the void of a family presence had taken an emotional toll on her. She walked into the next patient's room, which was vacant. Mr. Marino was in physical therapy. She was deep in thought, in a place much deeper and more cerebral that dumping bed pans and changing soiled sheets. She did these seemingly proletarian tasks with pride. Her ability to take care of the patients at the home gave her a sense of belonging, purpose, and pride, as if they were all her children.

Meadow also saw each and every patient as herself one day. Old, riddled with health deficiencies and without a home.

She made a personal promise to herself to not delude herself. She knew that without children, without a family, and with her alternative lifestyle she was setting up, in a way, a self fulfilling prophecy. Meadow did not want to be alone one day in a home with strangers caring for her needs. She took her job as seriously as parenthood, for she saw in them, her patients, her destiny.

Meadow went quickly but thoroughly in and out of each room performing her tasks with her mind continually thinking about destiny, sustainable love, and the concept of life partners.

I can't wait to see you Kelsey. Feel me missing you, feel me now, longing to just hold you, she thought as she closed her eyes and walked to the linen closet.

I know you can feel me, Kelsey, she added as she opened her eyes. But why aren't you taking my call? She pulled out her phone to redial Kelsey's number. Just as she started to pull up her "favorites," she heard her supervisor's voice.

"Meadow McKean?" Meadow stopped, placed the phone back into her pocket, and looked up.

"That would be me," she replied pleasantly as she smiled. Meadow and all of her coworkers, supervisors, and the owners of the home had close personal working relationships.

Her supervisor was jovial in tone when she asked, "I see you have requested to leave early today to take a patient home for two hours?" Her supervisor, Susan, looked up and frowned with a half heartedly before adding, "So big whoop, it's the seventy-fifth anniversary of a resident. Why should I let you go?"

Meadow replied with eager rebuttal to her friend and supervisor's cryptic question.

"Wow, since you put it that way, it seems dumb and frivolous to take the Marino's to their lifelong home of fifty-some years to have a quiet moment together to celebrate their love. I'm an ass, forgive me." She maintained a firm expression, although she wanted to laugh.

"Can I come?" Susan said as she leaned her right shoulder into Meadow's left shoulder.

"I know, Susan. Tell me how utterly sweet and insane that is. Seventy-five years and all she wants is to take him home to be within the all the memorabilia of the home that they built together." Meadow sighed wistfully, then snapped back to reality.

"Fuck, I sound like some romantic or something. I'm supposed to be a hard core dyke," she said and as she finished the words, she and Susan burst into laughter.

"But, seriously, is this a problem?" she asked, changing her tone slightly.

"No, I think it is great, and I wish my other LPN's were as personal and attentive as you. I thought you were leaving for vacation today, though? Does Kelsey know this?" she asked.

"I tried to call her. I'll call her again when I get to the Marino's home. She is already in Deep Creek," she said before she informed Susan, "I sent her flowers already to the trailer. I haven't talked to her yet. I'm sure she is settling in and cleaning the place to a clinical shine, if I know Kels."

"Well, this is a wonderful thing you are doing Meadow," Susan said affectionately. "I know Kelsey would think so, although she may kick your ass for being a day late for your much-needed vacation." Susan smiled then turned away from Meadow.

"Go, your shift is done. Have fun, make sure you fill me on Monday of all your, keyword here Meadow, relaxing, fun," Susan said as she walked away and held her right hand up in the air displaying a thumbs up.

Whew, Meadow thought. What a crazy day. I need to regroup, go get the Marino's, celebrate their much needed special day, go home, pack, sleep, and get up to drive to Maryland, and most of all get in touch with Kelsey."

She glanced down at her watch.

"Shit, I have to get back to Mr. Marino's room."

Meadow walked quickly down the hall thinking of calling Kelsey but not having the time. She reached their room to find Mr. Marino with his jacket and hat on, sitting in his wheelchair facing the door.

Mrs. Marino was sitting in the chair pulled beside of his wheelchair. She had a thin floral scarf tied around her hair, and a cream coat on.

"She looks so pretty," Meadow thought as she stood in the doorway and just looked at her for a moment. Mrs. Marino stood when she saw Meadow.

"Here we go, James." She skated behind her husband's wheelchair and placed her hands on the handles, pushing him forward.

Mr. Marino looked up at Meadow with a blank stare, as if questioning where they were going. His look was almost that of a frightened child going to the doctor's office.

Meadow stepped aside and allowed the two to pass in front of her as she stepped up and walked beside them.

"How long has it been since Mr. Marino has been home last?" Meadow asked Mrs. Marino after the confusion he had just displayed.

Mrs. Marino hesitated then said, "Oh, I don't know. It has been a long time, too long."

Meadow hoped she had not placed a dark veil over the auspicious event.

"Doesn't matter how long it has been, for that is the past. We have today and this wonderful event and we are taking you home, right Mr. Marino?" She placed her left hand on his left should as she spoke.

Mr. Marino was wearing a camel colored wool coat. His eyes remained fixated forward as he watched each seam of the long linoleum floored hallway slip beneath the wheels of his chair. His forefinger and thumbs continuously rubbed the rim of a brown wool fedora on his lap.

When the three reached the front receptionist, Meadow walked over to the girl as she instructed Mrs. Marino to wait while she grabbed an aide to help them out.

Meadow instructed Megan, the receptionist, to call one of the aides and have them wheel out Mr. Marino to her car.

She turned back toward Mrs. Marino.

"I will take Mr. Marino in my car. Why don't you go get your car and pull around here in front of the door and we will follow you to your home. Where is it?"

"It's about forty-five miles east toward the mountain," she replied.

Meadow's heart sank slightly when she heard the distance but remained upbeat and altruistic.

There is no way I'm making it to Deep Creek this evening, she thought. Kelsey is going to kill me.

"Meadow, you need my help?" Ryan, one of the aides, called out.

Meadow turned her head and noticed the smiling aide walking quickly toward her.

"Yes, Mrs. Marino is getting her car and pulling around here. I am taking Mr. Marino home." She looked down at him staring forward while still fingering the brim of his hat.

"It's the Marino's seventy-fifth wedding anniversary," she said loudly as she placed her hand once again on Mr. Marino's shoulder.

"Ryan, wait here with Mr. Marino while I get my car."

The short walk gave Meadow yet another opportunity to reach Kelsey, who surely was settled into the trailer by now.

She reached into her pocket and pulled out her phone, but as she pulled out the phone her car keys tumbled out with it, falling to the ground.

"Shit," Meadow said quietly as she reached down in a rushed stated, with her eyes scanning the home screen on her phone for the redial button. Just as she hit redial she realized that Mrs. Marino had already pulled around to the entrance and she glanced back to see Ryan pushing Mr. Marino to her car.

She stood up and placed her phone back in her pocket as she called back, "Ryan, no, no. He is driving with me."

She turned and quickly walked to her car, opening the door with her key fob.

"Damn it, Ryan.," she mumbled as she started her car and quickly placed it in reverse, backing out of the spot.

With seconds barely passing, Meadow reached the entrance just as Ryan was shutting the door of passenger seat, where Mr. Marino was sitting.

"Shit," she said as she frowned out of the window.

She placed the car in park as she beeped the horn, catching Ryan's attention.

She opened the car and jumped out.

"Sorry, Ryan, but I want Mr. Marino to drive with me. For legal reasons, I have to chaperone him home." She briefly explained the legalities to Ryan, although she was not obligated to. Meadow was flustered at the temperament of the last few minutes and did not want to confuse Mr. Marino anymore than he already was.

She looked at Mr. Marino, who was now wearing his hat upon his grey slicked back thick head of hair. His hollow face hinted at his once chiseled features. She watched as Ryan helped him out by his arm, Mr. Marino struggling to leave the safe confines of their car. She rushed over.

"Here, let me, Ry," she said quietly to Ryan.

"Mr. Marino, I want you to drive with me. See," she pointed behind them. "There is my car. I want you to drive with me so I know how to get to your home, okay?" She spoke calmly to Mr. Marino and evoked a calm demeanor as he stood up and shuffled alongside of her back to the passenger side of her car.

"Ryan, grab that door for us," she called out as she watched Ryan step quickly, open the door, and stand behind it.

Meadow moved quickly through the next few steps and did not let out a deep sigh of relief until Mr. Marino was in the car with his seat belt on. Mrs. Marino had been once again briefed and she was behind the wheel placing the car in drive.

"Here we go, Mr. Marino," Meadow said brightly as she drove forward, following the dark gray late '80s model sedan with spoke wheel rims.

She tried to make conversation to ease any stress that once again welled up within the fragile dementia patient.

"That is one fancy car, Mr. Marino. I can tell you took very good care of it." She had to speak loudly into the quiet, awkward cavity of the car. She did not expect Mr. Marino to answer, so she reached forward to turn on the radio.

"I bought that car once I retired from the mill," Mr. Marino said to the amazement of Meadow. She smiled, wanted to clap her hands but let out a small laugh of surprise and thought of anything relevant to say to keep him engaged and speaking for the first time, to her recollection.

"Wow, you must have saved a long time. Is it a Cadillac?" she asked.

"Yes, it was Maureen's dream car. I always promised to buy her one when I retired." He spoke quietly as he stared forward at the car's tail lights. While the two remained stopped at a red light, Mrs. Marino assiduously looked into the rear view mirror, checking on the welfare of her husband.

The two continued to have casual conversation over the course of the next forty minutes, though Meadow's attentions drifted away from the conversation several times and to her partner.

Kelsey is still at large, she thought. Or is it me that is at large? She questioned herself as she tried to pass the time until she could use her cell phone again. Her care for her passenger's safety prevented her from attempting to use the phone while they were en route.

The gray sedan's right turn signal flashed in front of her. Kelsey looked to the right and saw a driveway leading back to a stone house.

"Is this your home, Mr. Marino?"

She glanced over to see his reaction.

He leaned in his seat and moved his head forward to catch a better view of the house that stood in front of him.

"Indeed. Mrs. Marino and I built this house in 1947 when I got back from the war," he proudly announced. "Her uncle was a stone mason."

Meadow placed the car in park and looked out at the large stone house that was in perfect condition.

"It is beautiful," she said, her eyes moving over the stonework, onto the wood framed windows and to the large side porch and yard.

Meadow had not thought about the house or attempted to picture the size of it, and she would have never imagined the grandeur of this home. She walked over and opened the door for her driving companion.

"Here we are Mr. Marino. You're home." Her eyes filled with tears as she said the words.

She reached down and gently helped the frail but now excited man to his feet. He wobbled left and right for a second before he reached down and caught the passenger door with his hand. He was so busy looking at the house that his mind was moving ahead of his physical abilities.

"Here are you Jim," Mrs. Marino called out. "We're home." She walked over and Meadow handed over his right arm to her and fell back to walk slightly behind the two. She remained alert and held her right arm slightly forward as to offer Mrs. Marino assistance with her husband.

Meadow thought as she watched as the two slowly walk to the door, she and he need to have this minute, arm in arm as if they are the only two people in the world. In truth, right now, they are the only two that matter. Meadow watched as she found great inspiration from their interaction.

To have so much love after all these years, to just want your hearts companion to have the gift of love and comfort, home, is so amazing. Meadow did not think of Kelsey at that minute, for she was consumed with the reverberating emotion from the elderly couple.

The three reached the large wooden double door. Mrs. Marino reached into her purse, unlatched the clasp on the top, and pulled out a set of keys. She placed the key into one of the brushed brass locks and pushed it open.

Inside was beautifully preserved oak polished floors. Two large banisters formed a half circle that followed through to a huge set of stairs that led to a upper balcony that overlooked the foyer where they stood.

Meadow felt as if she was visiting a historical home.

"Mrs. Marino, this home is breath taking," she said out loud as she continued to look around in wonder and awe.

"Thank you, Meadow," she humbly replied as she took off her husband's hat and coat

"Come, let's go sit in the drawing room and I'll make some tea." She lovingly took her husband by the hand.

"May I make a phone call?" Meadow asked as she saw an opportunity to leave the two alone.

"Go right ahead, you can go into the dining room if you would like some privacy, just there to the left." Mrs. Marino's voice echoed out from a distant room.

Meadow looked to her left and saw a small hall that lead to a dining room. She pulled out her phone and walked through an entranceway that had wood hand-carved columns that formed an arch to the dining room.

When she was inside, she paused before calling Kelsey once again. Along the side of the room was a large fireplace, and the ceiling boasted an amazing spray of ornate plaster work framing the corners and center crystal chandelier.

The long table was set for two, not on each end, but across from one another, more intimately. One of the settings had silverware the other did not.

Meadow walked over to the chair where the partial place setting was and saw a picture of Mr. Marino on the chair. She reached down and picked it up. She held it to her face as she tried to envision this was the body of her patient. He was dressed in a military outfit, standing on a beach.

He served in the military, Meadow thought as she looked at the photo. Her eyes fell back to the chair and draped over the seat was a ribbon. Faded purple-blue ribbon clasped a gold colored heart with purple enamel surrounding the side profile of a man.

This must be a purple heart, Meadow thought with excitement and enthusiasm. Mr. Marino a war hero? She thought about her patient as she had so many times, quiet, meager, and weak. She now saw a brave, handsome hero.

As Meadow stared, memorizing the items in front of her, the phone she had inadvertently placed back in her pocket rang.

A jolt shocked her from her intense concentration as she dropped the medal.

"Shit, what is with me today?" she said as she quickly bent down to pick it up. As she did she removed her phone and looked at the screen displaying the name Kelsey with a large toothy grin.

"It's about time," she blurted out before saying hello.

There was a pause, silence, then a rustling sound as the call disconnected.

Meadow looked down at the phone to see three seconds blinking on the screen.

"Damn, we got disconnected," she said as she redialed the phone.

The phone rang, then rang again before continuing to ring six times to voicemail.

Meadow moved the phone away from ear and a strange feeling of nausea overrode her preceding emotions.

"What the fuck?" she said, louder than she realized.

"Are you okay?" Mrs. Marino called in from the other room.

"Yes, yes, I'm fine. I'm sorry, it's this phone," Meadow said as a blush of embarrassment changed her complexion.

"Can you come sit with Mr. Marino so I can make us some tea?" Mrs. Marino called out.

"Yes, of course," Meadow replied as she walked toward the foyer, following the voice from the other room.

As Meadow entered the sitting room, the decorous surroundings no longer distracted her. Her reddened cheeks flushed of color and left her body in a perched ominous physical and mental state.

She entered the room and sat beside Mr. Marino, trying with all moral conviction to focus back on the couple.

"Are you alright dear?" Meadow vaguely heard the voice.

"Are you alright, Meadow?" Mrs. Marino called out again to her.

Meadow looked up, "Yes, it's just—" she looked at Mr. Marino, then at the elderly woman in the glory of having her heart's companion home on their wedding day after so many years.

"It's nothing but an annoying cell phone," she replied then started to say, "You know how they are," then caught herself.

Meadow thought, there is no way Mrs. Marino has a cell phone.

Mrs. Marino walked out of the room and returned within seconds.

"Here try mine," she said as she handed a cell phone to Meadow.

This day will not cease to amaze me, Meadow thought as she took the cell phone from the graceful older woman.

Meadow tried Kelsey's number and the same chain of events played out.

"She must not have reception," she said to herself, trying to convince her instincts that her premonition of nefarious events was incorrect.

Meadow sat back and refocused her attention to Mr. Marino. She had so many questions for him.

"Mr. Marino, were you in the military?" she started.

"I was in the army, served at Normandy. Cold, cold water," he replied as his mind focused, then drifted.

Mrs. Marino appeared in the entrance way with a tray.

"Mr. Marino is a purple heart recipient, saved two members of his unit after their boat was sunk. He had his pelvis shattered but sill pulled those men to a nearby boat." She spoke as she sat beside her husband, whose mind was not engaged within the current conversation.

Meadow looked at his wife, who beamed with pride and said, "Your children must be so proud of you?"

"After his injuries, we were not able to have children. Instead, we spent seventy-five years paying attention to one another."

What a wonderful mindset to have, Meadow thought. Kelsey and I will have one another to focus on. We will fill our lives with one another like the Marino's.

Where Meadow's recent months were filled with moments of emptiness due to her inability to have children, the Marino's had seventy-five years of moments filled with love solely for one another.

The next several hours compelled Meadow. She watched the couple's interaction and body language while listening and learning from the lost old man, war hero, and devoted husband. She observed the loving reverence from the strong, sophisticated, and now independent woman and wife. As solitary souls, they were incomplete, lost on the various currents of their lives. Together they healed each other, completed one another and formed one soul.

Meadow's concerns over her lack of communication with Kelsey had been washed out of her mind by the flood of memories shared by Mrs. and Mr. Marino. She felt blessed that she was able to participate in their anniversary. She did not look at her act as a charity or part of a job responsibility. Meadow found a quiet, calm resolve to her current moral and emotional conflict.

During the quiet drive back to the nursing, Mr. Marino slept while her mind raced.

I can and will experience all the joys of life although Kelsey and I live alternative lifestyle.

CHAPTER EIGHTEEN

Still Shackled

"If we are not accountable, we have no true sense of belonging."
E.H.

Kitty's eyes welled up as she recalled the last directives from Smithton "Lock the door and don't talk to Strangers."

She turned as her emotions rushed squeezing air from her lungs. Her breath became short as she tried to keep ahead of the panic that was overwhelming her. She felt a tingling sensation on her skin as a hot wave swept over her face.

She ran over to the corner where she found sanctuary. She threw out hands and pressed them against the wall, fingers spread wide, hoping for stability.

"Breath, just breath Kitty." She coached herself, as she attempted to control her intake of air.

The attempt to calm the panic attack was not successful. She began to gasp for breath as she squatted down.

"You are not gone Daddy. Where are you? Please come back to me." She thought as she lost control of herself.

She repeated her father's words to her when he would leave her alone in the house,

"Lock the door Kitten and don't talk to strangers." He said as he kissed her on the forehead.

The strong and secure sense of stability was replaced by two walls of an abandon strange structure.

She vividly saw his wide, embracing smile that revealed his large teeth with a small space between the two front ones. She played the film in front of the dark canvas of her closed eyes.

Kitty smiled briefly, as she saw the whimsical shuffle of his feet and the rocking of his hands when he grabbed her to dance with him. She threw her arms around his waist and pressed her cheek onto his chest. She heard the rhythm of his heart and felt the addicting, comforting rush of love within hers.

Kitty fell to a fetal position on the ground. She was surrounded by darkness and cold. Her ethereal vision of her father was gone and felt the cold hard intimidating surroundings of the jail cell.

"I'm scared." She cried to quiet open space.

"Trooper Cantoniski, I know he is patrolling this street. Daddy what am I gonna do? Help me?" She begged for her father's guidance.

Kitty was malnourished, fatigued and mentally drained. Her body was unable to stay awake after the physical and mental drain of this recent panic attack. She fell quickly into a REM sleep.

"Daddy, can you hear me? It's Kitty. I'm in Miami, on vacation. Somethin' bad happened." She spoke through a gargled cell line.

"What is it Kitten, What happened?" Bob asked in a calm but concerned voice.

"We checked into this hotel that has two floors. Smithton was out doin' somethin', I heard someone outside of the door, I wasn't sure if it was Smithton, I opened the door n' this..." Kitty heard her father on the other line reply,

"Kitty, can you hear me?" He said in a faded voice.

"Daddy?" She spoke louder into the phone. The phone was silent as she eagerly waited to hear his voice.

"No." She yelled out in frustration. She looked down at the phone and tried to dial the number again.

"3-1-4,"She paused, "I can't I remember the number?" She yelled out in a frenetic state.

"This has always been my home number. What's wrong?" She screamed as she kept trying different combinations. Every time she tried a new combination the operator would come on following an unnerving familiar tone of an incomplete call.

"The number you have dialed has been disconnected, please hang up and try your call again." She repeatedly heard.

Kitty felt lost, desperate and alone. She opened the door to the hotel room and looked out of the room to see if Smithton was coming back.

The floor had become a tumultuous ocean, hundreds of feet below.

She knelt down and looked closer, thousands of shark fins circled below, swimming in interlocking circles, crowded, and caroming into one another.

Kitty stood up and went back into the room and closed the door. She picked her cell phone again and tried to redial her home number.

This time the call went through. She wiped her forehead in relief as the phone on the other end rang.

"Hello," a man's voice called out.

"Daddy, what happened?" She quickly asked.

"Who is this? The voice asked in a bereft tone.

"Daddy, it's me Kitty, can you hear me?" she yelled.

"This is not funny, my daughter died last week." The voice said as he hung up the phone.

Kitty looked up with confusion.

The tone of a rap/dance song breeched the silence of the room. Kitty heard the tone from the phone in her dream. The sound continued as she stirred then awoke to hear the sound resonating in barren rooms.

She sat up and looked around trying to ascertain where the sound was coming from. The tone stopped.

She stood up as her eyes scanned the room. She walked around sifting through the long fibers of the shag carpet.

"There it is again." She said to herself intimating hope of finding the phone.

She followed the sound down the hall and into one of the back bedrooms. Her eyes scanned the carpet until she saw a cell phone on with the green and white battery exposed. She walked over and picked up the phone. She reassembled the back cover and turned the phone over as she powered it up.

Meadow was the name displayed on the screen.

"Meadow?" What the fuck Smithton, are you fucking around on me, again?"

Sadness overcame her as she began to cry. She stared at the phone trying to figure out who Meadow was or could be. The possible explanations terrified Kitty. Striking at her fear of abandonment.

"Maybe it was here before we got here. I'm freakin' maybe for nothin'." She thought with a small sense of respite.

"It must've never ringed before?" She said to herself trying to convince herself that it had been in the room all the while they were squatting in the trailer.

Kitty's eyes glanced around the room for other objects that could possible still be in the room. After a second of scanning the run she saw the back panel of the cell phone. She briefly wrestled with the back until she slid it onto the back of the phone.

She looked at the phone for several minutes not sure what her next move should be.

"Should I listen to the voicemails? It's sayin' 4 new voicemails." She walked over to her corner of the room hoping she would find some comfort in the space that had become a secure place for her.

She envisioned violet wallpaper. She could see her white lace runner under her glass mock oil lamp and all the posters of her teen heart throbs taped on her closet door.

She folded her legs under her body and sat down facing the wall, holding the phone in her lap.

She added up all the factors of the recent events, the cops, the dream, the ring, and now this phone. Collectively they were all causing her to doubt Smithton and her life with him.

Kitty had always trusted that Smithton would take her away from their small southern hometown. He promised her to care for as he promised Bob on his deathbed that he would care for Kitty and carry on.

She was never sure what carry on meant, she always thought it meant with the concrete business.

Smithton dropped that business as soon as all the equipment was sold. When the last of father's tools were sold she began to regress and remove herself from the reality that Smithton was doing her more harm and not taking care of her.

"What is up with this ring?" Where the fuck did he get it and why is it so big. I don't even like it." She thought. "Smithton had to know I would not like this ring."

"He knows I like girly, pretty stuff. This is like a man's ring." She paused, "That's it, he probably got into a fight with some D or some tweaker and took it after he kicked his head in."

Kitty felt eased with her postulation of the ring eliminating the scenario that it was from an affair of his.

Kitty hit the home button again on the cell phone. The picture of a woman standing in front of a red explorer pop up as the wallpaper.

"Who the fuck are you?" She thought, "Are you fuckin' Smithton?" She asked now removed from ease.

Her body started feeling light headed. Lack of food, lack of sleep and fumes from Smithton's cooking were causing presentiment within her.

"Where the F is he, BTW?" She yelled out. She stood up and walked to the bathroom.

She entered the bathroom and leaned over the sink looking down at the floor.

The floor was streaked with maroon lines from the aftermath of a rag saturated with a cleaning product.

Kitty focused harder on the surface of the floor.

"There are more black hairs?" She said as she knelt down. She saw several black hairs rolled together and left stuck to the toe kick of the vanity.

She quickly stood up and turned back to the sink and turned on the water.

She turned her head and held her mouth under the running water drinking it in quickly. Her hair, chin and shirt were getting wet.

She stopped drinking and turned around, water still running.

She knelt in front of the tub and ran her hand around the side. A ring of the same pinkish hue was haphazardly cleaned down.

"That fuck had a bubble bath with some ho, in this tub while I was in jail." Kitty grew enraged. She was not normally jealous or paranoid but she had too many factors adding up to an affair.

All of the external factors mixed a dangerous cocktail with her emotions, fueling an incendiary temperament that she could not control.

She stood up and walked out the bathroom.

"I'm outta here." She screamed as loud as her lungs would allow. Her body shook with emotion.

She opened the door and slammed it behind her, rattling and reverberating from the frame and flying back toward her. The door rested along the frame but not closed.

She stopped on the porch as her mind ambushed her standard temperament. She felt her rage pushing her thoughts in agonizing directions.

She turned to walk off the porch and noticed a sedan pulling into the trailer park.

"Fuck, the cops, they are here for me again." She jumped off the side of the porch reacting in a frantic paranoid state.

She ran behind the bushes alongside of the trailer. She squatted down and tried to control her breath that raced with her pulse.

The sedan did not turn into the trailer court, but continued forth down the road.

"Git it still K." She said to herself as she leaned her back on the aluminum siding and slide down onto her buttock. She placed her head in hands and closed her eyes.

"God, help me get this in control, please." She begged. The sun had turned its back on the day and a grey shade was falling over the sky. Shadows appeared and trees grew black and stark. She opened her eyes and saw a round object on the ground. It appeared at first site to be a ball. At second site it appeared to be a pumpkin, there, just at the bushes edge off the porch.

She reached out and pulled it to her. It was stuffed with flowers.

"It's a flower arrangement." She thought as she lifted up the bent carnations broken by the fall off the porch.

Kitty continued to glare at the arrangement with complete confusion. She thought,

"Smithton does not have money to git this for me."

"Besides, he never got me flowers?"

"Daddy, I remember every Valentine's day you bought me a lil' heart shaped box of candy, the one with like 6 pieces. I hated the bark one." Kitty's thoughts were sporadic.

"You always bought me a red carnation." Her fingers lifted up and broke off a red carnation from the disheveled arrangement. She placed the flower in her pocket.

Kitty sat back and smiled as she glowed with the feeling of love. She looked up and noticed a small white card on the ground beside the arrangement.

She lunged forward stretching her fingers out to pick up the card. She moved back and sat with her back against the trailer. She rubbed the card along her jeans removing mulch and dirt that had adhered to it.

Kitty held the card up but could not read the writing in the dim light. She stood up and walked over to the next trailer. Light was flooding out of a window high off the ground.

She ran over and turned her back to this trailer looking around for any possible onlookers.

There was enough light for her to read the card.

She mouthed the words as she read,

"I miss you already and counting the time until we can see each other and spend quality time alone together. Whatever happens in life, I want it to happen with you as my partner.

Your,

Meadow

She stopped and read the words again.

"Meadow, there is this fucking name again, Meadow. Who the fuck is Meadow?" Her voice screamed inside her head.

She pulled out the phone and looked at the call list.

She read the name that appeared several times,

"Meadow, Meadow, Meadow." She pushed the voicemail icon and read the name of the caller,

"Meadow."

Kitty pushed the voicemail icon to listen to the last voicemail.

She heard a woman's voice. A concerned woman saying she could not come tonight but would come in the morning.

"What is going on? No, No, No? What will happen to me?" She began to panic at the thought of losing the man who was keeping her down. Down was a place thought, ambiguity was Katherine's enemy.

Kitty heard cracking of sticks and crushing of leaves off into the tree line 40 feet away from where she stood.

Like prey to a predator she froze, then ran, back toward the trailer.

"The siding is off the bottom over there, run Kitty, hide under it, NOW." She said to herself as she sprinted to the one spot of the trailer where the skirting had been removed. She crawled into the small breech in the siding that surrounded the trailer. She lay flat on her stomach, folded her arms over her head and rested her forehead upon her arms. Her nose ground into the moldy dirt. She held her breath and waited. She heard footsteps approach the trailer.

She saw four legs run past her. She rolled over once, getting closer to the edge so that she could see from outside the bottom of the trailer.

She saw two men in black hooded sweatshirts, get out of the car in front of the trailer.

She leaned over dangerously close to the edge to see the car.

Kitty saw a red explorer. The two men started the car quickly and drove around the circle of the trailer park and out, screeching wheels once on the main road.

"Why do I know that car?" She thought as her body grew limp caused by the extreme drop in her serotonin levels.

Kitty had been on an extreme highs then extreme lows for over 48 hours. She allowed herself to fall into sleep, under the trailer where she dreamt once again.

Kitty was on a highway, the highway formed a rollercoaster. The car she was driving was out of control, racing around bends on a steep hill. She frantically turned the steering wheel but the car tittered close to edge never falling off the rails. Below the track was unknown to her.

She stopped the car after seemingly hours of panic. She choked then started to cough uncontrollably.

Kitty held her hand to her mouth and felt her hand dampen. She pulled it to her face to see blood. She choked again. Her teeth ached.

"My molars are loose." She said.

Her fingers grasped her molar, as she placed her forefinger and thumb around the large tooth, it fell into her hand.

Horrified, and in disbelief Kitty looks at the object that have fallen into her hand.

"My teeth are falling out." She screamed as she reached in and pulled out all the teeth in her mouth.

Kitty lay twitching, shivering and anguished amongst insects and night predators alone under the trailer.

CHAPTER NINETEEN

Heteronomy

"No two ice crystals are the same, each driven by currents, bonding as they are pushed together, constantly changing." E.H.

Kitty reached up and brushed a feather off her cheek as it tickled her skin and again, barely a touch on the miniscule hairs on her cheek. She opened her eyes and realized it was something crawling along her face.

She tried to sit up, hitting her head on a metal surface above her head. She lay back down slapping at her cheek, hair and neck.

Within seconds, she remembered she was underneath the trailer, on the cold, damp, moldy ground. She looked for the breech in the metal skirting so she could roll back out of her tomb-like surroundings.

She rolled several times and saw the night sky. The stars light a beckoning, welcoming her back to life. She drew in a deep breath and sat up.

She looked to see if she could see Smithton's truck. As she crawled closer to the edge of the trailer she saw the tailgate of the truck. She stopped and crawled back.

"I want to see what he is doing and wit who." She crawled over to the side of the window the revealed the living room. She moved just her right eye over to the window, her nose serving as the border as her other eye remained closed and against the metal siding.

The slates in the blinds allowed only a small space of vision into Smithton's world.

He stood back to the blind, head down over the small table in the corner of the room.

"He's cooking." She said to herself dejectedly as she looked to the rest of room for answers to her question.

"Who is with him?"

She found the room empty.

She turned her body away from the window.

"I don't want to go in there. I don't want to deal with the fumes, the allegations, this Meadow skank." She struggled with facing her reality and like a small animal of prey, found herself in flight mode.

Kitty turned and walked around the back of the neighboring trailers until she reached the road.

Hunger stabbed at her stomach from the inside. Her muscles quivered from low blood sugar levels. She looked down the hillside and onto the large, long dark building below. The streetlights shown on the dumpsters with the lids popped open from overflow.

"I know they throw away perfectly good food." She walked down the hill determined to take it for herself.

With the open wounds recently left on her psyche, Kitty walked on the dark hillside stepping over litter with legs straddled wide to avoid tumbling down the steep embankment. Kitty found herself sprawled with legs wide grabbing as weeds to hold up on the hillside.

Her hands stung and itched as she gripped tightly onto thorn and thistles bushes for balance. The hillside tapered off offering her aid from the steep grade.

She shuffled her feet trying to stop her downward momentum. She failed in her attempt. Her poorly fitting shoes and wounded feet could not support the speed of her body. She slid and fell forward ultimately rolling several times down the hill until she hit an old tire thrown over the hillside.

The small of her back caught on the curve of the tire. The cold stiff rubber felt like a mallet hitting her side.

Kitty let out a cry and lay on the ground looking into the stony soil.

"I've got to get up, keep goin' Kitty you're almost there." She coached herself into getting off the ground and forging ahead, following the light.

A flashlight that was the full moon cast light casting a shadow on her every move. No one honest was out at this time of night. The sound of approaching cars caused a tsunami of panic within Kitty.

She was not confident that she was camouflaged by the hillside. She gauged the distance of cars based on the sound of their tires. Once close she would fall to the ground stiff with fear, until she was sure that the car had passed.

"I know one of these cars is the cops." She thought at each headlight that approached and passed.

The back of the food store appeared to her as a mirage. She crawled toward it desperate for food and refuge then suddenly as if in a dream. She was about to engage in an act she could have never imagined herself doing. Without a thought of regret she stepped out of the weeds and onto asphalt toward the dumpsters.

She ducked underneath the illumination of the spotlights. She moved quietly with determination against the wall to the nearest dumpster.

Kitty was craving any food containing sugar. She reached her destination and ran to the dumpster. She reached up with her hands bracing the edge. She threw her left leg up and over the side.

Her muscle control was lacking due to malnourishment. She struggled to lift her torso over the edge but eventually succeeded.

Kitty fell into a bed of paper, rotten produce and spoiled milk. The acerbic smell did not affect her. She dug her hands through the debris as in a pool of water.

Suddenly appearing in front of her was a package of opened and crushed chocolate chip cookies. Frantically she grabbed the wrinkled bag and opened the foiled end.

"Oh thank god," She spoke out as she picked out several cookie pieces and stuffed them into her mouth puffing her cheeks.

She chewed, little. The chocolate melting on her tongue caused her to reminisce on happier times.

Kitty's held her hand out and picked the chocolate and vanilla swirled soft custard cone from her Dad's hand. The hot summer sun melted the frozen dessert to her desire.

"The cone is the best when the ice cream causes the bottom to become soft and squishy." She thought.

Suddenly, Kitty looked up, past the plastic top of the trash container, up to the vast black sky. She saw her father's face, just his face, eyes fixed upon her.

She stopped and the reality of her frail, craving body, scavenging trash from a store dumpster in a strange city, in a foreign state, struck her.

Moral Embarrassment and reality collided shattering the frantic state she was in.

"Daddy?" She cried out.

"Oh, Daddy, what has become of me? Please help me." She cried as her body slumped down onto a pile of trash.

She pulled her legs up and cradled them as she cried hiding her face in her knees as if that concealed her presence and actions.

"I've gotta get outta here." She said suddenly,

"I gotta get out of this dumpster, now."

Kitty sat up and crawled over to the edge of the dumpster. She threw her leg over and slid down the edge.

Once on the ground she walked over to the side of the dumpster, looking out into the woods. She slid down and grabbed her knees once again cradling her face as she sobbed uncontrollably into her knees.

"I'm a loser vagrant." She sobbed. "Smithton's not takin' care of me." She screamed internally.

"But, what would I do? How would I make money to live n' eat," Kitty then answer her own question, "Why does it matter, he's not doin' it."

Fear of being alone, having to stand on her own, Kitty was having revelations long past due. She only heard her own words resonating within her mind. The approaching car did not disturb her thoughts.

The cars headlights illuminated the dumpster and her small frame huddled along the side.

Kitty cried uncontrollably and was now on her knees with her face down on the ground.

Kitty stopped, she felt firm hands on her shoulders, lifting her off the ground, up and off the ground.

She looked up to see Trooper Cantoniski. The recent experience with the police was the current root of her mental dissent. She looked at him in shock and an overwhelming sense of panic.

Depending on herself terrified Kitty for she feared failing. What she did not see was that her dependency on Smithton was causing her failure.

"I don't wanna spend in the cracks. Those dark places where the sun doesn't see and there are no sounds."

"Ms. Hepburn, funny seeing you here." The trooper said as he looked at her.

Kitty did not speak. The pulse points within her body were racing. She merely swallowed as she looked down at the ground, avoiding eye contact with him.

"What are you doing here? I thought you were on your way to Grandma's house?" He asked with a tone of sarcasm.

"I'm sorry." She said. Kitty was apologizing to the trooper, to her father, to herself and to Smithton.

"What are you sorry for Katherine?" He asked.

Kitty did not answer.

"Are you sorry for trespassing?" He asked.

"I am just hungry." Kitty replied.

"Why don't you go home and have a meal? Where was that home again?" The trooper was questing Kitty in a teasing tone instead of grilling her for answers.

Trooper Cantoniski had two daughters. He felt fear when he looked at Kitty. He understood that the wrong person at the wrong time can change the course of your destiny.

"Katherine, there are 3 things that can happen here. I only want 1, see I'm not greedy." He placed his flashlight on her sunken cheeks and then on dark circumferences around her eyes.

He saw the potential of this being one of his little girls one day as he looked at the diaphanous young woman, shrinking down under the revealing illumination of his intrusive light.

Kitty felt the beam of light exposing her guile and desperateness.

"I don't care anymore." She thought to herself,

"Just tell him what he wants to hear. I can't do anymore." She thought with her head bowed low as she lifted her eyes to his face.

"What do you want from me?" Kitty asked.

"Information." He replied. "I know your either cooking, using or selling meth."

Kitty was offended, "I don't use meth."

She then replied, "I don't have any information to give, I'm here because I'm hungry. You picked me up the first time cause I was hungry. Like I asked before, is being hungry a crime?"

Trooper Cantoniski looked at the crushed bag of cookies grasped within her hand. The compassionate paternal side of him sparred against his professional obligations. His mind repeated,

"This young girl is starving and on the streets, this could be one of my girls."

"How about I take you to the diner and we can discuss your predicament there?" The trooper softened his stance slightly, removing the beam of light from Kitty's face.

Kitty replied,

"Do I have a choice?" She did not to be seen with him. She was petrified of going back to the holding cell.

"You do not." He sternly said as he turned off the flashlight and placed it back into the metal holder on his belt.

"Let's go." He said as he rounded her up.

"Back of the car." The trooper said as he opened the back door, just as he done before. The difference was that this time he showed more humanistic characteristics in opposed to militant.

Kitty did not speak, she merely followed him to the car.

"I knew he was watching me. How am I gonna get out of this?" She started a barrage of questions to herself, "What am I gonna tell 'im. What if Smithton sees me? Why is this happenin' to me?"

The two were in the car for less than 15 minutes before arriving at the diner. The trooper's radio constantly blurted out the aggressive, abusive, illegal and accidental happenings in the small town.

Kitty listened for fear that Smithton would on the list.

"If he was gonna take me in, he would'a radioed it in by now." She said to calm herself.

Kitty instinctually reached for the door handle knowing by experience that was removed from the backseat of the patrol cars.

She sat, shaking her left leg, up and down nervously while she bit the skin around her pinky finger.

Trooper Cantoniski opened the door and let her back into the night air. Kitty took a deep breath but did not relax.

"We'll talk and you can eat, food, not remnants left in a garbage dumpster." He said as the two walked toward the diner.

Kitty did not speak, with her head down, dirty hair falling over her petite face, she followed him.

Kitty felt humiliated. Her preservation instincts now removed her mind from the real time moment.

"I'm sorry Daddy. I know I keep saying that, but I am." She said as she stood in front of her father.

He replied sternly,

"You can't get these grades Kitten. You want to go on out of here and be something, make something of yourself. You know, move away from this small town."

Her small voice replied,

"Daddy, I don't want to disappoint you, and, I don't ever want to leave you. I'm supposed to take of you, this is my job." She said with head still hung low.

Bob walked over the kitchen cupboard and opened the door removing a deck of cards.

"Sit, we'll go over these flash cards again." He said as he removed the cards and sat at the round wooden table in the small kitchen.

For the next few hours, Bob held flash cards of mathematical equations in front of Kitty.

"What do you want to eat?" The trooper asked breaking through the membrane of her thoughts.

"What do you want to eat tomorrow?" Kitty thought once more she regressed back to her secure place.

Trooper Cantoniski handed Kitty a menu.

"Ms. Hepburn, what do you want to eat?" He asked once again.

Kitty looked up and said,

"Meatloaf."

The trooper waved for the waitress, who was very familiar with the trooper, over to the table.

"Can I have a meatloaf dinner, coffee dark and…"

Once again he looked to Kitty, "What do you want to drink?"

"Milk." Kitty replied as she placed her hands across her body and held her elbows. Her face a mere foot higher than table as she slouched down.

Once the waitress walked away Trooper Cantoniski turned his focus onto Kitty.

"I know you have what I want, information. I can guarantee you will not be prosecuted. If you don't co-operate now, once an arrest is made, you will be charged for distributing, making or carrying methamphetamine." Trooper Cantoniski did not speak softly with Kitty. "Look, I know you have a family somewhere that does not know what you're doing." He looked at her with his light brown eyes framed by years of wisdom.

Kitty looked down at the table. She did not immediately answer him. She thought about what he said and the possibility of Smithton getting caught. They had done this in several towns free from police.

She looked up and said,

"I don't know what you are talkin' about."

Her facial expression told otherwise to the trooper.

He sat back and cross his right leg over his left, pulling down his pant leg and taking a deep breath.

"Well, you eat your meal. When your next meal comes due, or the one you miss on top of the next one you miss, call me." He reached into pocket and pulled out a business card and snapped it onto the table in front of Kitty.

She looked down at the black and white card.

"You'll call me sooner or later, this guy doesn't care about you Katherine." The trooper said in the same tone he would use with his daughters.

Kitty's meal arrived and she ate quickly barely tasting the food.

When she was done the trooper reached into his pocket and pulled out some money. He placed 20 dollars on the table and got up.

Kitty just watched him with wide eyes,

"I can't get a ride home with you." She thought.

"Pay for dinner and keep the change." He said as he put on his coat.

"Until we meet again, Ms. Hepburn." He said as he walked away from Kitty.

CHAPTER TWENTY

Surely Unsure

"Memories choose a time, place to surface undetermined by us."
E.H.

Meadow returned home late after dropping Mr. Marino back at the nursing home. Overcome by fatigue she did not attempt to call Kelsey another time. She had assumed that she received her prior messages and was awaiting her arrival the next day.

Meadow's sleep was disrupted with disjointed and unnerving dreams that night. She dreamt of being on a city sidewalk and seeing Kelsey in a window on the top floor. In her dream she attempted to enter the building and take the elevator to the floor where Kelsey stood, but the elevator would not come down to the ground floor.

Meadow opened her eyes at 4 AM, again at 5 AM then when she repeated the action at 6 AM she succumbed to the daylight as if there were forces at work awakening her prematurely.

Meadow had packed a bag the night before allowing her to move quickly through her morning routine.

The cool late autumn air set off a wave of chills that passed over her body. She frowned as she saw a white skimming of ice coating all the windows of her car.

"It's gonna be a long winter if this shit is startin' already."
Meadow said as she entered the car and turned her defrosters
up to full blow and maximum heat.

She sat with shoulders pressed forward, her hands tucked
under her thighs and shaking her thighs to generate for warmth.

"I need to try Kelsey again. God, I hope she is not pissed.
It's possible." Meadow said to herself as she pulled her cell
phone out of the duffle bag that was sat on the front passenger
seat.

The phone rang off as usual. Meadow left a voicemail,

"Kels, I'm on route. It's early so I should be there in 3 or
so, hours. Expect me around 10."

Kelsey placed the car in drive and navigated to DEEP
CREEK despite frosted windows and an unsettling feeling
within her mind.

The drive was long and tortuous. 1 hour into the drive
Meadow had already called Kelsey's phone five times, leaving
but 1 voicemail.

"FUCK KELSEY, don't play games, I'm stressin' here."
Meadow screamed out as she drove to the upbeat music on
her CD.

Meadow contemplated the possibility that Kelsey was
actually mad at her for not coming the night before. They had
many trysts over each other's seemingly professional values.
Ironically, Kelsey despised when Meadow placed work in
front of a social event yet she was guilty of the same offense.
The relationship would be much more paregoric if they held
each other in the same regard, with all respects.

Meadow's mind tripped over the latter subject then onto
the next ominous one, children.

For the last year, this had been an overexposed subject where
blame was placed onto one another at various opportunistic

points. Meadow was aware that the truth of the problem lay within her.

Meadow banked on Kelsey maintaining patience with the subject matter. It was hard for Meadow being inferior as a woman.

The ability to have children is innate. The inability to conceive children renders one defunct. Meadow tried, while being heterosexual and again through in vitro fertilization while homosexual. Failure in this primary area of femininity and womanhood caused Meadow grave insecurity as a woman and as of purpose in this competitive world. Kelsey remained supportive but Meadow was cognizant that this patience would abate at some point, mainly at the age spike that they both were in.

The drive for the next three hours was painstaking. Nausea and diarrhea caused Meadow to make unscheduled stops.

"Drug addicts, street whores and teenagers can conceive, yet I can't, where did I go so wrong in life to place this burden on me?" Meadow descended into an unhealthy self incriminating mode.

The thought of the act that result in millions on unwanted children annually, she could not logically satisfy her insecurity as to why she was unable to fulfill this natural process.

Meadow's mental deluge was interrupted by the rap ring tone on her phone, it was Kelsey's ring tone.

Her heart stopped, she grabbed her cell phone almost driving off the road as she looked down at the caller id to praying to herself that it was Kelsey.

She hit open and spoke with unbridled joy,

"I looovvvee you. I am so glad you called, where have you been doll baby?" There was silence on the other end.

"Kelsey?" She said softly.

"Kelsey?" She said frantically, "Is that you?"

The call was disconnected.

Meadow was 1 ½ hours outside of DEEP CREEK.

She pulled over and lost her ability to breathe normally. She knew something was wrong.

"Do I call 911?" I can't just call the police if there is nothing wrong. Oh God, help, what do I do?" Meadow lay her head down upon the steering wheel. She was caught in between frantic and stoic, scared and in denial.

"I should call Lee, maybe she spoke with Kelsey."

Meadow's blurred vision scanned through her contacts until she reached the 'L's. She hit Lee's number.

Meadow sat and waited for her to pick up.

"Lee, fuck me, pick up." She screamed.

Lee did not pick up. Meadow was left to leave yet another voice mail.

"Lee, this is Meadow, I have not been able to reach Kelsey. She arrived two days ago now, I guess, at the rental. Please call me back. I'm worried. I, I, don't know what else to do. Should I call the State Police in Maryland? GOD, that is so desperate if this is nothing major. Please call me back."

Meadow opened the door and threw up, stomach bile, onto the ground below.

As she looked up, wiping her mouth with her sleeve a car sped past her. She looked at the back of the car thinking,

"That looks like Kelsey's car." She stood up and tried to keep focus of the quickly moving vehicle. She noticed three heads in the car, that seemingly of me.

"That could not have been her car. You are losing your mind woman." She rationed to herself as she sat back on the seat and pulled her legs in then closing the door.

She closed the door and looked up, past the peripheral instruments of her car and to the sky, the new, bright forming sky with promise of a new day, a new day for many, but not for Meadow. Meadow was now in a vortex of negativity that fed on the fears that mounted as each minute of each hour passed by.

She drove. She did not call Kelsey again for fear of rejection or worse, the fear of admitting to herself that she was in danger or injured. Meadow wanted to get to the rental as quickly as possible to see if Kelsey was there, if she was all right, or if she even arrived.

Meadow squinted at each road sign as she slowed to a near stop, waiting to find the sign which read "Fennely Circle".

"This one must be it, I can see a Fen," She said as she approached the roach that circled back into the woods.

As she entered she counted the trailers to the left to assure she found the last trailer on the left. She saw two trailers. Meadow noticed a young girl limping down the side of the road close to the end of the circle.

She slowed down and rolled down the window.

"Hello, can you help me?" She called out.

The young girl turned around. Meadow was struck by the pale complexion of the young thin girl.

She shuffled over to the car in evident pain to one of her feet.

Meadow asked, "Are you alright?" She was characteristically concerned with any level of suffering in others.

The young girl did not answer and seemed hesitant to approach the car.

Meadow sensed this so she stopped the car and stepped out, stretching, maneuvering to show a sense of calmness to her reticence.

"I've been driving for a few hours and I am really tired. My girlfriend and I are renting the last trailer on the left for the weekend, is that it?" She asked as she pointed to the trailer beside the one her and Smithton were occupying.

Kitty responded politely, "Yes, that's it."

Meadow held out her hand, "My name is Meadow Panaelis."

Kitty looked at her and the name immediately registered, Meadow.

Kitty held out hand, "My name is Kitty. I think I have something of yours."

Kitty walked with Meadow over to the trailer where she sat the flower arrangement.

"Did you send a flower arrangement in a pumpkin?" She asked as she walked slowly.

Meadow felt an eerie ominous feeling.

"Yes, I did, two days ago. I sent it to Kelsey."

Kitty replied,

"It must've been left on our doorstep. Sorry, it's still there, you can have it back."

By this time Kitty realized that Smithton was inside and did not want to make him anymore paranoid than he already was if he was cooking.

"Your trailer is just there," Kitty pointed as she inched her away from them. "I'll grab it and bring it over." She said in a final effort to divert her from being in close proximity of Smithton.

Meadow turned and walked a few steps back to her car, she got it and pulled it forward and off the side of the road in front of the rental trailer.

Kitty quickly ducked down underneath the window and grabbed the pumpkin; she walked hunched over, under the next few windows until she was out of site from Smithton.

Meadow go out and tears filled her eyes as she saw the young girl hold the pumpkin half filled with flowers, some bent, some missing.

"She must've thrown it out, oh God, she left me. Why would she do this?" Meadow sobbed with her head down on the steering wheel oblivious to the Kitty's on looking.

"I wonder if she is alright." Kitty though to herself with her genuine concern for the suffering of others.

She walked over to the car where Meadow was slumped over.

She opened the door and asked,

"Meadow, are you ok?"

Meadow looked up and without forethought in a very aberrant manner spoke from her heart to Kitty, a total stranger,

"I think she left me?" Meadow looked into the space up and over Kitty's head.

Kitty reached out her hand and took Meadow's arm.

"Let's get you inside. I am sure there is a misunderstanding'. We'll talk about it." Kitty ushered Meadow, a total stranger, toward the trailer.

Kitty reached out and turned the door knob and the door was locked.

"Do you have a key?" She asked.

Meadow whose mind was racing as her thoughts seemed to block the reality of the world from her vision.

"I think it's in the flower pot just there." She pointed down to a flower pot.

Kitty knelt down and finger through the dirt and felt a metal key. She picked it up saying proudly,

"Here it is. Let's get inside and figure this out k."

Kitty unlocked the door and pushed it open allowing Meadow to go through first. When the two were inside, Kitty placed the flower arrangement on the table and stood up toward Meadow,

"Are your bags in your car? Why don't you go sit down, I'll get them." She offered to Meadow.

Normally Meadow would not be so acquiescent to accepting guidance and assistance for a total stranger but in the middle of the current mental crisis, normality had been rewired.

"Yes, I have a duffle bag in the car." This is all she said as she walked through each room of the trailer looking for signs that Kelsey had been there.

The trailer was spotless. The shag entry rug was devoid of a footprint depressing the long green fibers downward under the weight of a shoe. The bedroom doors were still closed.

Meadow opened the first door, the beds were made and not a wrinkle was evident as if a bag had been laid on them.

She began to feel her pulse race and her breath hasten. She turned and ran toward the other door. She stopped at the door and placed her hand on the door knob,

"Please god, let her things be in this room, PLEASE god," She begged. Reality stung her cheek with the hard blow that the room had never been used or entered.

Meadow sat on the bed and tried to think of the last few days.

"What did I say? What did I do?" What did I miss?" She asked herself over and over in a monotone unfulfilling vain.

Meanwhile Kitty opened the car door and pulled out the duffle bag. Wrought with guilt and riddled with sadness for how she would feel if it were her in the same position.

"This is her girlfriend's phone. What do I do?" She thought of how she could offer her comfort without lying to her.

Kitty asked herself, "How did her phone get into our trailer?"

She turned and looked into the trailer occupied by Smithton.

"He better native been firkin' her. God Smithton, why do you always fuck things up, why?" She said as she walked back to the trailer beside theirs.

It did not dawn on Kitty that Meadow and Kelsey was a couple. She mistook girlfriend in the platonic sense.

Kitty was consumed with anger toward Smithton.

Meadow was consumed with grief over the loss of her lover.

Kitty was preoccupied with how to give back the cell phone without incrimination.

Meadow was preoccupied with planning on how to find Kelsey to win her back.

Meadow opened to sound of Meadow's sobs from the back bedroom.

Kitty could not resist the opportunity to look around and compare the nice appointed trailer with that of the sparse one they occupied.

She walked to the back room and sat the bag on the floor. She sat on the floor in front of the anguished woman. She did not speak at first. She did not know what to say to a woman. Kitty had not had a female figure in her life for entirety. Especially one that was older.

Meadow looked up with a look of hope in her eyes,

"Let me try and call her again, maybe she'll answer."

Kitty panicked. The cell phone was still in her pocket, and it was on.

"Give her some time, maybe she'll cool down." Kitty knew this was bad advice but she did not want to have to answer as to why she had her girlfriend's phone.

Meadow did not head Kitty's advice.

"Where is my phone? I think it's in the car." Meadow said as she jumped up and walked toward the front of the trailer.

Kitty turned and pulled out the phone and tried to power it down before the woman reached her phone and hit redial.

Kitty hit the off button and anxiously waited for the signal to appear to turn off the phone. It seemed to take minutes to power the phone off but eventually it was shut down. Kitty's fingers fumbled as her panic grew.

"There, the phone is off." Kitty said as the screen grew dark.

Kitty looked up and walked to the door, she stopped,

"I'll throw the phone under the bed as if it fell out in here." She walked back over and tried to slide the phone under the bed. It stuck on the carpet and did not go deep enough for concealment.

Kitty knelt down and pushed the phone in farther with her hand.

"What are you doing?" Meadow called out as she entered the room with her phone in her hand, Kitty knelt under the bed.

"What do you see?" She asked.

Kitty grabbed the phone and pulled it out,

"Is this your friend's phone?" She asked with sure conviction of guilt written upon her face.

Meadow ran over to her and took the phone from her hand,

"YES, that's it. Was it under the bed? How did you find it?" She asked not with interrogation in her voice but with joy.

Kitty responded,

"I saw somethin shiny when I was sitting here on the floor." She looked away from Meadow's face.

Meadow turned it on and sat on the bed.

Kitty wanted to find a way to exit the trailer without appearing suspect of any wrongdoing that would bring focus onto their trailer or onto Smithton. She had already started a series of events into action that would inevitable bring a negative reaction to Smithton and to her survival.

"Meadow, let me go home and tell me boyfriend where I am, you know how men can be, and I'll come back over so we can sort this, k?" She looked at Meadow who was not paying attention to anything but the phone log on Kelsey's phone.

"Ok," Meadow replied with preoccupation to her mind.

"Thank you Kitty." She looked up and grabbed Kitty's right hand. She held it for a minute. Then let it go, returning to the cell phone belonging to Kelsey.

Kitty pulled her hand away and placed it in her pocket.

She walked out of the trailer feeling as if the ice she was standing on was getting more diaphanous by the second. Falling into deep icy consuming water seemed inevitable.

Kitty closed the door and walked the few steps over their trailer. She stopped at the door and hesitated before opening it.

"Wing it, he'll be tripped miles high." She said as she walked in to find Smithton smiling at her, beads of sweet rolling down his forehead as his eyes were rolling around the room.

He had cooked boiled the solids and the condensation had formed in the plastic tubing. A slow consistent drip was draining through a coffee filet on the adjoining table.

Kitty held her nose,

"I'm gonna go to the back room, I'm not in for tweakin' right now." She said as she walked over and kissed Smithton on the lips.

He did not answer her. He smiled and soared back to his utopist world.

Kitty did not want to question him until she thought of the right questions. Smithton was very good at turning around her words and molding them into his words and returning them back in question format aimed at her.

She needed to think about all of the events that had transpired within the last few days and make sense of them somehow. She also needed to sleep.

As she lay on the floor and closed her eyes she spoke to Bob,

"Dad, please talk to me this dream and tell me what to say, what to ask and what to do."

She quickly passed from consciousness into unconsciousness, although when conscious she was still oblivious to the deviant events taking place in the other room.

CHAPTER TWENTY-ONE

On the Grind

"If we had the ability to still frame time and keep only those memories, never experiencing what happens next." E.H.

True to the last string of Kitty's REM sleep, her collective unconscious attempted to shake into reality and out of sleep.

Kitty's eyes fluttered as she slept.

"Daddy, bring the mirror closer so I can comb my hair." Kitty asked of her dad who stood just outside of the jail cell where she sat.

"Daddy, why aren't you speaking to me? My hair is a mess and I need to see me close up in the mirror." She said a second time.

"Kitten," She heard Smithton from outside the cell in the hall.

"Smithton, can you take that mirror from Daddy so I can comb my hair?" She asked with disgust.

"Kitty, look, look what I have for you." Smithton said as she walked closer to the bars.

He was holding a bundle of white blankets in his arms as if he were carrying a baby.

Kitty got up from the floor and walked over to see what Smithton was carrying.

"What is it Smithton?" She asked before reaching the bars.

"You are silly, it's our adopted baby." He replied.

Kitty walked over, peering between the bars. She placed her cold and bruised hands, one on each bar and leaned her face into the cold metal.

As her cheek touched the bar, the razor sharp edge split the skin on her cheek. She pulled her head back and covered her cheek as she cried out in pain.

"Kitty, never mind that, look at her." Smithton said to her as he witnessed drops of blood seeping through her fingers and onto the concrete floor.

Kitty leaned closer to the bars without touching them this time.

Smithton held the bundle up to her. He pushed away the blanket from the babies face, Kitty gasped as the sight,

It was her, her face, without a body, just her head.

"Daddy," She screamed as she looked for her father in the hall.

The mirror crashed to the ground and glass flew onto her face, Smithton's and the babies.

Kitty awoke, sweating and feeling physically ill.

She sat up and tried to piece together the strange dream without luck.

"What the fuck is goin' on?" She said as she realized that the fumes from the cook were starting to affect her physically.

Kitty felt her pulse and mind racing, she felt detached experiencing the events as if she was a mere bystander. She spoke up and said to Smithton, "I'm buggin' here. Step back, talk to Smithton." She said to herself as she lay back down on her back.

"I know he's bangin'," She thought as she looked at the popcorn tiles on the ceiling. "I just don't know wit who, maybe this Kelsey crab."

Kitty's street slang became thick when she was high. When she spoke to people outside of Smithton, she was guarded not to use the phrases which drew a stereotypical connotation about her mentality.

Kitty looked up as the door opened. Smithton walked through it and closed it behind him.

"Do you feel okay Kitten?" He asked her lovingly as he squatted beside her, brushing her damp hair off of her face.

"Smithton, are you bangin' 'round on me?" She blurted out as she felt false confidence.

He looked at her then down at the ring still circling her left thumb, then back at her face.

"No Kitty, are you trippin?" He said, "I knew the fumes would git to ya."

Kitty replied,

"No Smithton, I found a cell phone belongin' to some crab named Kelsey. Who is Kelsey Smithton?" She sat up as she spoke with eyes tearing at the thought of losing the only stability left in her life.

"Kitty, I don't know a Kelsey, no one, straight." He laid down dirty worn carpet with her, pulling her body into his.

He slowly kissed her cheek.

Her eyes stayed fixated on the bubbled white ceiling tiles.

"Where'd you git this ring?" She said calmly unaffected by his affection.

"From the D, he had a whole bag of 'me. Fuck me Kitty, I did somethin' straight for you, and this is the sugar?" Smithton turned her concerns around and threw them back at her as sharp offensive jabs.

Kitty had her answer. Smithton was unable to make direct eye contact with her. Years of experience seasoned her to his responses. This particular response spoke of his guilt.

"The next thing he'll do is get ragin' hot, git up, and leave." She said to herself as she smiled behind stoic lips.

Smithton continued, "Ya know Kitty, I'm humpin', I have murk to be doin'. Later." He said as he got up and walked to the door.

Kitty merely looked at him without speaking.

"Don't push 'I'm too far, he's so tweaked he could hit me." She thought to herself as she said,

"Fuck you, lyin' poot." She screamed as she sat up.

Smithton reacted immediately to the insult to his word and manhood. He rushed over to her and reached down with his large thin, dry hands and grabbed her by the throat.

Kitty gasped as airflow to her lungs dissipated.

Smithton picked her childlike frame up off the floor by her throat.

With his right hand his open handed struck the side of her face then released her body.

She fell back to the ground and sprung to her feet.

"Fuck you Smithton, you think your big gangsta now?" She screamed as she pushed past him denying her timorous.

As the male and only figure in Kitty's life, Bob instilled within her a level of tomboy. He never wanted his little girl to be victimized. A position he knew of first hand in dealing with her mother. This was just one of the sacred secrets Bob kept from Kitty throughout her young life. In this relationship, that lesson actually served her ironically.

Whether Kitty was bruised, bleeding or swollen she played the role of Bob's strong Kitten, at least on the exterior. The paradox was the internal hurricane swirling within her being, ripping apart her strength.

Kitty felt her face swelling, tears falling and stinging her face, she kept walking, out the door, down the short hall, through the lab and out the front door.

She knew from experience that if she did not leave he would, leaving her feeling discarded and without value.

"Where the fuck am I gonna go?" She said to herself as she stepped out into the cold night air.

She walked toward Meadow's trailer and saw the lights on.

"I never went back like I said." She kept walking toward the door.

Evidence of a domestic incident did not thwart her progress nor stop her from showing up on Meadow's doorstep.

As she reached her hand up to knock on the door, it opened. Meadow looked out at Kitty with shock and opened the door inviting her in warmly and with love.

"Honey, come in. What is going on?" She said in a soft welcoming voice. Although this woman was in a state of turmoil herself, she set her torment aside and opened her door, heart, and mind to Kitty.

A woman had never showed Kitty this kind of sacrificing, pure care before. Kitty took a second and glanced at her face.

"I want to carry this look of love with me, for all my time." She thought as she stepped into the trailer out of the dark damp air and away from Smithton.

Simultaneously she wrestled off the symbolic commitment ring she wore on her thumb and left it in her front pocket, liberating her up and lifting even further away Smithton and their derelict life.

Meadow looked at Kitty's swollen face and was fully aware of what had occurred. She did not want to ask Kitty about the events. Meadow wanted to give this young fragile woman a thermal of air enabling and encouraging her to spread her wings and speak confidently, openly, without fear of preconceived labels.

"Sit, want some tea?" Meadow asked.

Kitty thought, "Tea? I don't think I was ever offered a cup of tea. Hell, I never had a cup of tea."

"Could I?" She timidly replied before saying, "I hope I am not puttin' you out there. I know you have a ragin' bag of 'yer own stuff."

Meadow smiled at the sincere gesture offered by the young girl.

"Let's just have girl talk." Meadow said encouragingly.

She turned her back and went into the kitchen suddenly realizing she had no clue where anything was, or if there was even tea in the kitchen.

Kitty saw Meadow opening then closing cabinet doors and it dawned on her,

"This woman just arrived here."

Kitty stood up and walked into the kitchen with Meadow and said,

"Who doesn't luv rootin' through others stuff, neebishing?"

The two laughed together.

The two found cups, tea bags and sugar. Time elapsed and the two were sitting at the kitchen table sipping hot tea.

"Does he often hit you?" Meadow blurted out after her temperament could no longer refrain approaching the palpable issues.

"Only when he is tweaked or sneaked." Kitty replied.

She noticed a look of bewilderment of Meadow's face and realized that she did not understand what she had just said. Kitty rephrased her reply, "If he is high or caught lyin'."

"What drug does he do?" Meadow asked.

"He cooks," again Kitty hesitated then reworded her thoughts, "makes methamphetamine, to use and sale."

"Do you use?" Meadow asked with consternation.

Kitty replied quickly, "nooo," with a street sarcastic emphasis. "I'll snort here and there, blow ya know, coke."

Meadow tried not to lecture but was unable to offer motherly advice to this lost soul that desperately needed it,

"A man that hits a woman has no foundation of morals. Abuse against woman is contagious. Do you have children?" She asked.

Kitty did know where the words came from, she had never really thought them let alone voiced them aloud.

"I am infertile. She felt tears well up within her eyes. I was raised by my dad. My mother left us when I was a baby. I started havin' sex real early, got a ragin' infection and didn't know what to do. Nor did he. So we did nothin'. Ends up, it was an STD that damaged all my stuff, so now I have birth control."

Kitty cried as she spoke the words. Meadow teared up as she heard the story similar in ending only to her own story.

Although Meadow's mind was consumed with Kelsey, she had a spot for this young girl also. The two had not stopped talking, after an hour or so Kitty felt compelled to stop and focus on her new friend. She said,

"Look, I know you have a lot on your mind, I should go."

Meadow looked at her with panic, "No, you most certainly are not going back over there tonight. You will sleep here and deal with that in the morning."

Kitty imbibed the maternal advice and did not offer a rebuttal.

"You can sleep in other bedroom, on the couch, with me, wherever you feel comfortable." Meadow added.

Kitty wanted to say, with you, but felt insecure.

"I can sleep where ever you want me too." She replied,

Meadow sensed her hesitance and spoke up,

"Well, I could use the moral support and warm body, I think you should bunk with me."

Kitty smiled and the two walked back to the bedroom that had not been utilized.

Kitty followed Meadow's lead. As Meadow kicked off her shoes, so did Kitty. As Meadow lay her head down so did Kitty.

Meadow wrapped Kitty up from the outside of the comforter and brushed back her hair.

"Sleep young one." She whispered.

"You sleep too, I'll help you find your friend in the morning, it will be ok, ok?" Kitty said as she yawned and closed her eyes.

Meadow stayed up watching Kitty for a short while, crying over the recent events, and worrying about the future of her life and love, or lost love.

CHAPTER TWENTY-TWO

Supposed Reality

"Fear influences perception, insecurity induces fear yet love can eliminates fear and insecurity or evoke it, Love is two faced." E.H.

"Hello, my name is Meadow McKean, I would like to report a missing person." Meadow's voice quivered as she spoke the words she never imagined contemplating let alone speaking.

"I'm not sure, the exact time, she was set to arrive at a vacation rental we booked 2 days ago. I have not heard from her since. Yes, I'll hold." Meadow turned and sat down on the kitchen chair and placed her brows onto her right palm and started to cry.

"Yes, my name is Meadow McKean, my partner is missing and has been for 2 days now." She repeated the information.

"What are you talking about wait another 24 hours? That is absurd." Meadow's voice was loud and forceful.

Kitty stirred as she heard the loud voice coming from the other room. She sat up to listen to her new friend's conversation.

She placed her hand on her cheek, which was now black with surface blood.

"Yes, we are lesbians, does that really matter?" Meadow screamed, "NO we are not having a lover's fallout. Can I have your supervisor please?"

The room fell silent.

Kitty got out of the bed and shuffled into the kitchen. She pulled out the chair adjacent to Meadow and sat down, folding her feet up setting them on the seat of the wooden chair and hugging her legs as she stared intently as Meadow.

"My number is 412-223-7899, I expect a call from him before noon or I will personally come to your station and file a complaint." Meadow removed the phone from her ear and slammed it down on the table.

"Can you believe that they want my Kelsey to be missing for another 24 hours? She could be injured laying in a ditch somewhere, hurt, bleeding or worse. Then they question our sexual preference? Missing is fucking missing whether you're a lesbian or not." Meadow screamed as she stood and paced the kitchen.

She stopped and looked over at Kitty, let me get you some food. Lee said she stocked it for us. Meadow opened the refrigerator door and pulled out a carton of milk.

"I have no fucking idea where things are." She mumbled as she opened then shut multiple cabinet doors until she found a bowl, cereal and a spoon.

She placed the items on the table in front of Kitty and prepared a bowl of cereal for her, just like her dad did every morning of her life.

"You look like you haven't had a meal in a week Kitty, when is the last time you have eaten?" Meadow asked with those large loving and emoting blue eyes of hers.

Kitty replied,

"It's been awhile, my last meal was with a nark cop."

She looked up, "Hey, maybe I can call him to help us. I have something he wants, maybe he will start a search for Kelsey?" She said without thinking out the consequences of such an action.

Meadow stopped her, "Kitty, I think you have enough domestic issues back home, getting your boyfriend busted would cause a lot of changes. I think you need to move but we need to talk through those steps first." Meadow thought of Kitty's well being.

"Let's go looking for her ourselves Meadow. Why not?" Kitty said with new found hope.

Meadow replied,

"Let's see if this supervisor calls me back. If he doesn't, I will show up there and file a complaint and go looking myself."

Kitty ate so quickly that milk dripped down her chin with each spoonful. Meadow got up and pulled a paper towel off the roll and handed it to Kitty.

"Meadow?" Kitty asked quietly, "Can I ask you a question?"

Meadow looked at her as she sat down again, "Yes you can ask me anything Kitty."

Kitty was unsure how to ask her questions to Meadow, she stammered with the beginning words,

"I, I didn't realize that when you called Kelsey your girlfriend, that she was really your girlfriend." Kitty spoke up quickly as to not give Meadow any misconception that she was judging her or was disapproving of her, their, lifestyle.

"I think that's cool n stuff, I'm just curious, have you never been with a guy?" She asked shyly.

Meadow explained,

"I was married, for a decade of my life. I thought that what was I was required to do. He was mean and controlling and mentally abusive." Meadow looked at Kitty to gauge her reaction.

"I was very unhappy, and then one day I just left, with nothing. I wanted to start a new life, the life I felt I was born to live." Meadow began to feel overwhelmed with emotion as she spoke but did not want to deny Kitty an explanation.

Kitty asked, "Did you have children?"

"No, I was unable to have children. Kelsey and I were going to adopt." Meadow broke down and started to cry once she realized what she had just said, "Oh my God, Kelsey and I are going to adopt, it's been a hard and stressful ordeal for us. That was one of the reasons we booked this weekend." Meadow was sickened at the slip of past tense usage.

Kitty sensed that the timing was not right so she did not Meadow any more questions about her past or current life.

Kitty saw the pain in Meadow's face. She saw the fear in her eyes when she spoke about Kelsey. She had never seen anyone show such unprovoked emotion for another person, male or female.

"God, could you imagine having such a relationship." She asked herself. "I'd give anythin' to have such a bond." In her short life she had only seen relationships between men and woman as destructive, violent and using.

"I wonder if it'd be like bein' with your best girlfriend all the time?" She thought with innocence and naiveté.

Kitty looked up Meadow and spoke up with new found courage.

"Let me go tell Smithton I am going to help you today. Maybe you can come, maybe he saw her pull up or somethin'." Kitty asked.

Meadow's mind was fragmented and disorganized.

"I need to find a notebook and write down a game plan, what she was wearing, driving, tattoos…" She stood and pointed to her left hand. "We both got ring tattoos on our left ring finger." Meadow held out her hand as Kitty looked at the small Celtic looking intricate band around her ring finger. She added,

"I also bout her a ring that she wore overtop of it."

Kitty grasped the band in her jeans pocket and held it tight as if she could make it disappear. She did not say a word to Meadow about her recent gift, out of respect.

"The ring Smithton gave me was stolen. It doesn't mean the same thing." She thought as she held it tight.

Meadow's phone rang and the two jumped as they stared at the phone.

Meadow picked it up and spoke,

"Hello." She said tacitly.

Meadow started to have a conversation with someone unrelated to the current crisis.

Kitty looked up at Meadow as she spoke,

"I'll be back." She whispered.

Kitty's was growing more anxious with each passing minute. She felt a panic attach swelling within her chest shutting off air from entering her lungs. Her nerves were raw and her fear augmented with each minute that passed now that the sun was up. She knew Smithton would accuse her of being with another man. Coming home the next morning was a risky act for Kitty. Experience taught her that he would be paranoid, irate and inconsolable.

The cereal that had just settled within her stomach was now churning. She stood up and placed her bowl and spoon in the sink. She put away the milk and set the cereal back on the counter, looking at the box one last time, reminiscing about her days before cereal became a luxury.

Anger, sadness, and anxiety consumed Kitty as she walked out of the kitchen. The door that stood in front of her was closed, small, and ominous. She reached for the door knob and hesitated. She looked back at Meadow on the phone. She felt awkward, as if she was caught in the space between today and tomorrow.

Kitty opened the door and stepped down onto the step that displayed the decorative pumpkin.

"I use to love decorating pumpkins with Dad." She thought as she walked away from the illuminated pumpkin that represented a lifestyle that she no longer lived.

"I liked being with Meadow. That was the most normal I have felt in years." she said as she continued on her way.

She wanted to stop, wanted to turn, but she did not. Kitty could not turn and walk away from the only remaining tangible aspect of her life that was directly connected to her father.

CHAPTER TWENTY-THREE

Malleable

"Who creates puzzles and determines the configuration of the pieces?" E.H.

"On the duff?" Smithton said as Kitty opened the door to the trailer.

Kitty did not answer. She was prepared for his wrath. She accepted the consequences of her actions when she decided to stay next door. She was not willing to accept condemnation for actions in which she was not guilty.

"No," she replied. "Look at my face, are you flyin'? Are you so fucked that you don't remember hitting me?"

Smithton looked at Kitty's face and saw an angelic, unattainable, unapproachable figure. His mind would not process the facts.

"I was worried about you, Kitten. Where have you been?" he asked as he attempted to assuage her and redirect the initial introduction.

"I slept in the shed, Smithton. I was afraid to come back in here with you cookin' and tweakin' and freakin'," she said as she wondered where the extemporaneous response came from.

Smithton did not reply. The fumes had saturated into the surface of their cocoon. He had portioned and bagged the crystals. His internal mechanism had tempered. He walked over and took her by her left hand. As he did, he felt her thumb and noticed that the ring was not there.

"Where is your ring?" he asked as he held up her hand up to her face and his.

Kitty looked at him as her mind searched and scanned plausible comebacks.

"Yeah, that ring," she said without rehearsing her response.

"What up, Kitty?"

She looked at him and already felt the positive effects of Meadow on her persona.

"You mean, 'what's up?'" she replied.

Smithton looked at her with a razor sharp glare intended to strike at her with intimidation and conditioned fear.

"What is up, Kitty?" he replied smugly.

Kitty bought seconds more of forethought with her last exchange, enabling her time to think of how she wanted to respond to his former question.

"Funny about that ring, where'd you git it?" she asked as she pulled her hand away from his clamping grip on her hand.

"Why does that matter? It was a gift. Who gives a shit where I got it? I found it." He paused. "Where is it?" He grabbed at her hand.

Kitty looked at him and played this game using his rules and tactics. "Why aren't you askin' where I've been for days, Smithton? Why is the ring your one focus?"

Smithton played directly into her tactics just as she normally did into his.

"Right, then where the fuck have you been shackin'?" he asked.

"You must be so high Smithton, have you checked the back bedroom? I sleep better there." Kitty played her cards with a solid stoic face of sincerity.

Smithton hadn't actually checked the back bedroom so he found himself lacking a response. He looked at her without any fears about the recent events that took place in the back bedroom and asked of her, "Who moved in next door?"

Kitty replied, "I have no idea." She said keeping her loyalty with Kelsey. Kitty was conscious not to ever discuss Meadow's. However, Kitty wanted to get information from Smithton. She waited a minute or so then asked, "I heard two guys in the food store talking about a missing girl from this trailer park." She waited to see his reaction more so than hear his response.

He replied, "And?"

Kitty was annoyed with this response, so she jabbed back.

"And what, Smithton? Someone is missing. I think it is weird that you find a ring and stuff. Weird stuff is goin' on, it's makin' me nervous."

Smithton's paused giving himself enough time to manufacture a response, he under estimated Kitty in this incidence.

"How would she know where I got the ring?" he asked himself before answering, "She wouldn't."

"Kitty I don't have time for you, quit lettin' your mind tease you. Anyway, I don't have time for this. I have to meet my D-man." Smithton reached into his pocket and pulled out some folded up money and threw it at Kitty, striking her on the chest.

Kitty was filled with frustration, he did not give her any information she could use. She did not want to push the subject and give her hand so she let the subject die.

She knelt down to collect the money. As she was on all fours he replied, ""I'm sure this is what you want from me."

He turned away from her and walked toward the door, "Later." He yelled back at her.

Maybe it was how he spoke to her, or his abrupt and apathetic closing sentiment, she could not keep stifled. She yelled out, "That's not enough, Smithton! I want to know what you did to this girl."

Smithton stopped and turned around. He rushed back toward her, grabbing her by the shoulders and shaking her small frame.

"Don't act like a snitch diggin' at me for info, Kitty. What the fuck? I told you I don't know and I don't care if you fuckin' like it or not, that is my answer." he said.

Kitty replied with courage, "No, you didn't say you didn't know. Are you sayin' you don't know?"

"Yes, that's it. I don't know and I don't care and if you're not gonna sport the band, give it back so I can sell it." He held out his hand, waiting for the ring.

Kitty knew that this was the only thing she had that linked Smithton to Kelsey. A part of her wanted to give the ring back as she still possessed a stronger emotion to protect the man who had been caring for her since her father died.

But a new emotion had cropped up, a feeling of strength and courage that she felt since meeting the formidable mothering figure that unconditionally cared for her throughout the night.

Kitty struggled before reaching into her pocket and pulling out the ring. She looked at it, then looked at Smithton, who was agitated and pale. Perspiration collected in small beads on the sides of the bridge of his nose. His upper lip was shiny from sweat. His pupils were black and large as his focus darted around her facial and body expressions.

Kitty thought to herself, "If I give him the ring, I have to get it back. I can't let him think I suspect any of this." She grabbed the ring and handed it to him. She was beginning to see his actions as neglectful, reckless, and decimating. She was confident she would coerce him into giving it back before he left the trailer, just by enraging him.

She looked into his eyes as they tried to fixate on her. She looked at his pupils as a camera lens that kept opening and closing as he focused.

"When you're ready to take care of me, you can give it back." She said with strong emotion and firmness.

Smithton snatched the ring from her hand seconds before grabbing her by the throat. He tightened his finger and forefinger down onto her larynx.

"Better watch who you're fucking with, Kitten. This is your life, too," he warned her.

Kitty reached around and pushed him back by his shoulders, an act that took Smithton by surprise and caught him off balance.

He stumbled then tripped up on his lack of secure footing, falling to the floor. Kitty felt a rush of adrenaline and empowerment. Her initial reaction was to reach down and help him but she refuted her instincts. She was aware that her face had to show her level of surprise as much as his displayed.

"I'm sorry, Smithton," she said firmly. "But don't ever fucking grab me by the throat again or I'll tell Bob." She spoke as tears started streaming from her eyes. She had a level of faith that her comment would restore sanity within Smithton.

He got up quickly, trying to recover his manipulative stance and said, "Go tell dead Bob I said hello and don't ever touch me again," he paused for a second before adding, "Kitten."

He turned and mumbled, "Fucking bitch," as he walked out of the room throwing the ring back at her. "Keep the piece of metal Kitty, I'm over it and you."

Kitty shocked that he actually returned the evidence. She kept her cool until he left.

"He has no idea I know anything," she said to herself, "or he would have never gave it back."

She placed her hands on her throat and started crying once her attention turned back on the abusive scene that had just ensued. She cried out loud,

"Daddy, please stop all this, please?"

The quiet space offered no reply or comfort. She buried her face into her knees and wrapped her arms around her legs, shrinking into the smallest form she could.

What am I gonna do? She cried to herself. If that cop sees my face he'll push me toward a PFA.

She wanted to feel the calm, loving support that she experienced hours before. There was a holding pattern to Kitty's life that was transforming violently.

"I don't wanna deal with this." she thought as she silenced her sobbing.

She looked over at the cut off plastic soda bottles and plastic hoses. She felt ashamed as she looked around the empty room that they were calling home. It was dirty, dilapidated and wreaked of sadness.

"This is one step away from homeless." she realized as she continued a healthy retrospective of her reality.

She reached into her back pocket, searching for the cell phone before realizing she gave it back to Meadow.

"Shit, shit," she mumbled as her mind raced. "How am I gonna contact that po?"

She realized that she was using the street slang she picked up from Smithton. She wanted to be less like Smithton and more like Meadow.

"How do I contact that cop, cop?" she said, correcting her latter terminology.

Kitty walked into the bathroom as she tried to plot her next move. She walked into the room and turned on the water, splashing some into her mouth before swilling it around and spitting into the rust-stained sink.

She walked over to the toilet and kicked the lid down, then sat on the closed seat as she stared straight ahead, searching for the answers. Kitty placed her elbow on her knee and bit at the chewed down nail on her middle finger. Her eyes glanced down at the ground and over the long hair that was the last voice of Kelsey's life.

"Smithon may be a prick but he's no killer." She said to herself as she tried to apply logic resolute to her unanswered questions. "Maybe she was in a wreck or somethin'?" She paused, then thought, "I need to talk to Meadow again."

She stood up and walked out of the bathroom, down the hall and out of the mobile lab. She stepped out into the air that now turned damp, chilling and sobering. She looked over at Meadow's trailer only to find that her car was gone.

"Shit, she left without me."

Kitty was disappointed and disenfranchised. She sat down on the splintered wooden step. She had nowhere to go; she had no one to talk to.

"Daddy, what do you think I should do?" She asked once again, as if he would speak to her. She shut her eyes and imagined his face in her mind. She imagined him sitting her down and standing in front of her, strong, wise, and heroic.

She saw him speaking and reasoning with her

"Kitty, if a boy hurts you or treats you bad you have to do what's right. You weren't raised like that. You know better." He would say.

She recounted the events when she and a young neighbor boy broke up. He had pushed her once she said she didn't want his hand in her pants.

Kitty remembered.

She kissed his lips and felt the force of his tongue into her mouth. She responded doing the same thing as the two young tongues circled one another aimlessly.

She was pushed onto the basement floor of the unfinished house where they would meet. He began grabbing at her undeveloped breasts as he reached underneath her t-shirt.

Kitty once again did not feel aroused by his actions. She merely went along with the young, aggressive lead from her boyfriend.

His hands found their way from her shirt to her shorts. The top of her pants did not allow the space required for his hands to enter so he reached down forcefully to the bottom of her pant leg.

Kitty pushed his hand away but he grabbed her hand and forced his body onto hers, weighting her down. He grabbed her hand and forced it down his pants.

Kitty wanted to push him off her but she didn't. She wanted to stop his violation to her body but she did not want to be disliked. She was not aroused or engaged.

She felt a sticky wet consistency around her young boyfriend's penis. She had never felt a penis before and yanked her hand out once she realized that he had prematurely ejaculated.

Disgusted by the thought, she rolled away, stood up, and ran home to her father. The facts were not fully disclosed to her father.

Kitty shook her head as if to evacuate her first memory of a boyfriend, invasion and self-condemnation. She remembers the boy was absent from school the next day. She was relieved that she did not have to face him. She wanted to use her flight instinct and never see him again instead of dealing with him or the embarrassment she felt. From an early age, Kitty took on other's infractions, accepting responsibility for them instead of defending herself. She never tried to understand her actions or behavior; to her, they were normal.

The next time Kitty saw the boy, he had a broken arm. She never spoke to him, nor did she ever learn how the boy's arm was fractured. She was, in a private way, happy about it.

Kitty looked out onto the road and saw the passing of a car that resembled a police patrol car.

Just as quickly as her relapse into the closed, dark places of her memory occurred, they were forgotten.

"I'll get that cop to look for Kelsey."

She stood and walked toward the street, searching for the cop.

CHAPTER TWENTY-FOUR

Amnesia

"Don't allow your mind to interfere with your heart. Love is felt before thought." E.H.

The two of them laughed as they watched the music video. Kitty jumped onto the bed and twirled her finger around the air on the side of her temple.

"I'm goin' crazy!" she sang out as she and Smithton laugh.

Kitty fell backwards onto her back, kicking her feet on the bed as her stomach muscles ached from the usage. The two laughed uncontrollably.

Kitty walked along the narrow shoulder of the road, reviewing all of the conflicting information logged within her memory banks. The memories clouded her vision.

Come on, fucker, she thought. I know you're watchin' me. Come the fuck on and git it.

Kitty walked the entire mile to the strip mall in a clouded haze of conflicting emotions. She looked down and out onto the back of the food store, serving as the underbelly of the secretive meeting place for her and the cop.

Kitty looked into the windshield of the cars that sped past her, oblivious to her.

"Where these people are were going, who are they? How do they live?" She asked ash played this game to keep her mind occupied.

Kitty was experiencing fractions of normalcy that were conflicting with her abnormal existence. Bob had successfully built a home and supportive environment for his daughter after his wife left them. He never filed for a divorce from her. He never wanted to finalize the harsh reality, the end. Bob fell in love with one woman in his lifetime, Kitty's mother.

He was painfully aware that he failed her. He was young and conditioned into the mindset that a wife did not need friendship or support. A wife stayed home and raised children, period. She rejected the lack of time spent communicating or bonding, so after days, weeks and months of unsuccessful personal arbitration to restore their relationship, she left him. In reality, she left not only Bob but her child.

Kitty stepped over garbage as she around the back of the store. She walked to the back of the store where it was vacant. Carts, cars, woman and children cluttered the front of the store; the back of the store was desolate.

Kitty walked toward the curb, behind the dumpster where she once scavenged for food. Ironically, she glanced dismissively at the items now that her stomach was full.

She sat and waited. Trooper Cantoniski was off work this day, unbeknownst to Kitty. She stood, paced, sat, and then abandoned waiting.

Kitty walked back along the same narrow corridor that lead her back to the existence she was trying to flee.

Off into the distance, Smithton could see a girl walking along the shoulder of the road up ahead of him.

"That's Kitty. What the fuck is she is playin' at?" he said as he approached her backside.

Smithton pulled up alongside of her as she walked along the roadside.

"Kitty," he yelled out.

She turned and looked at him, angry that she was relieved to see him.

"Git in," he yelled out to her.

Kitty ran around the side of the truck that offered her sanctuary. She hopped into the truck, the music was blaring out a familiar song often played by Smithton. The song gave her a comforting feeling that he was reminiscing about the two of them. "Sweet Melissa" was one of her father's favorite songs, and that transferred onto Smithton. The song made her smile.

Smithton saw the large bright smile that lit up his world and overpowered any drug he could possibly take. He smiled.

The man made, self-induced iceberg separating them collapsed under the weight of their bond. The two had a strong connection forged out of the trials and tribulations they weathered in their short lifetimes.

Smithton sang out just as he did when the two arrived at the strange neighborhood and overtook the abandoned trailer.

"My sweet, Katherine," he sang, replacing the words of the song.

Familiarity took hold all of the conflicting emotions raging within Kitty. She felt a rush of emotion she had not felt for a long time.

She thought, this is my Smithton, he's back, thanks Daddy.

Kitty slid over to Smithton's side of the truck and placed her head on his shoulder. She watched the shoulder of the road as it came and passed behind the two of them.

She looked up at Smithton and saw the fragile, soft, and flawed man that stepped up to the call of being her father, mother, lover, and friend.

Smithton looked down at Kitty and smiled as she gazed up at him.

"I have a bag of sunshine for you, and before you craze on me, it was givin' to me by D. Reach into my front pocket.

Kitty laughed and reached her right hand into Smithton's jeans pocket. She felt a small bag familiar to her. She pulled it out to find a gram of cocaine.

Kitty laughed and sat up, looking at the white baggie as if it could to remove all the conflicting tides cresting within her.

She opened the baggie and placed it up to her right nostril. She sucked up as much powder as her nose could contain, then she sat back and waited for her demons to fly out the window and onto the side of the road.

The rush from the amphetamine did not inspire warmth, as Kitty hoped. Instead, he wanted to jump out of the car and run. She did not. Kitty sat with her head on Smithton's shoulder waiting for a miracle to occur.

This is what she knew: Smithton was home and he was all she had. The possibility of being alone stifled her into acceptance.

The truck drove into the small sheltered circle. The first vision Kitty experienced that answered her prayers was Meadow's car. Unbeknownst to Smithton, Kitty found the courage from the one person that could interrupt their lives.

Smithton and Kitty exited the truck and walked together into the trailer. Once inside, he grabbed her hand and stopped walking. He looked at her and breached the space and time between them.

"Do another bump," he instructed as he pulled out a card from his back pocket, his driver's license, and handed it to her.

Kitty felt incapacitated. She took his license and dipped the edge into the bag. She scooped a large amount of powder onto the edge of the plastic and held it to her nose.

Smithton softly and slowly placed his hands around her waist and pulled her frame into his. His right hand slid up her back and onto the nape of her neck. He kissed her slowly with all the emotions he was capable of exhibiting. She felt his love. Whether it was her childhood fairy tale wishes or merely an abated moment, Kitty succumbed to Smithton's touch.

She kissed him back, hard, grasping and pulling his t-shirt into a knot within her fists. They fell to the floor tugging and ripping at each other's clothing.

Grime and history was erased as the two of them fell together. Smithton made love to Kitty without guilt this time. Kitty made love to Smithton high on cocaine, numb.

Kitty's mind was not on Smithton; he did not embody security. She thought of Meadow and felt the love that Smithton was attempting to show her. Kitty was not engaged in an affair, yet this other person commanded her attention.

Once Smithton climaxed, he rolled off of Kitty.

"Want onto?" He asked.

Kitty looked over at him. "No, I love you Smithton," she said with her familiar conformity.

Smithton held out his hand, magically, and opened his palm. He displayed the ring.

"Kitty, marry me," he asked softly.

Kitty was stunned silent. These were words that Kitty desperately longed for, yet she felt different. She felt as if she was standing on a small desert island looking out and into endless blue water fading into blue skies without difference.

Kitty reached out and looked at the ring. She rolled over and kissed Smithton as she thought, "Daddy, this is what you wanted so it is what is right, right?"

Kitty's father prearranged her and Smithton uniting before his death. She felt she was betraying her father's wishes with all of her recent train of thought.

"When's your next deal, Smithton? Take me? I'm sick of hangin' and trackin' round here." Kitty strategically moved her rook.

Smithton abandon his paranoia with Kitty this time and spoke sincerely, "In a dozen or so." he replied, meaning within the next twelve hours.

"That lady next door is a risk, Smithton. Her friend is missing. I met her today." She casually said.

Smithton perked up his attention, "Does she know anything 'bout us?" he asked.

"No, but I don't want her askin' 'round or stirring up shit," she replied as she wove a tapestry of premeditated questions and answers.

"Then sort it out, Kitty. As I said, this is your life, too." Smithton replied.

"I need to go sort her out then," Kitty said feeling relieved that she now had a clear escape route. The stress of the game she was playing was causing her to feel physically ill. She spoke through grit teeth and said,

"I love you, Smithton."

She hoped to bring the conversation to positive closure.

He looked at her and could tell there something different about her. This new change evoked concern within him. He wanted to keep her with him, but did not. He wanted to let her out into the world to see if she would come back to him.

"Beware of strangers, Kitten," he said as he lay on the ground with his hands folded behind his head. He felt a certain sadness that he had never felt before with her. He hoped that his new move and this latest deal did not ruin his future with the only person he had left in his life.

Smithton's high was fading. His mind and loyalty fleeted and concerned itself with immediate gratification, as usual.

Kitty looked at him as he was reaching into his pocket, looking no doubt for his bag of high. She felt the tug of conflicting patronage stronger than ever. She was seeing him from a different vantage. She turned away from Smithton and looked toward the door. As she turned the door knob he called out, "Kitty, stay." He did not want to lose her just yet.

He held up a bag of white powder hoping to drawl her back in. Smithton spent his life relying on providing drugs to either lure or retain friends and lovers fully knowing they were duplicitous.

"Come git high with me?" he asked as he smiled at her with eyes that at one time ignited the emotions of true love within her.

She did not answer him. She was focused on the road outside of the plastic blinds. She could see that Meadow's car was not there.

"She isn't waitin' 'round for me." she thought to herself.

She turned and looked back at Smithton, who was still lying on his back with his arms and legs folded, still smiling with his coy and confident boyishness.

Kitty turned and walked back toward the man who was her universe.

"Snow or crystals?" she asked him.

"Now Kitten," he smiled as he shook the baggie in front of her. "I know my princess does not want crystals. I got you a bag of blow."

Kitty smiled dejectedly and walked over to him and plopped down onto the floor. Smithton pulled out a small piece of vinyl that he cut from the skirting of the trailer.

He dipped the end into the bag and scooped up a large amount of white powder and held it up to Kitty's nose. She hesitated, her conscious battled and begged of her to deny the offering but she succored and snorted the powder through her nostrils.

"It's been awhile since I did blow. Where'd you git it?" she asked as she immediately felt the rush from the amphetamine.

"I asked for it, swapped my black for it, for you." He reached over and pulled her by the back of her head into him and kissed her.

Kitty sat back against the wall and walked with the high along its path. Her mind did not think of Kelsey, or Meadow, or Bob. She talked with Smithton about the things they always talk about when they were high.

They talked about where they wanted to go, what kind of house they wanted to live in, and what type of truck they wanted to buy when they made their way back down south.

CHAPTER TWENTY-FIVE

Abandonment

"The innocent fail to see finality when realists fail to see continuation."
E.H.

Meadow's eyes looked around the now familiar roadside looking past the pavement in front of her car and onto the roadsides. The fear inside her told her quietly, nagging that she was looking for signs of death.

She looked over the hillsides and into the thick brush, fearing to see Kelsey's face or body.

The thought of death took her mind immediately to her father. She looked up at the dark gray sky.

Why do I look to the sky when I want to think of you? It's not as if you are looking down on me, is it?

Meadow searched for answers from places that were not accommodating her questions.

"Come on Kels, I'm losing it here. Talk to me, where are you?"

She pressed forward with tears in her eyes and knots in her stomach. She tried to envision Kelsey's face but couldn't. The street became familiar and Meadow knew she was close to the road where the trailer was. She tried to imagine Kelsey driving up the same road.

"This is the same path you took," she said with agony and desperation. "Where did you go, Kels?"

Meadow was now in the familiar territory of the trailer park court. She kept coming back to it instinctually, though unwilling to admit that this was her final destination.

The path winded around white, green, and tan aluminum trailers that were dirty, used, and neglected, standing in stark contrast to the golden field of abandoned hay fronds that stood against the last cutting of the harvest.

Meadow looked at the field, acknowledging its vastness as it reached upward and met the sky. She thought of Kelsey as she looked out into the field. Kelsey's spirit swept over the field, blowing dried dead fronds onto the windshield.

Meadow pulled into the trailer park and alongside the trailer. She noticed a truck parked in front of the trailer where Kitty lived.

Maybe they're home, she thought as she put the car in park, turned off the engine, and glanced out the window.

Maybe she talked to that cop, she thought as she walked toward the door on the side of the trailer.

Meadow glanced at the siding that was falling off and over at the dirty windows, then reached up and knocked on the door.

Kitty looked at Smithton and Smithton jumped up off of the floor.

"Fuck," he said in a loud whisper.

Kitty's nerves frayed as she felt responsible for the intruder, *Fuck, it's the cop*, she thought as she jumped up and grabbed Smithton's arm.

"What do we do?" she whispered as she held him back. "Don't answer it."

Smithton pushed her away.

"Stay here, Kitty," he said as he inched toward the window.

He stood with his back against the wall and turned his head toward the window.

"It's some woman," he said to Kitty.

Kitty's did not think of the woman being Meadow. She got down on her knees and crawled over to the side window. Her heart raced against the cocaine that was intoxicating her body. She was scared and frantic.

She reached Smithton and grabbed at his jeans.

"What do we do?" she asked as the knocking continued.

Smithton walked over to the door.

"I'll answer it," he said. "Stay against the wall and outta sight."

Smithton coughed and pressed his forefinger and thumb against his nostrils assuring that they were free of residue.

He opened the door a mere three inches and peered at Meadow.

"Yeah?"

Meadow looked at the thin young man with surprise.

This must be Kitty's boyfriend, she thought. He is not what I expected.

"I met your girlfriend, Kitty. Is she here?" Meadow asked with caution.

"Nah, she's not," he said as he started to close the door.

"Wait," she said, moving in closer to the door. "Maybe you can help me."

Smithton sensed the reliance of the woman and opened the door, stepping through it, moving her out the way with his presence.

"With what?" he asked as he closed the door behind him.

"Maybe you saw my girlfriend. She arrived here the other day." Meadow looked at the physical appearance of Smithton and figured he was definitely on drugs.

"Nah, I didn't see anyone. Kitty already asked me."

"So then you spoke to Kitty?" Meadow asked.

Paranoia toward Meadow mixed with annoyance toward Kitty rose within him.

"Yeah, she's my glad," he replied coyly.

Meadow looked at him, showing her confusion at his terminology.

"Girlfriend," Smithton said, then waited for her to reply.

Meadow pressed forward with her questioning, sensing he was spurious with his immediate answer.

"Did you see her car? It's a red Explorer." She looked at Smithton's eyes as they darted back and forth as he squinted at her.

"Nah. Look, I'll tell Kitty you banged the door." He turned and walked back into the trailer closing the door behind him.

Meadow stood looking at the door as it slammed shut in her face.

"What a fucking asshole." She though as she raged on.

"Should I knock on the door once again?" she thought, "I want to continue my questioning or leave it? This guy can turn out to be a fucking psycho for all I know." She thought to herself as she stopped knocking on the door.

Meadow thoughts turned toward Kitty and the volatility of the relationship. She did not want to endanger the young woman's safety any further than possible under her intrusion into their relationship.

Smithton locked the door behind him then looked down at Kitty, who was still on the ground. She overheard the entire exchange with anxiety. She feared Smithton's thoughts over the knowledge of the friendship.

External relationships were prohibited by Smithton at any of the transient dwellings. Their survival depended on anonymity.

Kitty braced for Smithton's wrath of incense. She sat still as her eyes widened and watched his movements.

Smithton walked over and grabbed Kitty by the back of her t-shirt. He wrapped the thin fabric around his fist and dragged her back to a spot where their presence was not exposed by any of the windows.

"What did you play at, Kitten?" he said as he pulled up. Her light doll-like frame was lifted onto her feet.

"She was asking questions Smithton. I told you." Kitty defended her actions under the fact that she had already informed him about the woman renting the trailer next door.

"Yeah, yeah. Kinda forgot to tell me you two were bro girls. That is a problemo, gitto, Kitty?" The veins in his forehead grew larger.

When Smithon was high and angry his meth street slang grew stronger. Kitty stepped back and tried to react with calculation.

"I am tryin' to keep her away from us, Smithton. I am tryin' to do what you taught me. What's the prob with that?" She exaggerated the word prob, mocking his street slang.

Smithton was defused slightly as he recounted the conversation that they had already had about her and her missing girlfriend.

"Is she a fishmonger?" he asked her. Smithton was very perceptive, although at times it was over intensified by his meth paranoia.

Kitty was aware that Kelsey and Meadow were lesbians but did not want to respond as if she was aware.

"I don't fuckin' know that, how should I?" she replied defensively.

Smithton reached into his pocket and pulled out several baggies of his product. He removed one bag and placed the rest into his jeans front pocket. He sat down with his knees bent and leaned his back against the wall. He reached down into his shirt and grabbed the silver chain. At the end of the chain was a name tag. He left it hang outside of his shirt while he untied the wire tie on the baggie. He dipped the name tag into the bag, then to his nose. He inhaled, then looked over to Kitty and nodded his head for her to get out her baggie of cocaine.

She did as she was told and moved over closer to him and sat beside him. "Where's your piece of aluminum trailer?" she asked with a mocking grin.

"I'm goin' big this time babe." He replied.

Smithton dipped the dog tag into her bag then up to her nose. She took a short, quick sniff then closed her baggie up. She did not want to make waves but had no interest in getting high with him or anyone for that matter. She felt a metamorphosis occurring within her.

Smithton left his product on the brown carpet in between his long bent knees, then replied with an unusually reserve tone, given the recent events.

"Well, I'm fucked now in this tin can. I was gonna meet my D for my uptown cook, but I can't leave now. You fucked that, Kitty."

"I'll watch her out the window to see when she leaves. If she's lookin' for her friend, she won't stay long." Kitty tried to be defusing and accommodating. She was filled with anxiety over the thought his next move.

"You don't go anywhere near a window. I leave when I see it neat," He snapped back in response to her offer of surveying the neighbor.

"Can I git up to git my backpack? I want to change my clothes," she asked him.

Smithton brushed off her request, waving his hand dismissively at the back of the trailer.

Kitty got up and walked to the bathroom where she had her backpack hung on a hook on the wall. She grasped the bottom of her worn t-shirt and pulled it up over her head. She did not stop to glance at her reflection in the large spotted mirror reflecting her thin frame. She had adapted a dismissive response to her appearance.

Kitty was cognizant that her once full, healthy frame was now thin and bony. Her once healthy rose colored complexion now pale yellow and sallow with darkened reflections under her distant eyes.

A large dark circle on her protruding hipbone did catch her attention. She stopped from removing her second hand store outdated jeans and looked closer.

A large bruise overlapped the alarming appearance of her emaciated frame.

"How did I git this?" she thought as she looked closer at the bruise. She touched the bruise then recoiled at the pain.

"Oh, fuck. This is from Smithton," she thought as she replayed the last few days.

She kicked off her jeans and walked over to the toilet. She picked up her foot and kicked down the toilet seat left up from Smithton. The outdated heavy plastic seat and lid slammed against the porcelain bowl.

Kitty sat down and brought her feet up to her chest in her standard comfort position. Kitty felt safest when she occupied the smallest space in the slightest of light.

She banged her forehead against her knees two times as she repeated tormenting, self derogating words.

"What the fuck am I doin'? What the fuck am I doin' Daddy?"

Answers did not come. Smithton did not notice she was gone for an extended amount of time. Her high was wearing off. The absence of food, water, and sleep was causing her to feel the exhaustion placed upon her body.

She moved to lay between the toilet and wall. She closed her eyes and entered yet again a collision of a conscious and her subconscious universe.

Her tired body lay on a soft sheet as she was covered with a soft warm comforter. Her head nested into a fluffy pillow.

A loud and firm knock on the door awoke her as she sat up. Smithton sat watching television.

"Smithton, it's the housekeeping service," she said with concern.

"They can't come in, you have drugs on the dresser." She jumped up and out of comfort.

"SShhhhhh," Smithton said. "She'll go away."

The two looked at the door as they held their breath.

The doorknob turned as Smithton jumped up and grabbed Kitty by the hand, pulling her away from the door as it was about to intrude onto their solace. Kitty ran alongside of him, scooping up the mound of baggies as she ran with Smithton toward the bathroom.

"Get into the tub," Smithton whispered as he locked the door behind them.

"Hello," they heard as the woman called out.

"Shhhhh," Smithton whispered.

Kitty huddled in the tub with the baggies clenched to her chest. Her heart pounded. She waited to hear once again, the turning of the doorknob. She was naked, petrified, and holding a large amount of drugs.

She heard the door open, she did not breathe in air as she tried to disappear.

"Become invisible Kitty, close your eyes and disappear." She tried to convince herself to remove herself from the room, from the dream that was turning into a nightmare.

Kitty tried to wake herself by shaking her head back and forth. She was not awaking nor was she disappearing from the tub as the door opened.

The metal rings of the plastic shower curtain drug against the firm metal bar hanging above her body. She looked up.

The familiar police officer stood in front of her.

"Get out of the tub, Ms. Hepburn," he firmly commanded of her.

Kitty did not know where Smithton was.

"Did they take him?" she asked as she stood up, naked.

The baggies tumbled onto the white porcelain surface.

The police officer reached in and grabbed her by the arm. Neither spoke as he escorted her out of the tub.

"Run, run down the hall and down the steps once you get outside." She plotted as she walked alongside of him without speaking or disobeying his demands.

The police officer opened the door and Kitty ran. She ran down the covered outdoor hall, past closed doors of occupied rooms. As she ran, she looked into the windows. She noticed couples lying in bed watching television, laughing and eating food from trays placed before them.

Kitty heard a deep barking off in the distance. She turned to find that she was running toward a very large black Doberman. She turned and ran as fast as her feet carried her. With bruised feet and shoes that did not fit, she was losing the race. The distance between her and the dog could not be gauged as the dog faded into the darkness of the night. Only white eyes and large teeth illuminated through the darkness.

Kitty reached the end of the hall and frantically reached for doorknob of the last door to the last room.

She opened the door and closed it behind her as she heard the nails of the dog's claws scratching at the metal door behind her.

"Thank God," she said as she relaxed and turned into the room that was not a room of the hotel. The room was a clinical room with a metal table in the center and large white operating light exposing a naked man on the table.

Kitty looked without fear as she walked toward the backside of a man who was working over the naked body.

"Is this an operating room?" she asked as she walked forward with curiosity.

The man in front of her wore a long green cotton smock. He was sticking a long thin needle into the cheek of the man on the table. The technician was depressing the needle and as he did, the cheeks of the man on the table swelled and turned pink, then red in color.

The technician removed the needle and aggressively plunged it into the other side of the sleeping man as he repeated the same steps that resulted in same affects.

Kitty stood beside the man on the table and gasped as she choked in air, unsuccessfully breathing.

"Daddy, what are they doing to you?" she screamed as she realized the naked man on the table was her father.

Kitty pushed the technician as she screamed to leave him alone.

The technician turned.

"Kitty, he is dead. He asked me to do this, all of this."

Kitty looked into the face of the technician in the green mortuary coat. It was Smithton in the clinical room, stuffing

Bob with fluid to swell his lifeless, cancer shrunken face with embalming fluid.

Kitty woke. She cried out, "Smithton."

He did not come. Kitty's memory lapsed and betrayed her, forcing her waking consciousness back to her father's funeral.

She could not remove the vision of her father, the man who stood as the only symbol she knew of life embodying love. She remembered his defeated body lying still and lifeless, with his appearance fake and deceiving, cheeks full instead of collapsed. Kitty remembered the strange color of his complexion that mocked the memory of her father's true appearance.

Kitty stood and ran out the bathroom, crying, searching for comfort. She called for Smithton again, but not hearing a response, she ran into the abandoned living room.

Kitty walked the perimeter of the small room, quietly calling out for Smithton. The room exposed no one. The room signified loneliness and abandonment to Kitty. She felt as if she had lost control of her reality. Her mind was not distinguishing between reality and nightmares.

"This is not happening," she cried out into the abandoned room. Her suppressed and untold fears overflowed from her disturbed sleep and now possessed her reality.

"What happens to me? Who takes care of me? How do I survive?" she mumbled as she shuffled her unwilling feet into the dark kitchen.

Kitty looked around the room and called out into the ostensibly deserted small space.

Kitty continued into the kitchen.

"It's cold out, dark; will he ever come back?" she asked herself the question she tried to avoid during saner moments.

Kitty quickly spun around as she hysterically feared being exposed. She realized she had not put on a tee shirt. She folded her arms over his chest and looked out of the window in fear. Her eyes calmed her fears as she realized that the round intrusive light was the full moon. Although officious, she rested her now delirious mind.

The full moon confronted and opposed the darkness. Its light offered Kitty hope.

She turned and looked out of the confinement of the kitchen walls and onto Meadow's trailer.

"Her car is there," she said as she felt a lift to her abated spirit.

She ran back into the bathroom and grabbed her t-shirt. She put it on as she ran out of the trailer, guided by the illumination of the moon to Meadow's door.

Kitty softly knocked upon it. Meadow opened the door.

"Come in, child," Meadow said as she felt relieved to see the young woman. She was concerned about while consumed with distraught over the two women that consumed her waking and sleeping thoughts.

Meadow felt like a mother, an unexpected saving emotion.

CHAPTER TWENTY-SIX

The Confrontation of Space and Time

"Total Perfection does not exist. Masked and alluring, for in reality no one reaches their own definition of perfection." E.H.

Smithton felt insecurity consuming his ego. His failures were nagging him. "I haven't failed anyone," he thought superficially, without diagnosing his selfishness. Smithton had friends that invested time in his life, yet he could not focus on their needs. His life was running from a high to a high.

"Did I failed Cee?" he thought as he sat at the red light, clenching and unclenching his fists.

Drugs and sexual pleasure caromed with her needs. This was the first woman Smithton used for his sexual gratification. He was not interested in her as a person. Once the car accident took her life, he vowed to only use women for sexual gratification.

Smithton cocked his head to view the light in the intersection for the intersecting turning yellow. He slammed his foot down on the gas pedal, jumping the green light.

"I know I'm dying Smithy. I just want to know that I was a good father and I did better than my dad."

Smithton replayed Bob's words in his mind. This was perhaps his most incensed demon. He never forgot Bob's pleas that he take care of Kitty and carry on the loving legacy that he tried to build.

"I failed you Bob", he thought before yelling "Fuck!" at having to stop once again at the next red light.

"I'm fuckin' sorry," he said to out loud. "Now what?"

He felt an interminable foreboding. Smithton gave up at this moment and succumbed to the demon that begged his attention, defeat, and self condemnation.

"It's all about ice and rage now, Smithton," he said out loud as he turned down the street toward the garage.

His addictions, sexual pleasures, and dark demon controlled his actions.

"I just wanted to be like everyone else, that's all I ever wanted." His thoughts turned toward his parents. His thoughts then became too deep for him to handle. He snapped out of his thought process when noticed that he reached the block where the garage was located.

He pulled up to the left large aluminum doors and idled his mind, memories, and truck. Of the two doors, one was manual and one was controlled electronically from within. He recalled using the left door the last time he was encapsulated by the D's bangers.

Smithton leaned forward and turned up the radio as he sang out using his rich, harmonious voice.

"And I have one more silver dollar."

Smithton sat taping the steering wheel and shaking his leg quickly, rocking his body uncontrollably back and forth, as his thoughts related to the words of the song that he held as one his mantras. Smithton associated with the words and phrases that spoke of desperation and an undying rouge attempt to preserve freedom of one's spirit.

After few minutes, the door lifted with the clanking of the electronic chains, prompting Smithton to place the truck into drive. His truck moved slowly forward into the garage bay.

Smithton placed his truck into park and waited once again with agitation to complete the mission. His mind was fixated on the whore over the sale of his product.

One of the D's bangers appeared in the passenger side window of Smithton's truck. The large ominous thug did not motion for his attention; the thug merely occupied the entire space of the window and waited for Smithton to acknowledge his presence.

Smithton realized that he did not prepare himself by removing his gun from under the seat. He leaned over and rolled down the window with trepidation.

"D wants your fat sack," the large black man said with a firm tone.

Smithton held out a plastic bag containing smaller bags of his product.

As the thug reached in, Smithton pulled it back an inch out of is reach.

The thug tensed his facial expressions.

"Where is my ho ass? She sits and hands passo producto."

The thug laughed as he replied with an islander accent, "Yo have Jones, huh mon?" He laughed as he mocked Smithton.

"Just git the ho ass dis ride and we pass this," Smithton replied firmly.

His tense desire translated to sexual desire, although the ability of him achieving a full erection was becoming problematic and only intensified his agitation.

The banger turned and yelled into the garage, "Aye, Niyah! Yo is jonesed. Come 'ere brass."

Within a minute or two, Smithton's embodiment of lust, redemption, furor, and sin appeared wearing the same shiny black and turquoise tawdry mini skirt she wore the last time he dehumanized her.

The banger spoke to her off on to side, and Smithton strained to hear but could not.

She opened the door as she flashed a familiar smile.

"Armstrong, you be wantin' dis?"

She laughed as she spoke and toyed with the devil, then sat down and slid her unwilling skirt along the seat and over toward Smithton, with the intention of receiving, passing, then pleasing.

Smithton smiled and as he placed the gallon zip lock bag onto her palm, he laughed back, enticing and seducing her.

"Yeah, downtown, Niyah." He looked into her face, past and beyond her eyes. This was an indication to her that he wanted her to give him a blow job. He smiled then said, "Niyah, is it?"

Smithton bridled his desires until the deal was done first. Niyah handed the bag out to the waiting thug, who was smiling as he thought of the inventible sexual actions between the two.

Once Smithton saw the bag exchange hands he yelled out, "Release homie. Bennies when I return."

For the first time in Smithton's drug career, starting when he was fourteen, he was releasing his product without the exchange of money. This was the first domino pushed to start his demise. Smithton felt as if he was caught up in a spinning cyclone that was sucking up all the pieces of his world.

He had a premonition that he would be busted and did not want to be caught with product or large amounts of money. If Smithton was going down, it was going to be on his terms, not the cops'.

Smithton's reckless mind was setting up a self fulfilling prophecy for its own expiration. Tonight's self gratification was not about money, it was about pushing his high to the maximum limits. He wanted a sexual release and he wanted to punish a woman for his failures.

Niyah was chosen to pay the price tonight for his failures, short comings, and betrayal. Smithton had prepared himself to make her pay the price for breaking his promise to Bob and ultimately, Kitty.

The heavy door rolled upward in disjointed sections, distracting his deviant thoughts. All of the muscles in this body popped but not enough for him.

He reached into his pocket and pulled out one of his reserve personal bags of meth. He held it between his forefinger and thumb and dangled it in front of Niyah.

"Move your lips over to my chest and pull out the chain," he instructed her.

She obliged him willingly. Smithton was the only male that sexually aroused her in uncountable months. She giggled and placed her lips upon Smithton's chest. She kissed his chest, feeling emotion as his flesh impacted with hers. She kissed him sensuously, hoping he would feel her emotion. She felt the ball chain within her teeth and slowly bit the chain concerned not to catch his skin, pulling the chain upward with her head.

"Niyah, you're the bomb," he said as he fatuously lured into a false rush of emotions.

"Now be a good brass and dip that into that bag and do daddy right," he asked of her.

Niyah did as she was told as the truck drove out the garage and onto the street. She was unaware of the destination; she thought they would drive to one of the several abandon buildings left derelict in the rundown neighborhood. After placing the dog tag under Smithton's nose, she was directed to do the same.

She laughed although, she wanted to be looked at seriously by Smithton. She wanted to speak up but did not want to risk changing the party atmosphere in the truck. She snorted another large clump of meth, then dipped the dog tag into the bag and held a large clump of the drug up to Smithton's nose.

"Other nose hole," he said as he turned his head. After inhaling this large amount of methamphetamine, his gag reflex caused him to dry heave.

"That's the score right there, bitch," he said with pride.

Smithton wanted to fly above reality. He was willing to overuse the drug to keep rolling. While he was high he was not faced with all of the mental inflictions he was experiencing.

"Where we goin'?" Niyah asked once she realized that they were out of the city blocks that she trolled and felt comfortable in.

"Do you trust me, Niyah?" he asked with premeditated calculated deviance and manipulation. He called her by name this time to evoke her emotions with the bait.

Niyah looked at Smithton and replied, "I do."

She unzipped his jeans and pulled out his limp penis. She bent over and began sucking the head of his soft penis, sucking harder attempting to give him an erection. She rubbed, sucked, and ran her tongue around the head of his penis without efficacy. Niyah began to feel insecure with her performance. She perfunctorily performed these acts daily. This was her business, and she was aware that she should give oral sex to climax in 5 minutes. Smithton was not getting hard and she had been working on him for over six to seven minutes. Stress distorted the atmosphere and the two began feeling each other's tension.

Niyah wanted emotional bonding with Smithton. She sat up and wiped her mouth and said, "Were too cranked, Armstrong. We need to come down some."

"Don't fuckin' tell me I need to come down, yo lips aren't suckin' hard enough. Git down on me and draw out my cum." He reached over and pushed her head back down onto his dick.

In truth, Smithton was aware he was not getting hard nor did he think he would be. When he snorted large amounts of meth, he was not able to get a full erection. Bringing to his attention was not a good tactic for Niyah. Not even Kitty could talk about Smithton's erectile dysfunction.

After a few failed minutes, Smithton yelled at her to stop as he approached the land fill where he dumped the road kill.

"Sit up and wipe your sucker," he said as he pushed her away and stuffed his half erect penis back into his jeans and zipped them up.

"Reach forward and grab my employee pass, right there." He pointed to a plastic card that dangled from a nylon cord on his rear view mirror as he spoke to her. Niyah did as she was told without asking any questions.

"He must work here," she thought instead of asking.

Smithton pulled up the guard house and rolled down the window and held out his badge as he yelled out, "I'm here to dump."

The small, thin, disheveled teenager was awkward and uncertain of the protocol to use at this time of night.

"I have to call the supervisor; I'm not sure if I can let you dump this late at night." His response sounded more like a question than an answer. Smithton noticed his eyes wonder into the truck to survey Niyah, so he thought to act quickly.,

"This is my wife. I apologize, dude, we were out at dinner and I got a call from the super to pick up a kill on State Rd. 48. He said to dump it tonight. You can call him, dude, but he won't be too impressed with you."

The young guard looked at Smithton and believed his lie.

"Is the burn still scheduled for tomorrow?" he asked the guard.

The young man started to walk toward the back of the truck, Smithton opened his door and stepped out as if was stretching.

"I have three in the back, guts hangin' out, legs snapped off two of 'em," he said as he tried to dissuade the guard from looking into the empty bed.

Smithson's voice remained calculated and aggressive, taking advantage of the youth's naïveté.

"I don't want my old lady to see it either," he added.

Niyah sat still smiling widely. She did not hear the contents of the conversation past the point when Smithton called her his wife. She was reading emotion into the premeditated response. She pulled at her skirt and smoothed the front then crossed her legs with pride.

"I need to check your ID, then I'll let you through," The young guard said as he held Smithton's ID under the scrutiny of his flashlight. He glanced up at Smithton once again, shining the flashlight into his eyes.

Smithton's held his hand up over this dilated pupils,

"Dude, you mind?" he said.

The guard could see that the photo on the ID matched the man standing in front of him.

"Alright," he said as the arm lifted.

Smithton could not resist questioning the new employee about facts he already knew.

"Is Phil in the trailer?"

The employee hesitated then stumbled over his words.

"No, he has been AWOL," he replied.

Smithton glowed with pride.

"Wow, that's weird. Who is in the trailer?" he questioned.

The unconfident man struggled to answer with corporate correctness.

"There is a temp from the city scheduled to come tomorrow morning and supervisor the burn, but there's no one up there now."

Smithton reveled in his moment of power. He sat back and hesitated before thinking of what to say.

"I'll handle this tonight. I'll dump, then stick around for a hour or so to make sure anymore dumps are placed right for the burn. They'll thank you tomorrow instead of firing your ass for fuckin' up the carcass placement, know what I mean, dude?" Smithton asked.

The young man with corporate aspirations was assuaged and eased by Smithton's offer to manage the hill while he stayed at the gate.

"Hey, that'd be great, thanks, man," he replied. Smithton's adrenaline pulsed with power and raced through his veins.

He thought, "I control the fate of this slut and the new guard is eating out of my pocket." He laughed as he got back into the truck and closed the door. He placed his hand out of the window and motioned a thumbs up to the guard.

"Stupid fuck," he said out loud.

Niyah looked over and smiled. "You are like a boss or somethin' here, huh?"

Smithton desired a velocity rush. He drove up the familiar hill, instructing Niyah to feed him more meth.

"Come on baby, reach into daddy's pocket and shed some sunshine."

Niyah knew exactly what he wanted and obliged him while lifting the grainy powder upward toward his nostrils, holding firm until he inhaled the large amount she scooped up.

"Now, one in the other hole, then one under the tongue," he said as she glanced over at the strikingly handsome man.

"This is suicidal ice; you sure?" she asked.

She had developed emotion for Smithton and could not help showing a humanistic side to her. She felt guilty in participating in giving him the excessive amount of meth. Although her instincts told her not to give him that large amount of meth, she did not have the moral constitutional restrain to stop herself or stand up to Smithton. She shoveled heaps of ice into the other nostril and under his tongue. She then proceeded in snorting two more lumps in her own nose.

The winding road seemed endless to Niyah as she felt the effects from the large amount of speed that she just induced. Smithton's mind was polluted with domination, anger, rage, and intense sexual desire. He could not focus past sodomizing the whore until he pulled out and envisioned cumming on the back of her head. As he looked over at Niyah, he no longer remembered her name, he no longer saw a woman, he saw an instrument that he would use to climax and satisfy his rage.

He stopped the truck abruptly as he could no longer contain his rush. Niyah's body jerked forward as the truck came to its halt. Smithton kicked opened the door and stepped out into the night sky. A clear black sky shimmered with dozens of stars. A full moon worked in Smithton's favor. The beauty of the sky was lost as neither one looked up to acknowledge the beauty of the night. Both looked down to the ground with thoughts of lust.

Smithton walked alongside of the truck until he reached the back fender. He leaned against the cold metal frame and waited for his prey. She did not immediately come and his mind pressed him to act violently and aggressively.

Calm it, Smithton. Her runnin' around will fuck this scene, he said to himself as he called out her name.

Niyah slid across the seat, ducking behind the steering wheel and out of the open driver side door. She stumbled out and into the cold night air. She staggered around the back of the truck and over to where Smithton stood.

"What's that smell?" she asked.

Smithton grabbed her and spun her around as he answered her question.

"It's the smell of decomposing flesh. That hillside is all dead, maggot filled road kill."

Niyah's stomach turned as she turned her head and could finally make out the mound of carcasses. Her stomach rejected the ungodly smells and sights, and she bent over and threw up on the ground. Her hands were on her knees. Smithton grabbed her by the back of her hair and forced her torso down onto the ground.

She did not have time to react. Smithton fell on top of her body and she coughed as the air was pushed out of her lungs by his force. He pulled up her skirt up and pulled her ass back onto his body.

"Niyah struggled. Smithton was trying to hold her down and pull down his zipper.

"Quit struggling cunt, you wanted this. You're gettin' me as I wanna give it, hard and in your ass."

Smithton succeeded in pulling out his penis that was half hard. He tried to stuff it into her asshole but it would not enter her.

Smithton could not deal with the lack of performance when he needed it most. He pushed her shoulders and body back down and flat onto the ground.

"Cunt, your gittin' my cum one way or other," he screamed as he held her mouth into the dirt, muffling her screams.

Saliva ran from the sides of her mouth as she attempted to scream. The dirt turned muddy under her drool and stuck to her lips and cheeks as he pushed her face down harder. Smithton took his left knee and began kneeing the back of Niyah's head, the blows forced her head to the side where he continued to thrust his knee down onto her jaw, crushing it.

The pain stifled Niyah. She could no longer speak or scream or move her head, yet her eyes were open and staring at the tall mound of flesh. The tan objects faded into a red haze as blood dripped from her open skull, clouding her vision and stinging her eyes. She closed them as she felt Smithton thrusting his hard penis into her ass.

She felt him pull out and scream with a sigh of release as he leaned down to her face.

"I told you I would cum on you, didn't I?" he asked her.

He reached down and with both of his hands twisted her bloody head, snapping her neck. He stood up and shook off his penis before placing it back into his jeans.

He grabbed Niyah by the back of the skirt and lifted her limp frame off the ground. Her neck dangled and swayed back and forth as he drug her body over to the far edge of the mound.

He set her at the edge and stepped onto her back and up to the next dead dear. He grabbed one by its atrophied legs and pulled the swollen animal down and on top of Niyah.

Smithton pulled carcass after carcass onto her body until the mound's edge had been expanded to envelope Niyah. The last buck he pulled down had its throat opened down to the stomach. The animals intestines were hanging out of its belly but still attached. Smithton used the intestines to cover any part of her body was even remotely exposed.

"No one will see this whore again, the burn is in hours. She'll be smoked," he said as he stood up and wiped his bloody hands along the fur of the dear.

Large black open eyes with a clouded haze stared in the hundreds at Smithton who stared back with enjoyment to see all of the death he could possess.

Smithton turned and walked back to his truck. He drove down the hill and waved at the guard as he smiled at him.

"I think it's time for some more ice, don't you, ho ass?" He laughed as he reached into his pocket and pulled out his dwindling baggie.

"Oh, Niyah, wasn't it?" he said as he looked over to where she sat an hour earlier.

He shoveled the crystal powder up into each nostril then made his way back to Kitty.

CHAPTER TWENTY-SEVEN

Free Fall

"Never allow yourself to be pushed off the platform, only you control the jump." E.H.

"Are you ok?" Meadow asked Kitty as she as she closed the door behind her. "Did he hurt you again?"

Kitty was emotionally distraught and weary.

"We need to talk to the cop about Kelsey. I have a feelin' Smithton knows more than he's tellin' us," Kitty said to Meadow. "I've known Smithton a long time; he worked for my father's company. My dad approved of him." Kitty sobbed uncontrollably as she spoke, breathing between sentences and crying.

"He has abandoned me," Kitty kept repeating.

Meadow led her into the kitchen, sitting her down at the table. Kitty stared down at the autumn leaf table cloth without response. Meadow spoke to her as she made her a cup of tea,

"What do you mean abandon? Did he leave you?" she asked Kitty.

"When I woke up, he wasn't there. In my dream, he left me. He was sticking my dad's body with needles." Kitty was nebulous with her response.

Meadow placed a cup in front of her and pulled a chair beside Kitty.

"What do you mean, honey? Your dreams are not real. Did he or didn't he leave you?" Meadow spoke with a soft, comforting voice.

"Meadow, I trusted him. I don't anymore. The drugs have changed him." Kitty knew she stepped one foot into the center of the spotlight. Once she stepped in with both feet, she knew that there would be no return.

Although Kitty had become increasingly fearful of Smithton and had an inner voice telling her he had been lying to her, she still loved the man she once knew. Kitty clung to that version of Smithton. She spent her time waiting for the return of man who was her best friend. He had been her best friend since she was a young teenager.

"I used to think that if I just did what he wanted and not made waves, he'd change back," she said as she finally took her eyes off the orange and brown fabric tablecloth and into Meadow's eyes.

"I've been waitin' a long time and he keeps just movin' me around. Now he's hittin' me and I am always hungry." Kitty's eyes begged to be rescued.

Meadow asked Kitty, "When is the last time you ate?"

"When I was here," she replied.

Meadow asked, "And the time before that?"

Kitty thought then replied, "Cookies from the dumpster behind the food store."

Meadow's heart ached for the young girl as her conscious became incensed even more at Smithton's neglect.

"Oh, honey," Meadow said as she reached her hands out and pulled Kitty to her chest and hugged her tight.

Kitty lowered her head and rested it onto her chest feeling shame and embarrassment. She could hear Meadow's heart beat and found it soothing. Meadow ran her hand down

Kitty's hair and rocked her as she cried. After a few minutes of unconditional love, Kitty calmed down. Meadow stood up and walked over to the teapot that was whistling loudly and poured Kitty a cup of tea, then opened the refrigerator door.

I haven't had time to shop, she thought to herself as she wondered what she was going to make Kitty to eat.

Meadow began opening the cupboard doors, looking for food items in the kitchen. She opened an upper cabinet door and found a box of macaroni and cheese.

She pulled it out and opened the box, pouring the dried noodles into a pot she found under the cook top.

"I'm making you some macaroni and cheese, okay, Kitty?" Meadow informed more so than asked.

Kitty looked up as she prepared the food.

"Meadow, there is somethin' really bad that I have to tell you," Kitty said quietly.

Meadow's heart fell to the floor as her mind jumped to the worst assumption.

She knows what happened to Kelsey? Meadow thought as her throat tightened, gripping the words from escaping from her mouth.

"What Kitty? You can tell me anything, sweetheart. In fact it is very important you tell me everything." She encouraged the young scared girl to purge her conscious.

"We are squatters. We move from trailer park court to trailer park court occupyin' abandoned trailers." Kitty looked away from Meadow and back down at the table as she pulled at the short frayed skin around her fingernails.

Meadow let out the air that she held too tightly as Kitty spoke.

"Is that it?" She wanted to scream, but realized that the sacred news shared with her had made the young girl feel dehumanized.

Kitty needed to show Meadow the ring. The metal was burning a hole within her nerves, causing her feel as if she was being dishonest with Meadow.

"Meadow, I have somethin' to show you that may hurt you." Kitty forged ahead with extreme trepidation.

"Trust me, Kitty, you have to trust someone and there's no one better than me."

Kitty reached into her pocket and grasped the ring in her palm.

"Smithton asked me to marry him a few days ago, and he gave me a ring." She noticed the look of surprise on Meadow's face, who clearly did not anticipate the conversation going this way.

Kitty continued. "He said he got it from a pawn shop." Kitty removed her hand from her pocket and placed her hand down on the table, opening her palm and letting the heavy ring fall onto the table.

Meadow gasped.

"No, no, no," she cried out as she picked up the ring. "Where did he say he got it this?"

Kitty replied, "He said he bought it. I was hoping it was not Kelsey's ring, Meadow. I'm sorry. It doesn't have to mean anythin' bad though." She tried to offer some hope to the woman who sat in shock holding the silver ring to her lips.

"Are you mad at me?" Kitty asked, fearful that Meadow was going to ask her to leave.

Meadow wanted to explain her thoughts in a way to Kitty that did not push her further into unwarranted self-condemnation.

"Kitty, this ring is not your fault. You did the right thing by keeping it and giving it to me. You are a bright and beautiful young woman who has suffered a great loss when your father died, leaving you at such a young age. Your father entrusted your well being to a man who is not doing that." Meadow paused, realizing her long dissertation was going to sound like a lecture, but this did not stop her from saying what she felt the young fragile girl needed to hear.

"Change is not going to find you, chase you down and tackle you. You have to make the move to change your life, and you did that, here tonight. I am very, very proud of you and I know your father is looking down at you right know, shining about you with pride and love."

Kitty started to cry as she visualized what Meadow was saying. She had not been talked to with such love, support, and encouragement since her father's illness.

Kitty slid off the chair and collapsed onto her knees, placing her head onto Meadow's lap.

"I love you, thank you. My daddy sent you to me, Meadow. You are an angel." Kitty's tears fell onto Meadow's jeans as she cried with every heartfelt word she said to Meadow.

Kitty stopped crying and looked up at Meadow. She wanted to give something back to the woman she saw as the mother she never had. Kitty knew that there was only one thing she had to give Meadow.

"Meadow, we need to go find that cop so I can give him what he wants so he can look for Kelsey." Kitty felt a rush of love within her body once she released the offer. She felt as if she was giving back to the woman who had given her everything.

Meadow looked down at Kitty and pulled her up softly by her shoulders and back onto her chair.

"What do you mean, ' him what he wants?'" she asked.

Kitty explained. "They know Smithton is making and sellin' meth. They busted me sayin' I stole food, but I didn't. I had the receipt. Daddy didn't raise a thief, but Draino was on the receipt so they knew. They took me to jail. He's followin' me."

Kitty gave Meadow so much information in one long sentence. Meadow stood up and sifted through the events and facts. She turned back to the cook top and opened the foil packet, dumping it into the pot containing the strained cooked noodles.

She spoke as she stirred the noodles.

"Kitty, if you do this you can never go back to Smithton, you know that, right? You may have to be on your own. This is a big, big move for you, honey."

Kitty did not hesitate to reply with the palpable response: "It is the right thing to do. I want to do this for you."

Meadow had never been the recipient of such a charitable act. She was moved to tears that this young girl was willing to give up everything and anything she owns and knows to help her find her partner, a woman she had never met.

Meadow brushed the tears from her eye and cheek, although Kitty had already noticed she was moved to this emotional state.

"Here, eat this," Meadow said as she placed the bowl of noodles in front of Kitty with a spoon.

Kitty ate the noodles without stopping between spoonfuls to talk. She had consumed the food so quickly at one point she started to choke.

"Slow down, Kitty," Meadow cautioned her.

When Kitty was done eating she looked up at Meadow and said, "Let's go find Trooper Cantoniski." She smiled, trying to offer Meadow hope.

Meadow replied, "I will not leave you alone Kitty. When we find Kelsey, we will take you in until you are ready to stand on your own two feet."

Kitty stood up and placed the bowl and spoon into the sink.

"Wait, I have his cell number," Kitty proclaimed as she bent down and slid off the oversized worn tennis shoe she was wearing. She reached into the shoe and pulled out a Band-aid. She opened the sides to reveal a small piece of note paper.

Meadow realized just how guarded and dangerous the cell number was to Kitty's preservation and safety. She was amazed at the steps she went to in order to securely hide the state trooper's cell number.

Meadow pulled her cell phone out and set it down onto the table. Kitty reached for it and Meadow placed her hand over top of hers stopping her for a moment.

"Are you sure you want to do this, Kitty? Kelsey and I will take you in even if you don't take this risk." Meadow looked deep into the girl's dark mahogany colored eyes that would one day shine again with health and vibrancy.

"Yes, my dad has already spoken to me about it. While I was on your lap, he whispered in my ear." She smiled. "He whispered, 'I am so very proud of you Katherine. You will always be my courageous little Kitten.'"

Kitty picked up the phone and made the call, and Meadow listened as Kitty arranged to meet the state trooper at the local restaurant. She heard Kitty say at the end of the conversation,

"I'll see you in an hour, I won't be alone; my best friend is bringing me. Her name is Meadow."

CHAPTER TWENTY-EIGHT

Prey

"At what point in time are coveted sins considered safe from the light of day?" E.H.

Kitty stared out window and into the darkness during the short drive to the diner. She was consumed with trying to explain to herself whey Kelsey's cell phone was in their trailer and why he had her ring.

I know in my heart that Smithton is lyin' to me about never seeing Kelsey. Maybe he stole her stuff out of her car to sell, Kitty thought. That sounds like somethin' he would do. He would deny ever seeing her because he doesn't want to get caught.

Meadow's mind was also consumed with Kitty's boyfriend and Kelsey's ring.

Maybe he mugged her once she was inside the trailer. That could be why the cell phone was under the bed maybe she dropped it when he mugged her? God, I hope he didn't hurt her. Meadow was not as ignorant as Kitty was to the capabilities of a methamphetamine cooker and addict. Meadow was aware that they would steal, become paranoid, and violent. This is what worried her.

She felt comfortable that Kitty would be safe from him now. She looked over at her as she stared out the passenger side window, looking fearful of the meeting.

Meadow reached over and put her hand on Kitty's hand and said, "It will be okay, honey. We will do this together. We have to know the truth about what happened. Don't we deserve that?"

Kitty looked over at Meadow and felt somehow responsible for her pain and suffering.

"I'm so sorry for this, Meadow, I'm so sorry."

Meadow's car reached the diner and she pulled into the parking lot.

"Do you see the officer's car? Is it unmarked or a patrol car?"

"His car is unmarked; it's blue. I think that's it over there." Kitty pointed to a sedan parked at the very end of the lot.

"Don't park in view, Meadow, park in the back. Smithton knows your SUV." Kitty spoke with fear in her voice.

"I will. It will be okay, Kitty." Meadow pulled into a spot on the other side in the back of the lot, strategically parked away from the unmarked police car.

The two walked quickly into the diner. Kitty looked around and saw the back of the undercover State Trooper. The two walked down the aisle and sat down in the booth.

"Hello, Ms. Hepburn," the officer said. Meadow looked over at Kitty, unsure of the inside joke.

"This is my friend, Meadow," Kitty said. "Her partner arrived at the trailer park three or four days ago. She had not been seen nor heard from since."

Kitty handed the trooper the ring, "Smithton gave me this ring. It belonged to her friend, Kelsey."

The trooper stopped Kitty at this point.

"Hold on there, are you setting the terms here or am I getting information from you?" The trooper looked over at Meadow.

"Have you filed a missing persons report?"

"I tried," Meadow replied. "They told me to wait. She called me when she was within a few miles, then I never heard from her again. We found her cell phone in the trailer. Her car has not been seen, either."

The trooper looked over at Kitty.

"What do you know about this? What does your boyfriend know? Have you questioned him?"

"I asked him where he got the ring, and he said he bought it on the street," Kitty explained.

"Well, he could have," the trooper replied.

Meadow sighed out of frustration.

"Her boyfriend is the last person to see my girlfriend alive. He is a volatile drug addict."

The trooper looked at Kitty and asked, "Are you willing to give me information that will lead to an arrest, and possible testifying against the Smithton Taylore? He is your boyfriend isn't he"

Kitty firmly replied, "Yes I will help, as long as you start an investigation to find Kelsey."

Meadow reached over and placed her hand over Kitty's trembling, frail hand.

The trooper asked Meadow, "Does your friend have any distinguishing marks like tattoos or piercings?"

Meadow grew paranoid. "Why do you ask that? She does but I want to know why you ask that." Meadow was finding it difficult to control her anxiety.

"What does she have, Miss?" The trooper asked calmly.

"She has a thick black ring tattooed around her left ring finger. It matches mine." Meadow held out her hand.

The trooper sat back and looked up into Meadow's eyes for the first time. He looked like he wanted to speak but was having trouble finding the words.

"We found a body part with this tattoo on it, today, in a parking lot a few miles from here."

Meadow broke down.

"Body part? She swallowed trying to dislodge the lump that formed in her throat. She forced the words from her mouth, "Was it a woman's hand?" Without waiting for a response she desperately yelled out, "You have to tell me. Please." She knew the answer as the police man nodded his head in affirmation.

Meadow turned white with a hot flash overcoming her face. Kitty felt helpless. She held Meadow's hand, trying to offer support. The truth was she was just as horrified to hear the news.

The trooper placed his hand around a mug of coffee in front of him. He looked up at the two women and informed them of the findings.

"There is a carcass landfill close by this parking lot. We think one of the hundreds of turkey vultures that circle the landfill for prey picked it up. Fate just happened to drop it in a public place so it could be found and hopefully identified.

"Carcass landfill? Like for road kill?" Kitty asked as her voice trembled and she braced for the response.

"Yes," Trooper Cantoniski replied.

Kitty spoke up bravely.

"Smithton took a job collecting and dumping road kill. I feel sick. I have to go to the bathroom." Kitty got up and tried to push past Meadow who sat at the end of the booth seat.

"I'll go with you, Kitty," Meadow said. She looked at the trooper.

"Give us a moment, please."

Kitty and Meadow walked briskly to the ladies room.

Once inside Kitty fell against the back of the door.

"Oh my God, oh my God, what did he do? What did he do?" She sobbed.

Meadow tried to calm her down yet, she was just as distraught, just from a much different vantage. Kitty was experiencing betrayal and unraveling a life of lies, while Meadow was discovering that woman she loved most in the world had been taken from her world by the boyfriend of the woman she was going to shelter.

The dichotomy was intense and the emotions extreme, but the two bonded together without ever lashing out at one another.

The two woman held each other and cried uncontrollably. After several minutes they dabbed their faces with paper towels and walked out of the bathroom and back to the booth where Trooper Cantoniski was patiently waiting.

The two sat back down in the same spots.

"What happens next?" Kitty asked. "How do we do this?"

"I need to take you into the station, get your real name, address, and have you make a statement. You have to give me names, dates, and specifics," Trooper Cantoniski explained.

He looked at Meadow. "And for you, ma'am, I need you to make an identification of the hand we found."

"Where is the rest of the body, Trooper Cantoniski?" Meadow asked with annoyance.

"More than likely it was burned with all the other carcasses yesterday. The landfill has scheduled burns. We have forensics going through the ashes for bones or teeth or other personal items, but it will take some time." He explained the facts with very little emotion, although he felt empathy for Meadow.

"Kitty, are you ready now?" he asked.

Kitty looked at Meadow with a look of panic in her eyes.

"Yes, we're ready," Meadow replied for her.

"Kitty you can do this. We will get through this, together," she said to Kitty.

Kitty reached over and hugged Meadow.

"Ms. Hepburn," Trooper Cantoniski said. "It seems to be a strike of luck that you found this woman."

He looked at Meadow and said, "She needs mothering." Meadow smiled at him and felt positive that the Trooper had humanistic traits and true empathy for her.

"Well, she found one," Meadow said. "Let's do this, Kitty."

The three got up and left the diner to set Smithton's fate into play. Kitty walked in a catatonic like state back to the car. She could not believe that Smithton was a murderer. She could not believe what had become of her. She was enraged that she vacuously followed him from state to state to be exposed, mistreated, abused, and lied too.

Kitty was in a state of shock but not in a state of denial. She knew what her father wanted her to do. He gave her the tools to make good moral, loving, and honest decisions. She had let him down when she let herself down by resorting to living off her primary needs for food and shelter. She never along this journey hurt another person or lied to Smithton. She would never place him in the level of danger he placed her in.

Kitty was living with a serial killer. Bob had allowed Smithton to take over care giving for his beloved daughter at the time of his death. Kitty was in shock that Smithton could disrespect her father in such an egregious manner.

"Daddy, do you see what is going on? I didn't know. I'm sorry, Daddy," Kitty mumbled as she sat on the seat with her head cocked against the side window.

Meadow gave her some space but not too much. She wanted Kitty to accept the reality without punishing herself for action that she did not control. She heard Kitty speaking to her father and apologizing, and she felt compelled to speak up.

"Kitty, your Dad knows you had nothing to do with this. He is watching over you. Maybe you had to go through this horror for some reason. It brought us together, right?"

Kitty smiled a slight smile.

"Yes, Daddy brought you to me." She paused, looking at Meadow. "Are you okay?"

Meadow hesitated.

"I don't think I'll ever be the same again. Kelsey was my soul mate, and she was taken from me, but this is something I have to deal with somehow."

Meadow thought about Smithton, Kitty, and Kelsey as they followed the undercover patrol car back to the station.

"Kitty?" she asked.

"Yeah?" Kitty replied as she looked over at Meadow.

"Smithton had reasons for not killing or really hurting you, remember that."

Kitty turned her head back to the window and tried to find the answer to her last question.

Maybe actually did love me. The drugs made him into a monster. Drugs took my Smithton just as cancer took my father. I don't want any more loss.

"Meadow, promise to never leave me alone."

Meadow understood why Kitty was asking this question and knew the answer that would calm her mind and give her some stability.

"Kitty, I promise I will never leave you alone."

CHAPTER TWENTY-NINE

Accepting the Fall

"Our highest love is protection against all preconceptions." E.H.

Smithton lay on the horn, breaking all protocol.

The large metal door opened quicker than usual and he pulled into the garage. The large black banger stepped out of the door ready for confrontation. Smithton got of the truck for the first time. His 9mm tucked into the back of his jeans, outside of this thin t-shirt.

"Yo, get my bennies from the D, pronto," Smithton yelled out. The Banger walked over to him, standing a solid foot taller and at least a hundred pounds heavier.

"Where Niyah be, ice man?" he said as he cocked his head and placed his hands behind his back with legs firmly spread.

This was a standard shot out stance for a banger, hands already on handguns behind their back with solid shooting balance.

Smithton laughed sarcastically.

"Yo ho ass is not job. She sucked and I fucked, then she pissed off." He smiled and placed his hands behind his back then added, "Not my biz where she is now. I say it again, banger boy: my bennies, pronto."

The thug turned around and stepped back through the door. The butt of two large 9mm guns stuck inside the waist band of his oversized jeans.

Smithton stood and waited with his hand on his gun. After a minute, the banger reappeared with a roll of bills in a rubber band. He tossed Smithton the roll as he said, "Here ya, now get goin'". He turned and walked back through the door and closed it behind him.

Smithton walked over to his truck and opened the door, the metal door clanged up and he stepped into his truck and drove out.

Smithton drove to the liquor store around the corner. He walked in and grabbed two 750 ml bottles of Jack Daniels and slammed them down on the counter.

He unrolled his money and looked at the teller and said, "How much you takin' me for?"

The teller looked at Smithton with disgust as he told him forty-seven. Smithton grabbed a fifty dollar bill and laid it on the counter. The clerk bagged the bottles and laid his change on the counter. It appeared as is neither of them wanted to address one another personally or even informally.

Smithton knew he was judged as a crack head the minute he walked into the door, and the clerk moved the cash register positioned directly in front of the security camera.

Smithton grabbed his bag and walked out of the store. Two doors down from the liquor store was a pawnshop. Smithton got into his truck and drove the short distance to the store. He walked in and over to the cage where the shop clerk sat.

"I'm here for my metal."

The clerk recognized Smithton, reached behind the counter, then laid them down before Smithton.

"You're ten days early," he said. "Price is the same."

Smithton did not respond. He pulled out his roll and counted out the bills. He slid them through the opening in the cage. Once the clerk counted the money, he placed his hand over the items and slid them out. Smithton picked them up and walked out of the store, placing them in his pocket.

He had been awake for almost two days. He had not known exactly how long he had been gone. He drove back to the trailer park and in front of the trailer in his usual parking spot. He walked out of the truck with one of the bottles of the Jack Daniels already half-empty. He wanted to hold Kitty and crash.

Kitty came out of the bathroom when she heard the door open and avoided eye contact with him.

"It's good to see my Kitten." He grabbed her and pulled her into him, hugging her tightly. Kitty did not speak.

"What's wrong with you? You know I had to dump my baggies." She looked up at him with tears in her eyes. Smithton looked at her and realized that she was upset with him. He turned and walked away, drinking from his bottle.

"Kitty, I need to crash. Lay with me, sweet child o' mine?" He laughed as he sang the words. "Can't we bitch later?"

Kitty stood still, not speaking to the man she could not help but miss, although he was standing in front of her. All Kitty could see was the young thin man that sat on her porch hours before his workday was scheduled to start and hours after it finished. Kitty felt the warm summer sun baking the paint finish as she sat on the step peeling away paint flakes, laughing with him, so intoxicated with love.

As Smithton stumbled to the floor to lie down, Kitty walked toward the kitchen, stopping when Smithton started talking to her.

"Kitty, please come in lay with me. I need to feel you. Remember you said you were marryin' me, so we can start conc—" he had stumbled on the word.

"Fuck it," he said. He reached into his pocket and pulled out the items from the pawnshop.

"Here, I think it's time you had this."

He held out his hand and dangled a necklace. Kitty walked over to him to look at what he had. She cringed as she hoped it wasn't another item belonging to Kelsey.

Smithton was slowly swinging the necklace. Kitty looked at the large gold ring that hung on the bottom of the gold chain. She immediate recognized it and slowly reached out to take it from him.

"Where did you get this? Why now, Smithton?" she yelled and started to cry.

"What the Christ? I thought you'd be happy. What's wrong with you Kitty?" he asked, perplexed at her reaction.

"I have been holdin' onto this for all these years. I pawn it every town we go so I don't do somethin' stupid with it." He reached out, grabbed her hand and pulled her down to the ground toward him.

Kitty was entranced by the necklace. Her muscles limp, she slumped to the ground with him.

"You said the other day that you'd marry me. It's time I give it to you then. That was my promise," he said.

Kitty wiped the tears away from her eyes as she clenched the necklace.

"I don't understand, Smithton," she cried as she covered her face with her hands.

"When your dad was dyin', he asked me to take care of you. I know I always haven't done that. I want to, I always intended to. He asked that I take it and when I was ready to marry you, I give it to you. He said it was your mom's."

Kitty cried uncontrollably. She could not understand his timing.

She closed her eyes and spoke to her dad, asking him why.

"Daddy, why now? Am I bein' tested or somethin'?" She could not believe that after all these years Smithton gave her such a priceless gift now, after what she had just done.

Before Kitty was able to respond, his cell phone rang. He ignored it. Kitty was startled at the ring and jumped. She sat up and just looked at Smithton.

As if in slow motion, Kitty turned her head as she heard the large bang that shook the trailer. Smithton's body quickly turned toward the door as five state troopers ran broke it down and charged at him. Two positioned themselves in front of him with guns drawn; one pounced on top of him, forcing his face to the carpet.

Trooper Cantoniski ran over to Kitty, grabbed her arm, and walked her to the side of the room.

"Don't say a word, Kitty," he yelled out to her.

"Stay down," another trooper commanded. You are under arrest, Smithton Traylor for murder in the first degree, assault, theft, possession of drugs and drug making paraphernalia, manufacturing methamphetamine, transporting methamphetamine with intent to sell—" The trooper rattled off another three or four violations.

Smithton just screamed for Kitty. He did not struggle; he did not resist. The trooper hand cuffed him behind his back, then pulled him up to a sitting position.

Smithton's nose was bleeding from being forced to ground. Blood dripped down his lip and chin.

"Kitty," he yelled. "I'm sorry. I'm sorry I fucked this up. I tried to do the best I could."

Kitty was hysterically crying as the trooper held her shoulders. She wanted to just collapse. The air in the room had been sucked out. Kitty felt as if she was being suffocated.

She felt desperate. She felt as if someone had reached into her body and removed her soul.

She looked up at the ceiling and saw her soul circling the ceiling. She wanted to repudiate all the events that unfolding horrifically.

It's going to be alright, Kitten, she said to herself. Tell him; tell him now before it's too late, she urged herself.

"Smithton," she yelled out.

"Katherine, do not speak or I will have to remove you from the premises," Officer Cantoniski yelled at her. Kitty looked at him.

"Why are treating me as if I did something wrong? Let me speak to him," she yelled as she felt a stab of betrayal from the trooper.

"How could you do this to me, to Daddy?" she yelled at Smithton as Officer Cantoniski tried to push her into the kitchen and out of the room.

Two other troopers were lifting Smithton off the carpet and onto his feet.

Everything was moving so quickly.

"Just stop a minute," she screamed but no one listened.

"Smithton, Daddy trusted you. You have to live this with. You lied, you lied to me, and you lied!" These were her last words before she was dragged into the kitchen. Kitty was consumed with hysteria. Small black and gray dots formed in front of her eyes.

Kitty remembered sitting on the chair with a paramedic shining a small light into her eyes. She jumped up, not sure of how much time had passed.

"Easy, sit down, miss," the man said.

She looked around the room for Trooper Cantoniski, but he was gone. Kitty pushed the paramedic over and ran out of the kitchen and into the empty living room. Kitty felt the world had abandoned her. She just wanted something familiar. She wanted to see Smithton.

She ran out of the trailer to find three police cars surrounding the trailer. She ran to the first one looking into the window, frantically searching for Cantoniski's face. Kitty felt despondent and hopeless.

Kitty ran to the next car and Smithton turned his head and looked at her. She threw her hands on the window.

Trooper Cantoniski rushed over to her yelling, "Katherine, I don't want to have to arrest you. Back away from the car."

"Why are you treating me like I'm the criminal?" she cried out to him.

Trooper Cantoniski's stature was firm and professional, yet every officer at the scene could feel Kitty's pain. She was young, scared, and confused. Trooper Cantoniski wanted to hug her but could not show her that type of personal attention.

"Please just let me say one more thing to him, just one thing. Please, Trooper Cantoniski," Kitty pleaded and begged him.

He looked into her large green eyes.

"Katherine, I will walk you over to car if you stay in control. You have one sentence, understand? One." He felt as if he owed her this; after all, Smithton would be a free man if it were not for her.

"Stand right here, Kitty. Do not move, or I will have to put you in the back of one of these cars, understand me?" he said as he held her small frame and looked into her eyes, wide with panic.

"I promise," she replied, filled with hope for first time since the troopers invaded her world.

There is no more freedom, this is it, she thought as she shook her head. Daddy, give me strength, please give me strength.

Trooper Cantoniski appeared with Smithton, who was now handcuffed around the waist with a chain than ran down his legs and to ankle shackles. He shuffled along beside Trooper Cantoniski.

"Katherine," he called out to her.

Kitty stayed where she promised.

Smithton was held a few feet in front of them. Kitty looked at Smithton, time, space, reality stopped. The world was white with his figure placed in front of this stark canvas.

"I will never forgive you for hurting me and leaving me, after all that happened between us," she paused as she started to cry. Kitty had one more thing she needed to say, she wanted him to clearly hear her.

She attempted to contain her composure as she started to gasp for breath.

"You betrayed Daddy, Smithton; you have to live with that."

Smithton did not answer her. He turned to Trooper Cantoniski and said, "Take me back to the car."

These acrimonious words blinded Kitty, the emotional blow could have never been imagined or anticipated.

"What?" she yelled at him, as he was being escorted away.

"How could he do this? What is going on?" She fell to knees and grabbed her hair. "I've lost my mind, what is going on?" Kitty never knew such infinite isolation. The abandonment was fathomless, although her nightmares placed her in training.

"Please don't leave me here on my own," she screamed.

Smithton stared at the ground as he heard Kitty's vociferous, inflictive cries and felt heartbreak with every moan, word, and sob. The pain she displayed was visual and visceral.

"Kitty, please stop," he said under his breath as he began to break down mentally. "Do you think I want this?" He looked up to the cry sky littered with ominous clouds.

Fuck you, Bob. What your daughter will never know is that you were the head of the organization. You fucking trained me, taught me your dirty little fucking ropes. Stay right there, Bob, on that pedestal within your lovely daughter's heart.

Tears fell from Smithton's eyes.

"I'm sorry, Kitten. I love you and did my best. I'm sorry I failed you."

Trooper Cantoniski opened the door and pushed Smithton's head down. He sat back down on the seat and placed his head as low as it could go.

"Kitty, I promise you: you will never know the truth about your life and your father."

The patrol car removed Smithton from the scene. Kitty sat on the ground and rain began to fall upon her head and face.

She looked up to the angry sky and longed for her father. There was nothing that would change her opinion or compete with her childhood memories.

"Daddy, you will always be my hero." Kitty said to herself as she got up, wiped her eyes and walked away from the trailer for the last time.

Would you like to see your manuscript become a book?

If you are interested in becoming a PublishAmerica author, please submit your manuscript for possible publication to us at:

mybook@publishamerica.com

You may also mail in your manuscript to:

**PublishAmerica
PO Box 151
Frederick, MD 21705**

www.publishamerica.com

CPSIA information can be obtained at www.ICGtesting.com
Printed in the USA
BVOW03s1731120114

341554BV00001B/70/P